Sam Davies

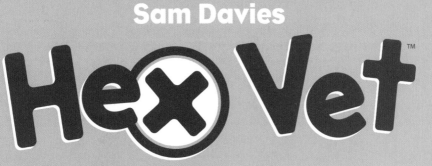
Hex Vet™

The Flying Surgery

kaboom!™

Ross Richie...CEO & Founder
Joy Huffman...CFO
Matt Gagnon...Editor-in-Chief
Filip Sablik.............................President, Publishing & Marketing
Stephen Christy.......................President, Development
Lance Kreiter............Vice President, Licensing & Merchandising
Arune Singh................................Vice President, Marketing
Bryce Carlson............Vice President, Editorial & Creative Strategy
Scott Newman..............................Manager, Production Design
Kate Henning....................................Manager, Operations
Spencer Simpson................................Manager, Sales
Elyse Strandberg..................................Manager, Finance
Sierra Hahn...Executive Editor
Jeanine Schaefer..................................Executive Editor
Dafna Pleban...Senior Editor
Shannon Watters...Senior Editor
Eric Harburn...Senior Editor
Chris Rosa...Editor
Matthew Levine..Editor
Sophie Philips-Roberts................................Associate Editor
Amanda LaFranco....................................Associate Editor
Jonathan Manning....................................Associate Editor

Gavin Gronenthal..Assistant Editor
Gwen Waller..Assistant Editor
Allyson Gronowitz...Assistant Editor
Jillian Crab...Design Coordinator
Michelle Ankley...Design Coordinator
Kara Leopard...Production Designer
Marie Krupina..Production Designer
Grace Park...Production Designer
Chelsea Roberts.................................Production Design Assistant
Samantha Knapp................................Production Design Assistant
José Meza..Live Events Lead
Stephanie Hocutt.................................Digital Marketing Lead
Esther Kim..Marketing Coordinator
Cat O'Grady...............................Digital Marketing Coordinator
Amanda Lawson..Marketing Assistant
Holly Aitchison...............................Digital Sales Coordinator
Morgan Perry..Retail Sales Coordinator
Megan Christopher....................................Operations Coordinator
Rodrigo Hernandez...Mailroom Assistant
Zipporah Smith..Operations Assistant
Sabrina Lesin..Accounting Assistant
Breanna Sarpy...Executive Assistant

kaboom! ™

ISBN: 978-1-68415-478-4, eISBN: 978-1-64144-617-4

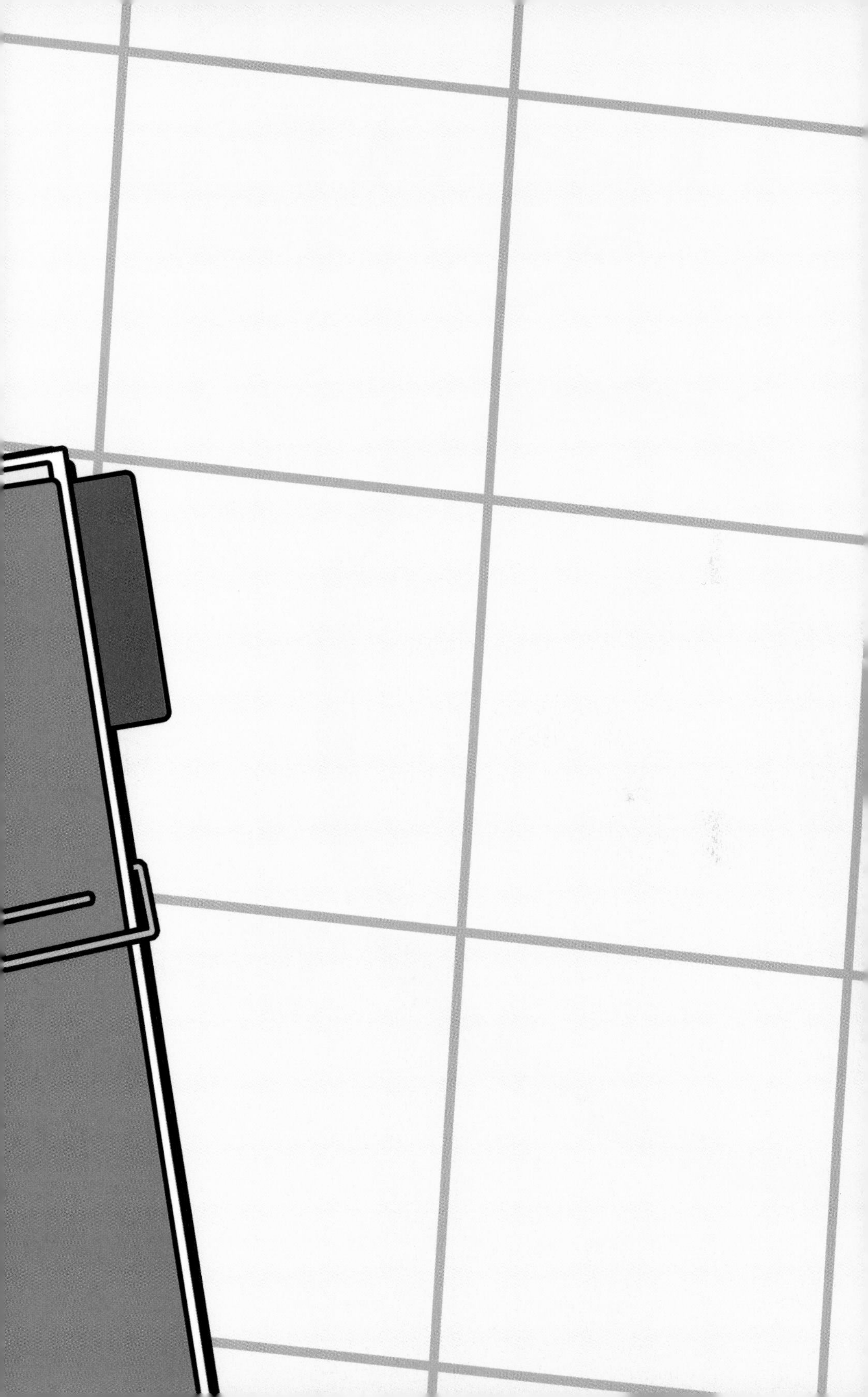

HexVet™

The Flying Surgery

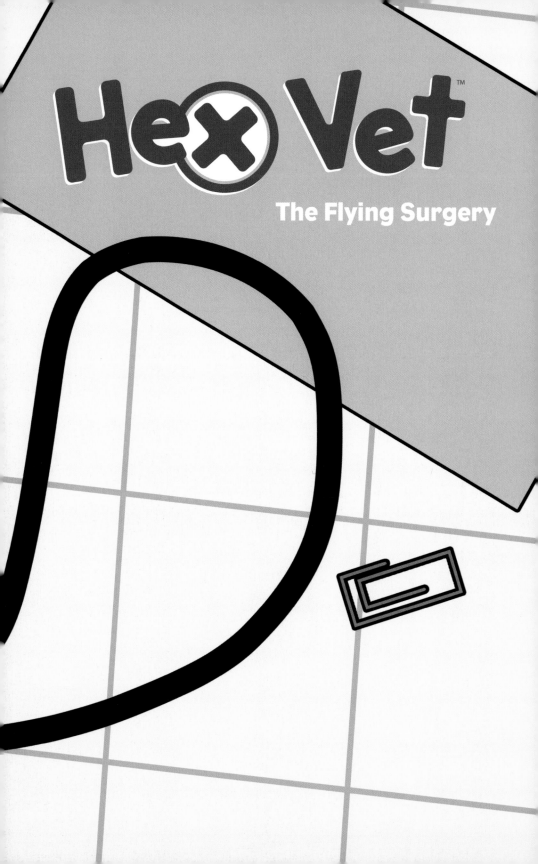

Written & Illustrated by
Sam Davies

Letters by
Mike Fiorentino

Cover by
Sam Davies

Designer
Jillian Crab

Assistant Editor
Michael Moccio

Associate Editor
Jonathan Manning

Editor
Bryce Carlson

Welcome to Willows Whisper Veterinary Practice

Meet the Team

Dr Talon

Nurse Chantsworth

Trainee
Clarion Wellspring

Trainee
Annette Artifice

Buggy the Bugbear

Friends of the Practice

Ornothea Fleetfoot

Renowned Explorer

Glenn Railion

Local Wildlife Warlock

Emilios the Griffin

A handsome bird

Augustus Wellspring

Volunteer

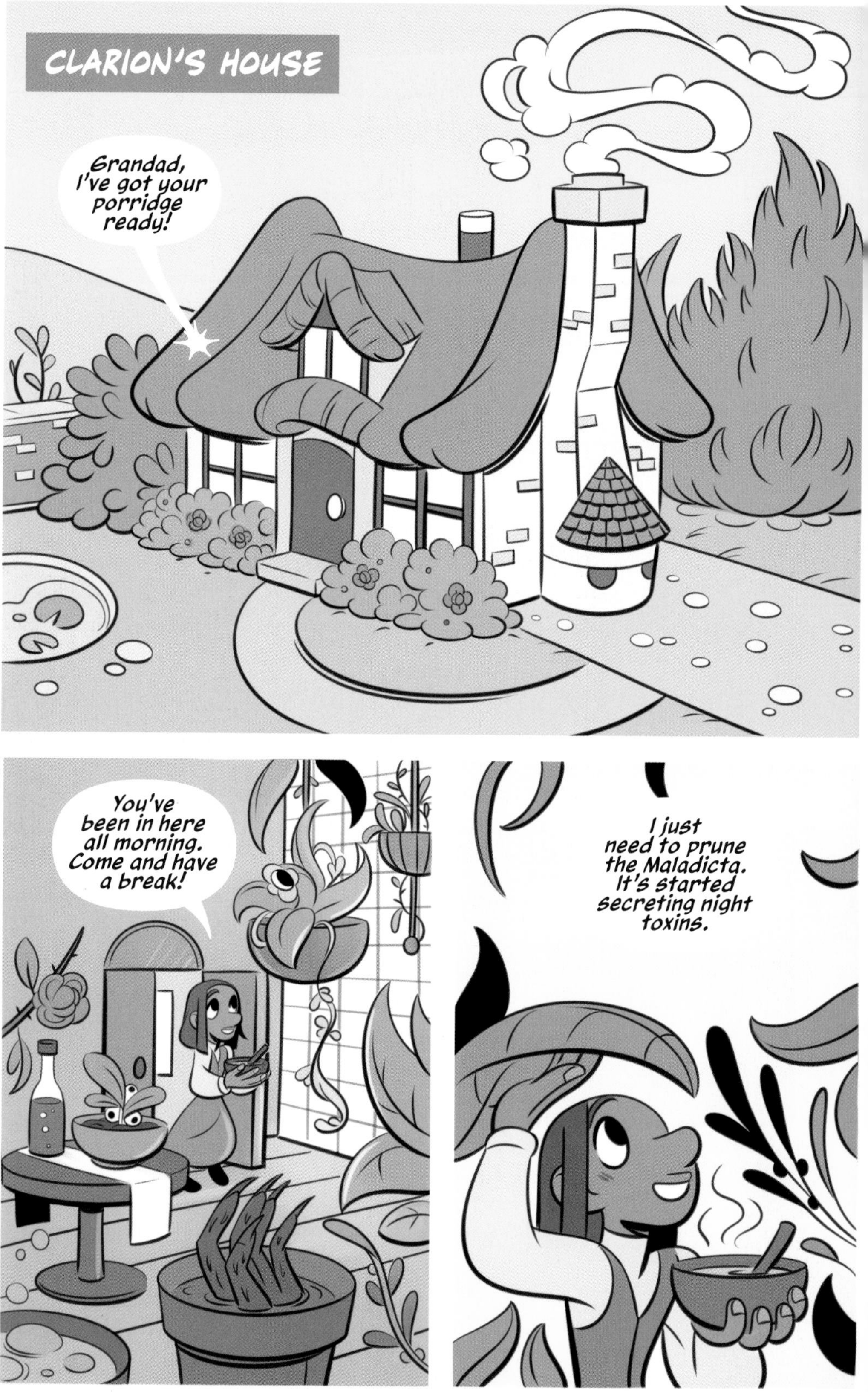
CLARION'S HOUSE
Grandad, I've got your porridge ready!
You've been in here all morning. Come and have a break!
I just need to prune the Maladicta. It's started secreting night toxins.

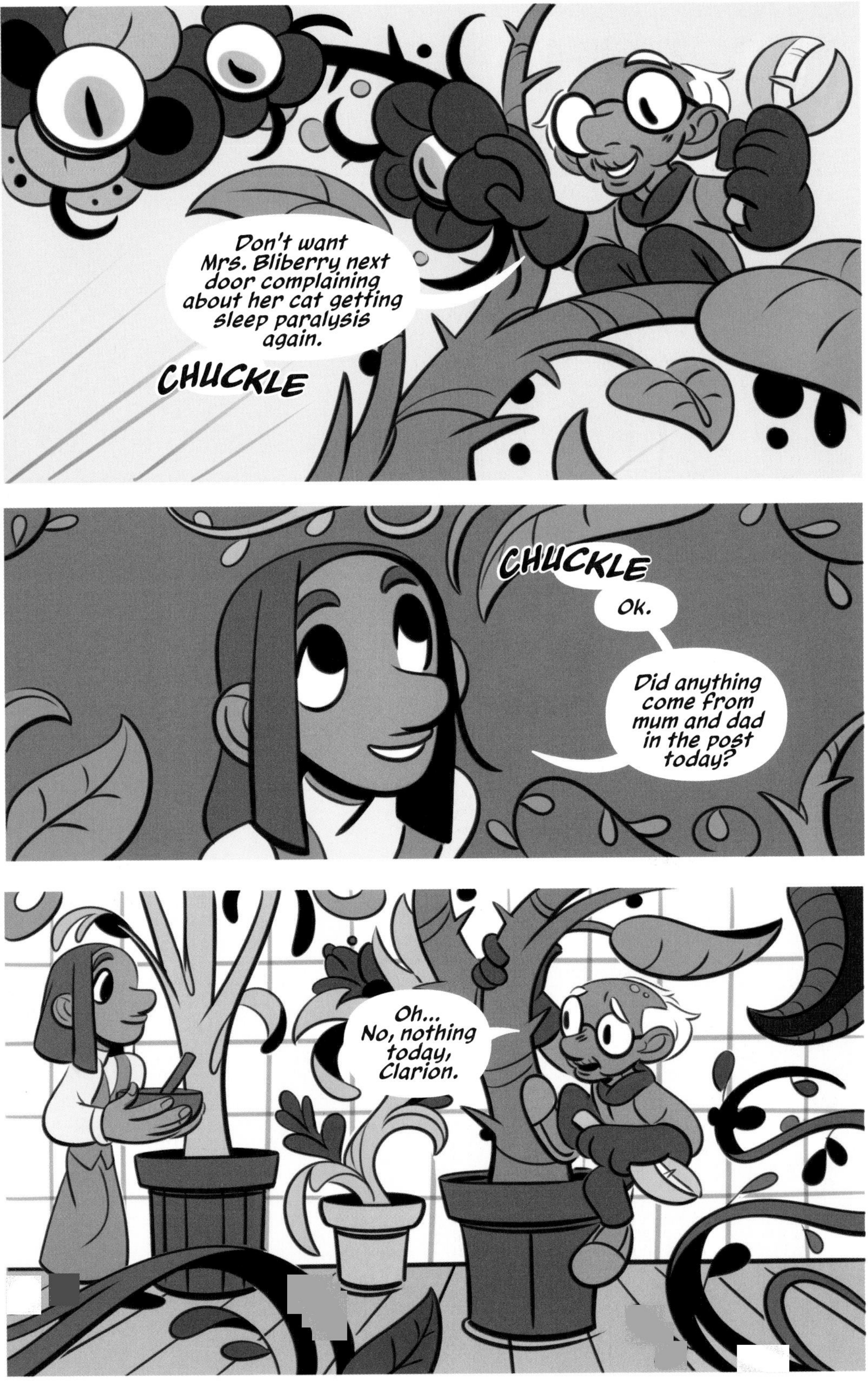

Don't want Mrs. Bliberry next door complaining about her cat getting sleep paralysis again.
CHUCKLE
CHUCKLE
Ok.
Did anything come from mum and dad in the post today?
Oh... No, nothing today, Clarion.

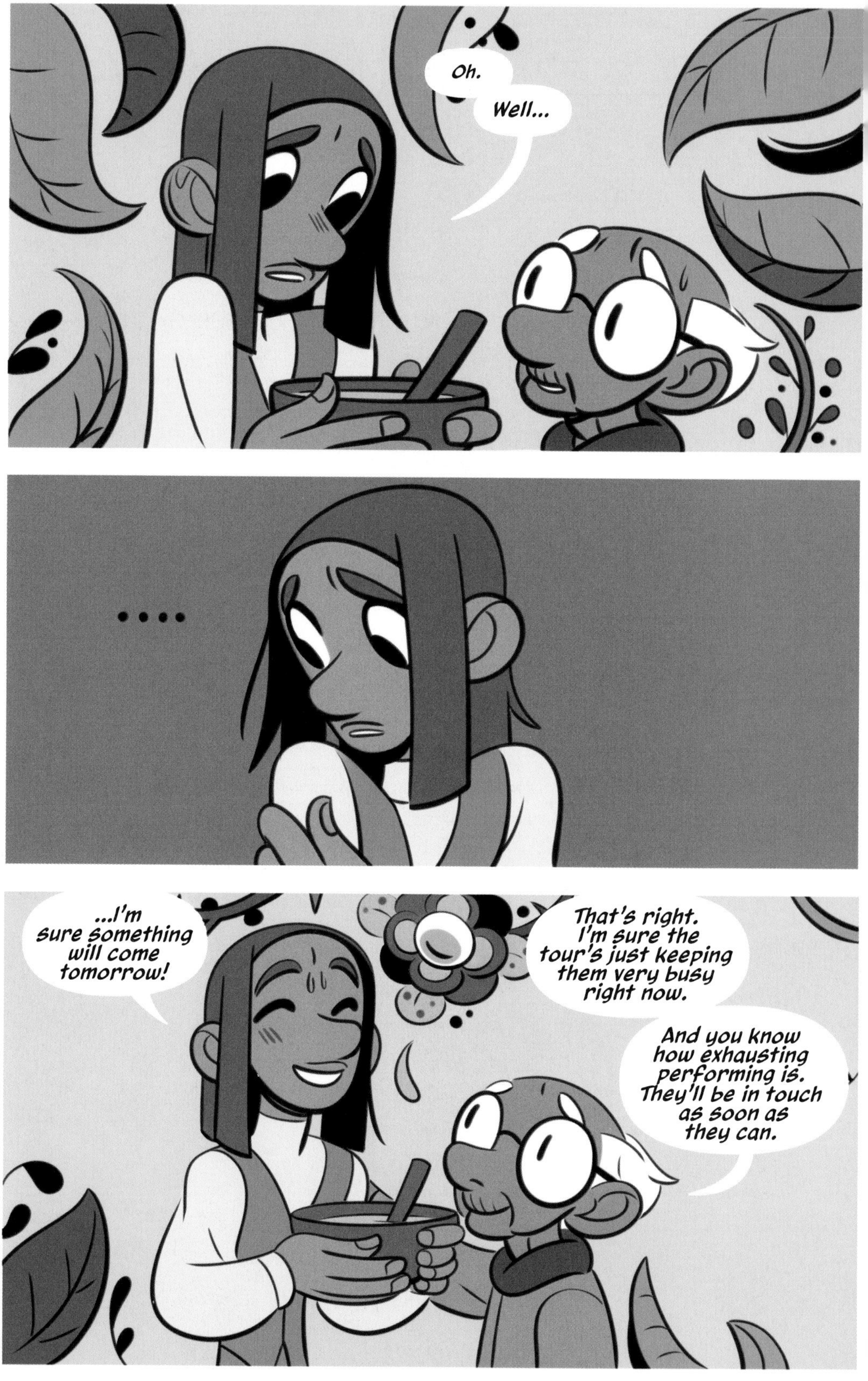
Oh.
Well...
....
...I'm sure something will come tomorrow!
That's right. I'm sure the tour's just keeping them very busy right now.
And you know how exhausting performing is. They'll be in touch as soon as they can.

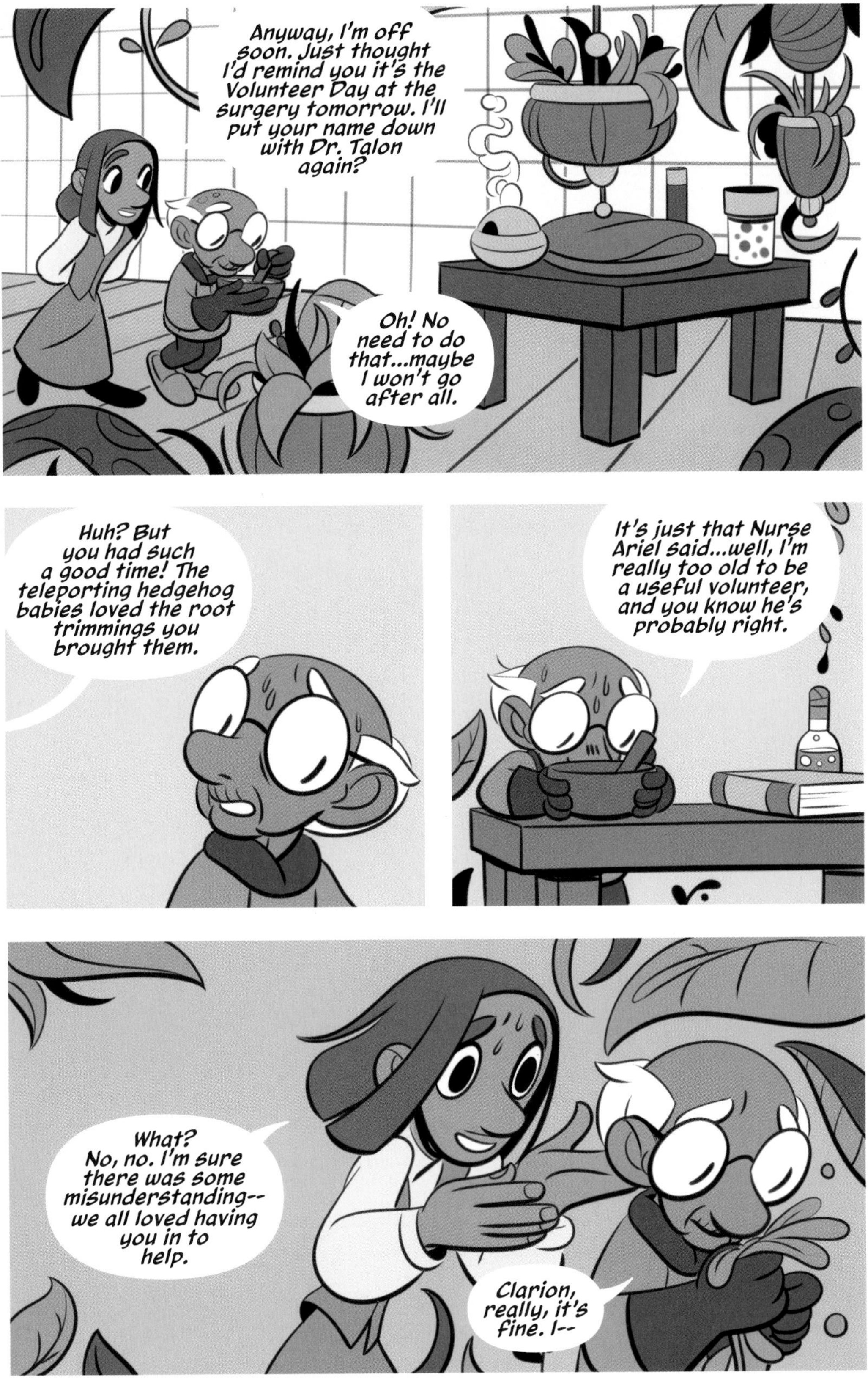
Anyway, I'm off soon. Just thought I'd remind you it's the Volunteer Day at the surgery tomorrow. I'll put your name down with Dr. Talon again?
Oh! No need to do that...maybe I won't go after all.
Huh? But you had such a good time! The teleporting hedgehog babies loved the root trimmings you brought them.
It's just that Nurse Ariel said...well, I'm really too old to be a useful volunteer, and you know he's probably right.
What? No, no. I'm sure there was some misunderstanding--we all loved having you in to help.
Clarion, really, it's fine. I--

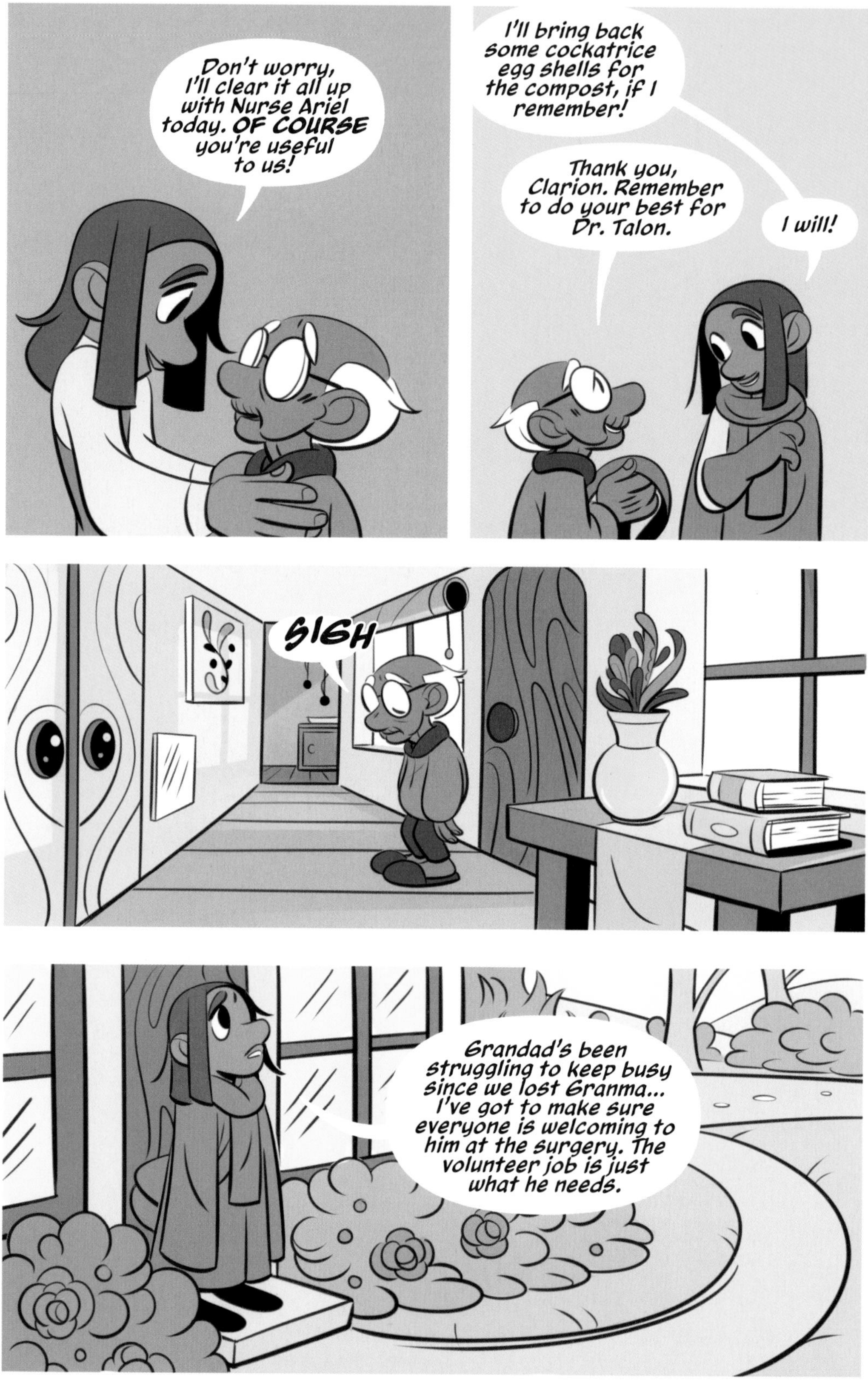
Don't worry, I'll clear it all up with Nurse Ariel today. OF COURSE you're useful to us!
I'll bring back some cockatrice egg shells for the compost, if I remember!
Thank you, Clarion. Remember to do your best for Dr. Talon.
I will!
SIGH
Grandad's been struggling to keep busy since we lost Granma... I've got to make sure everyone is welcoming to him at the surgery. The volunteer job is just what he needs.

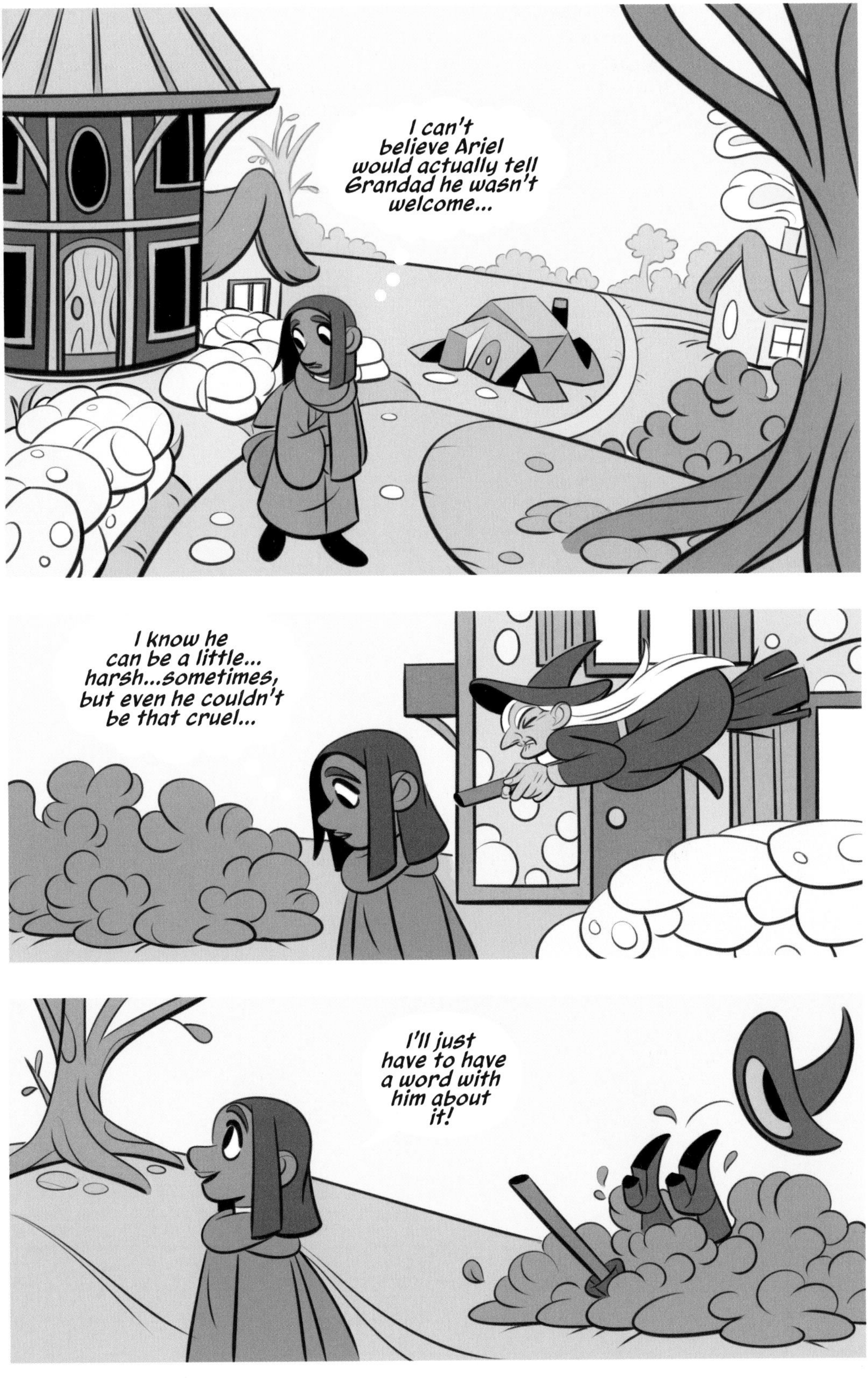
I can't believe Ariel would actually tell Grandad he wasn't welcome...
I know he can be a little... harsh...sometimes, but even he couldn't be that cruel...
I'll just have to have a word with him about it!

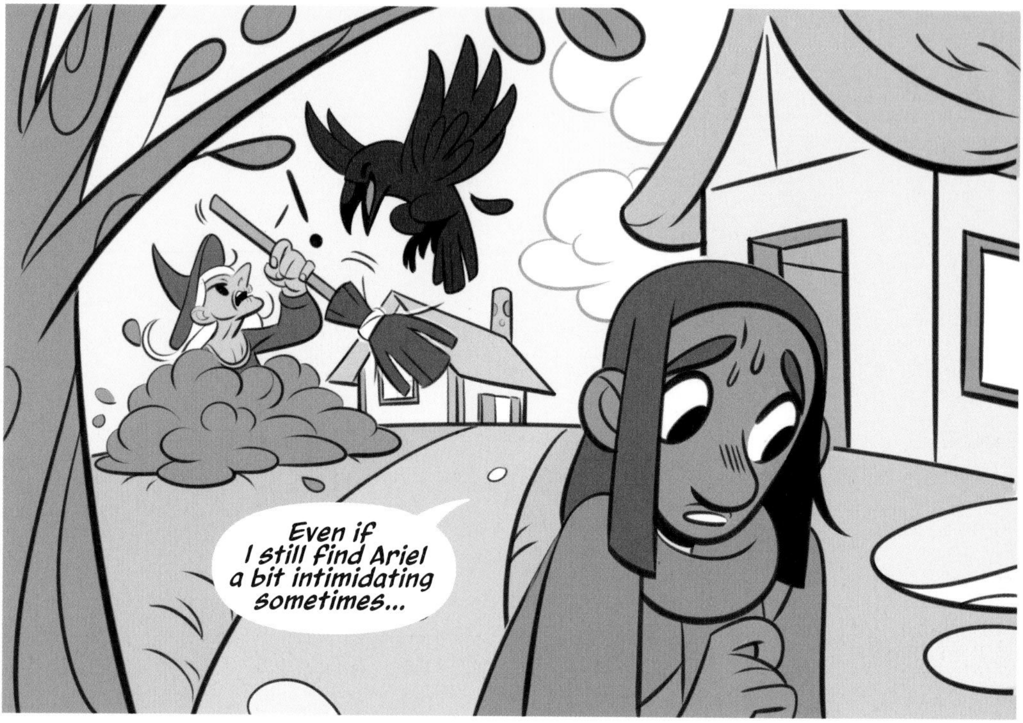
!
Even if I still find Ariel a bit intimidating sometimes...

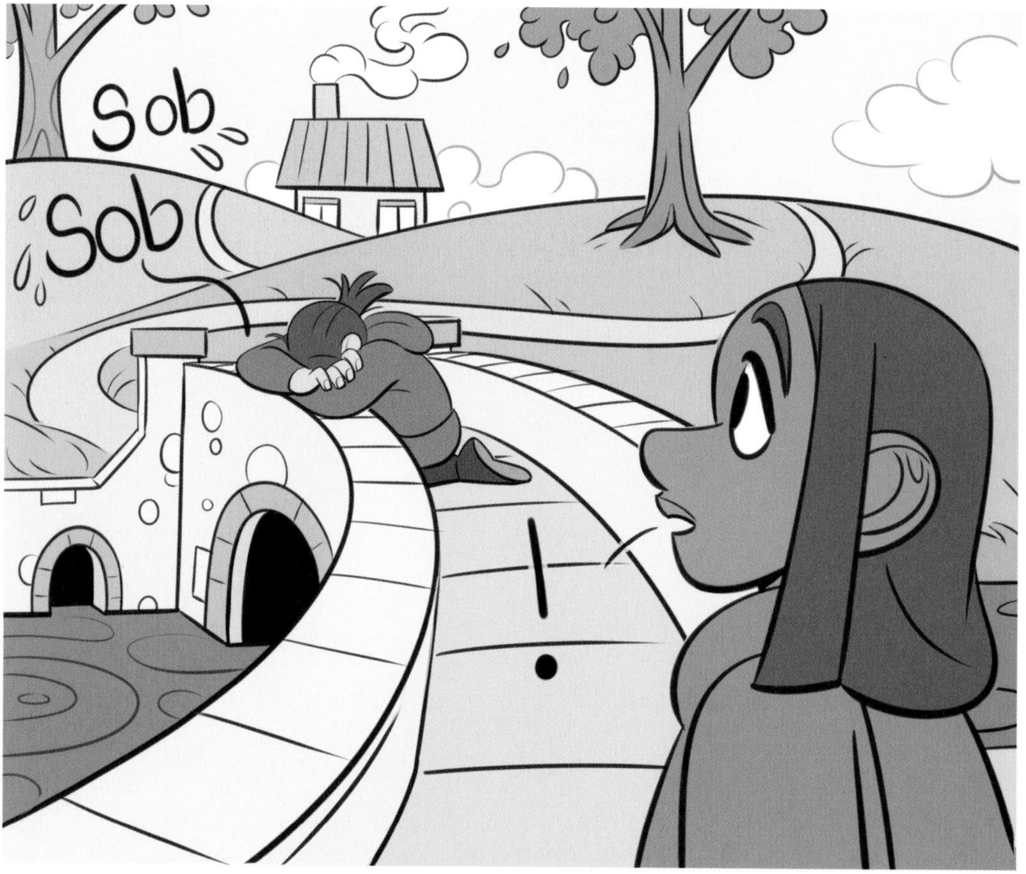
Sob
Sob
!

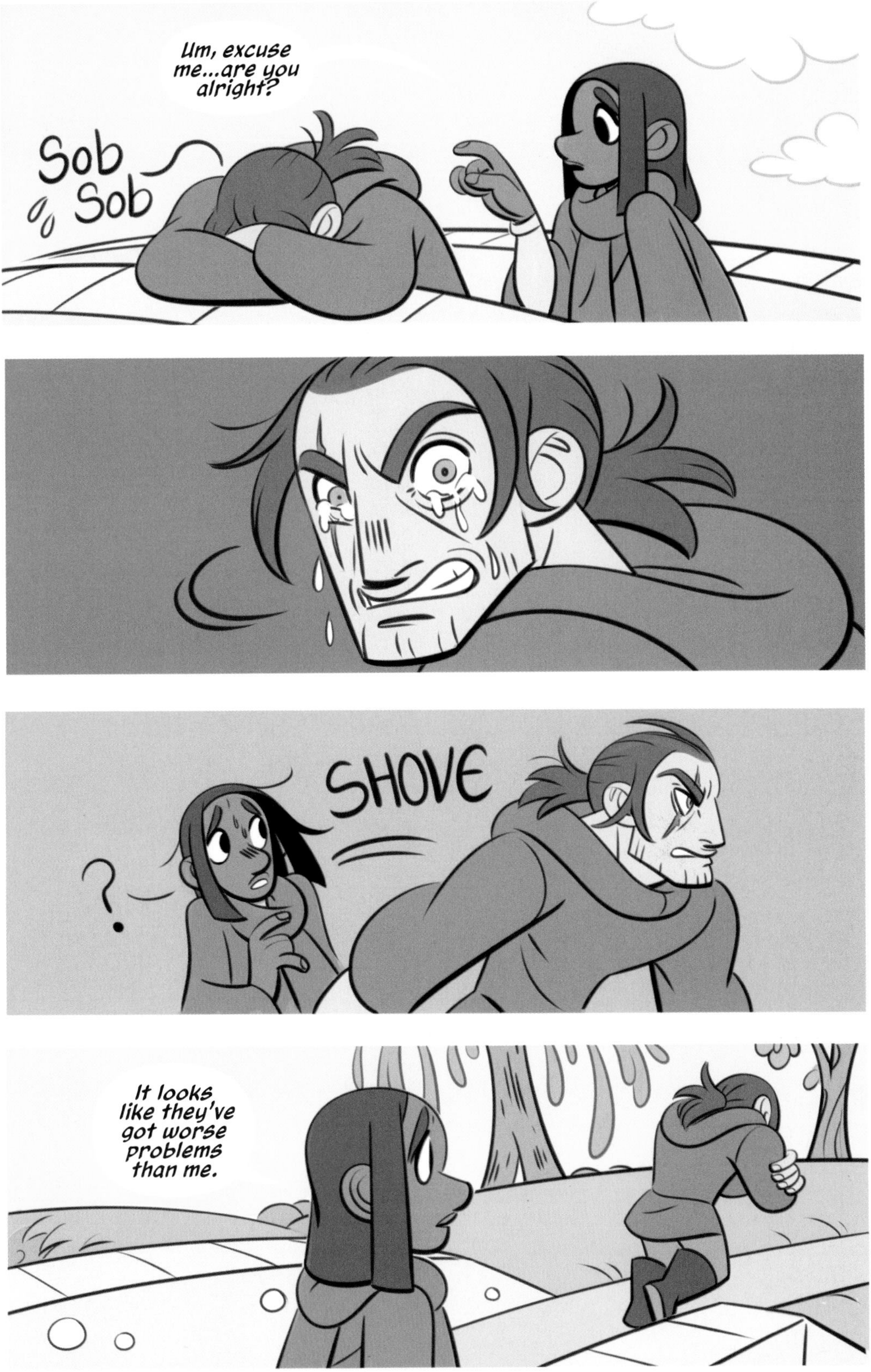
Um, excuse me...are you alright?
Sob Sob
SHOVE
?
It looks like they've got worse problems than me.

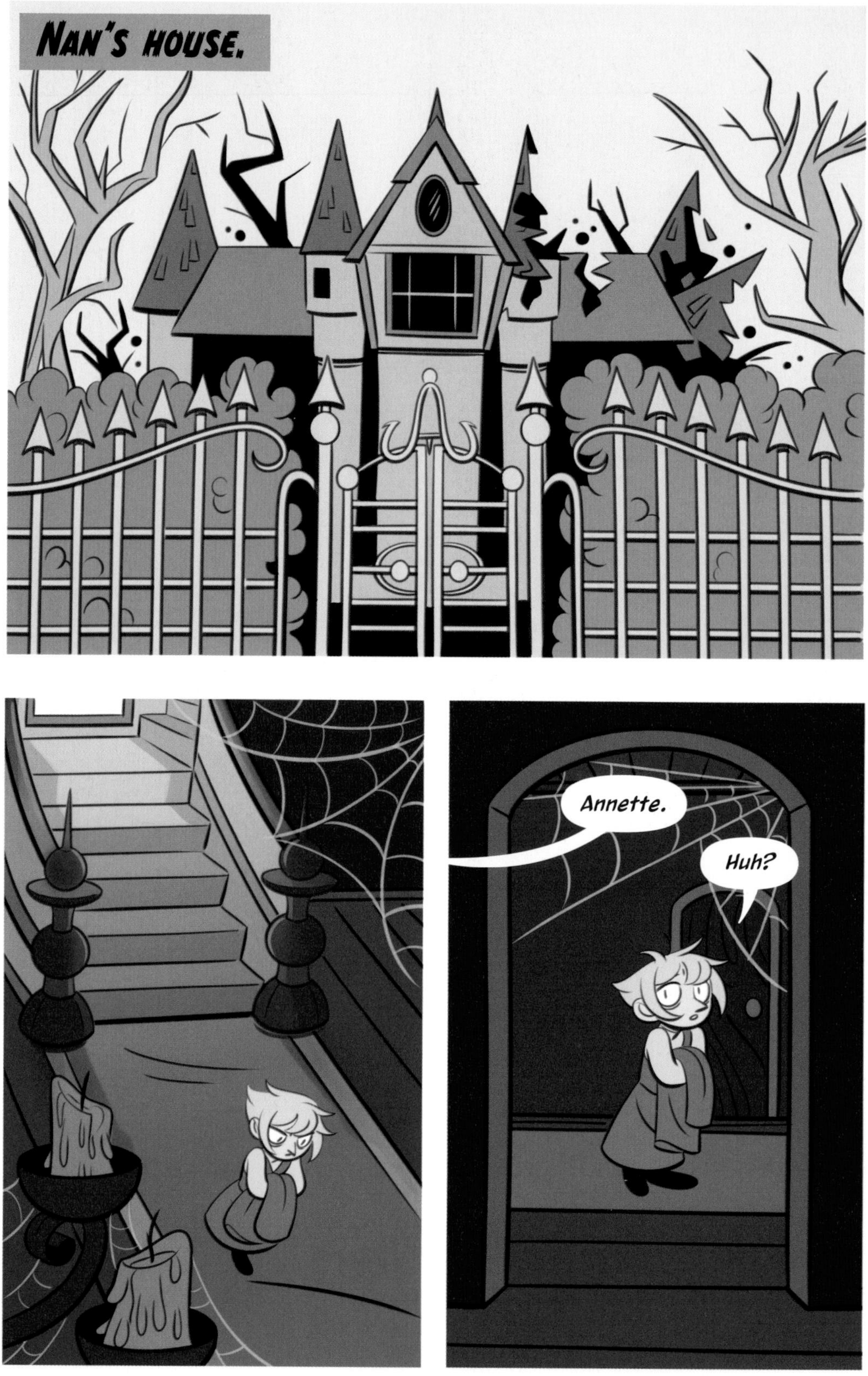
NAN'S HOUSE.
Annette.
Huh?

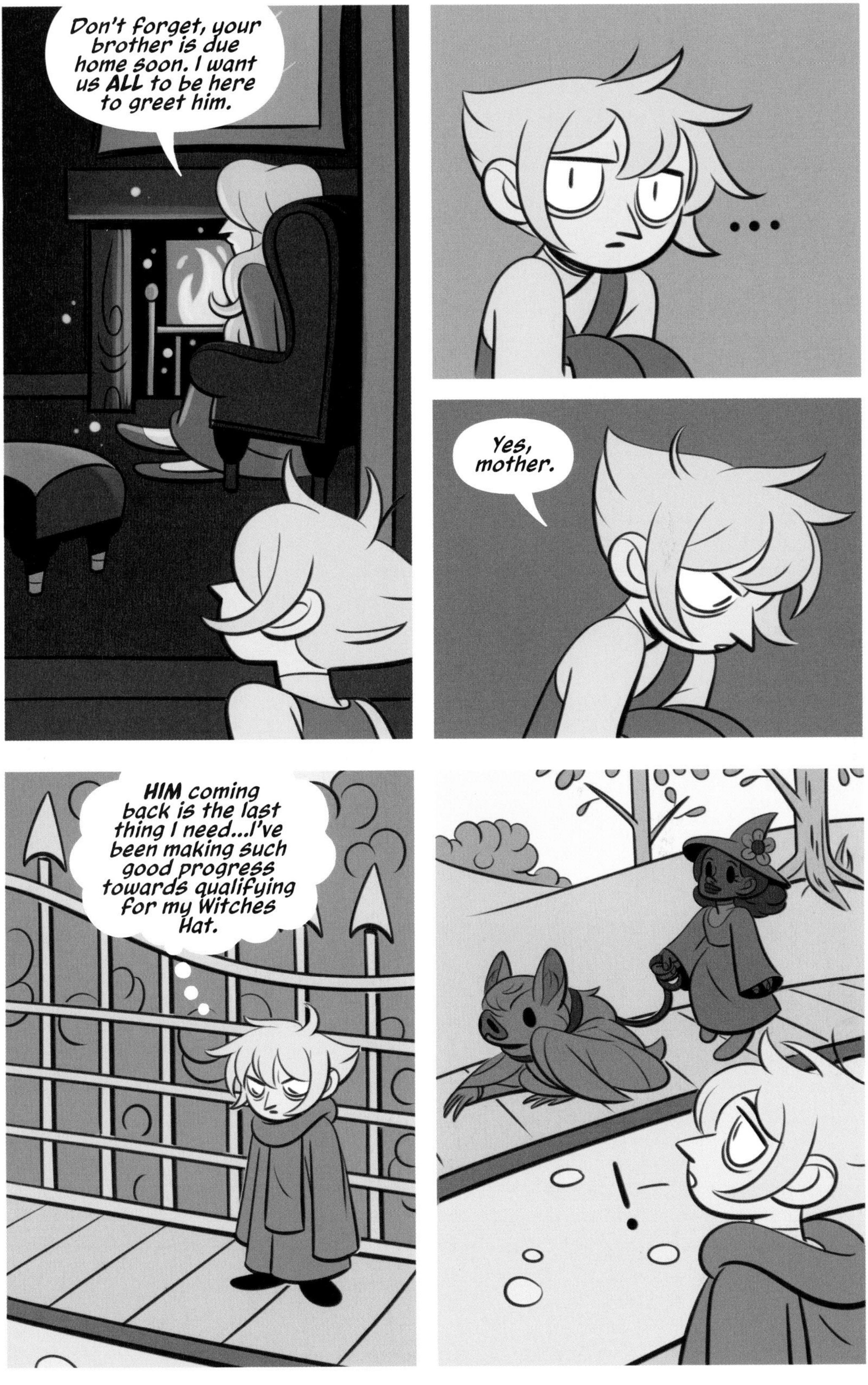
Don't forget, your brother is due home soon. I want us ALL to be here to greet him.
...
Yes, mother.
HIM coming back is the last thing I need...I've been making such good progress towards qualifying for my Witches Hat.
!

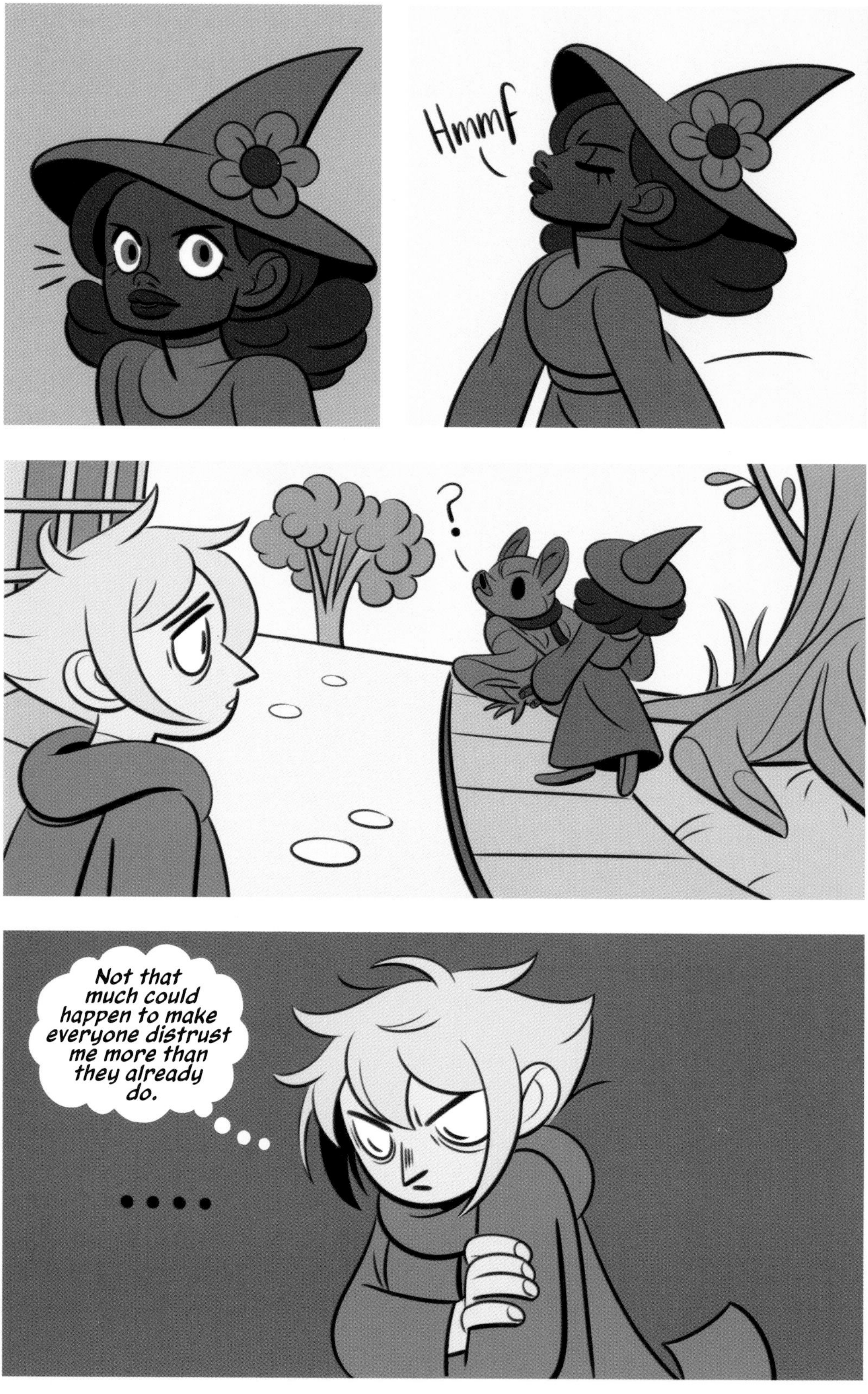
Hmmf
?
Not that much could happen to make everyone distrust me more than they already do.
....

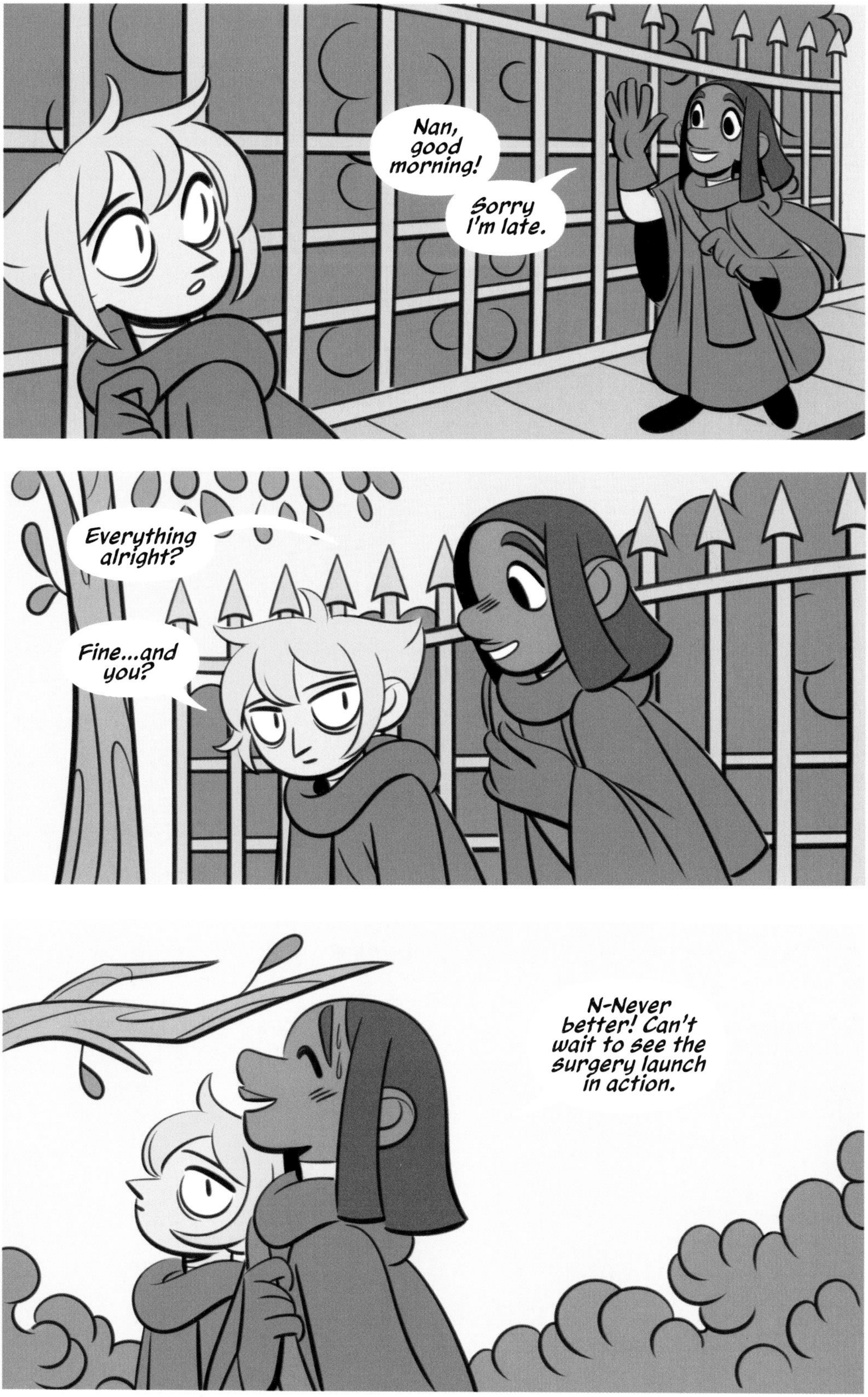
Nan, good morning!
Sorry I'm late.
Everything alright?
Fine...and you?
N-Never better! Can't wait to see the surgery launch in action.

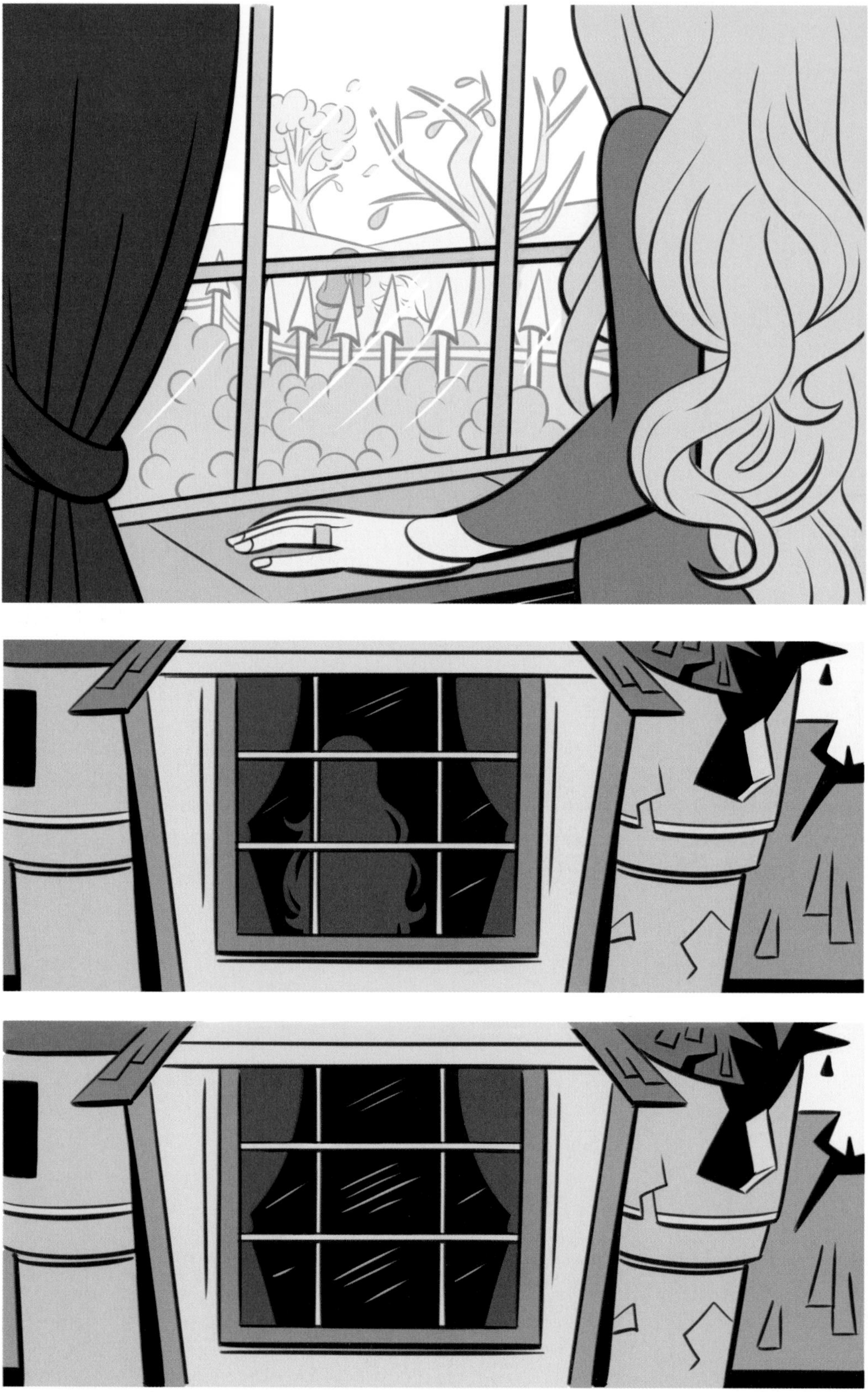

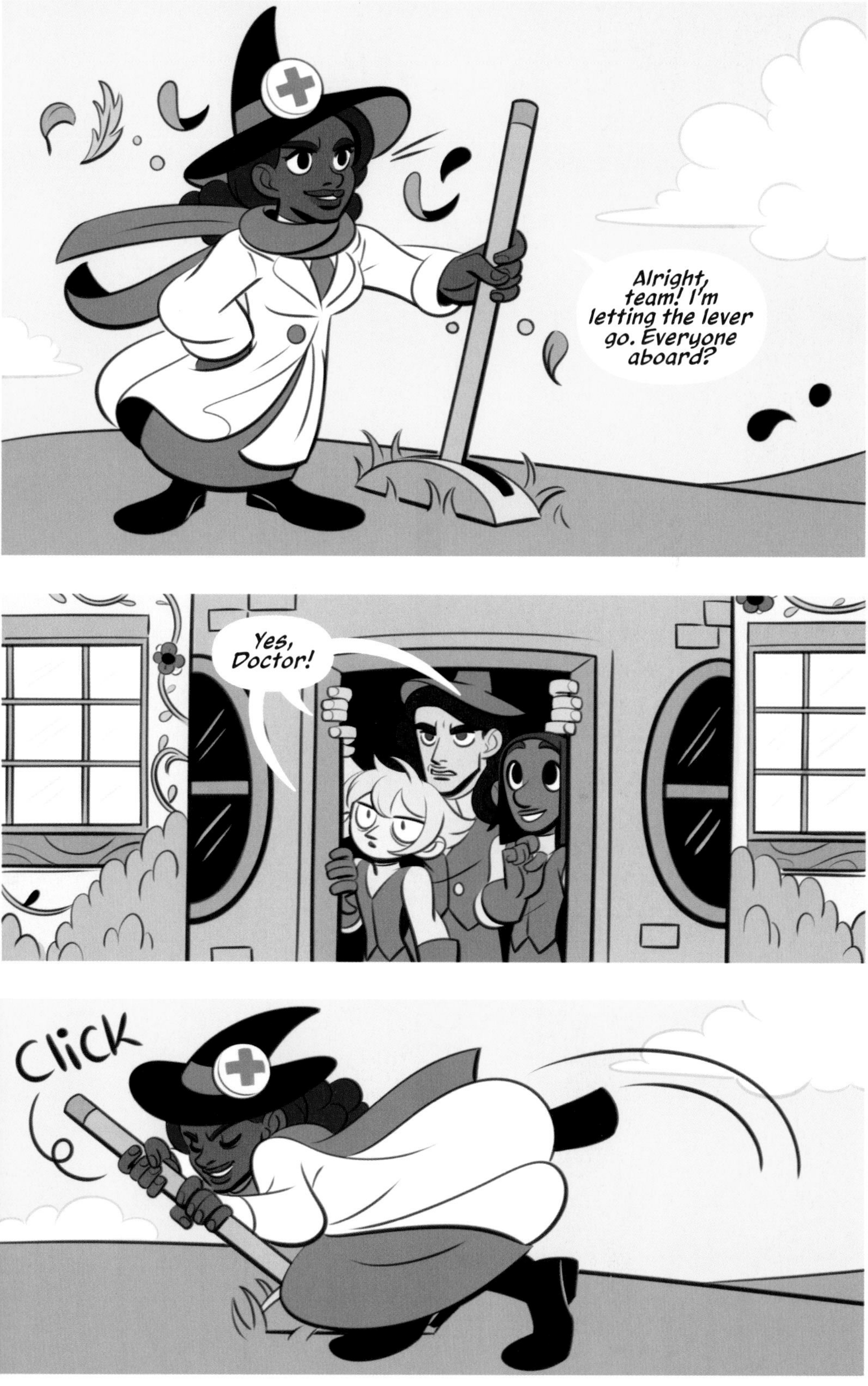
Alright, team! I'm letting the lever go. Everyone aboard?
Yes, Doctor!
Click

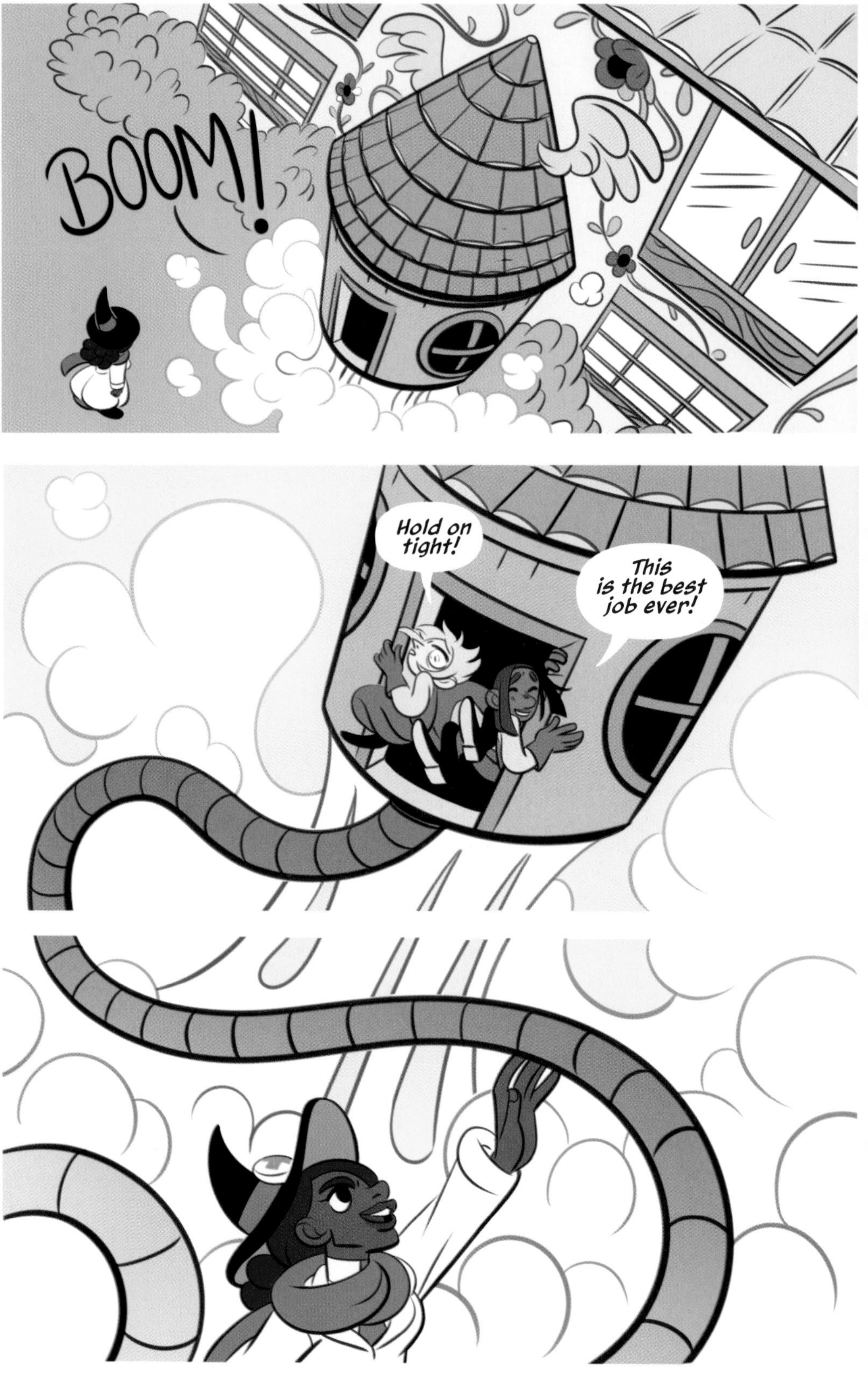
BOOM!
Hold on tight!
This is the best job ever!

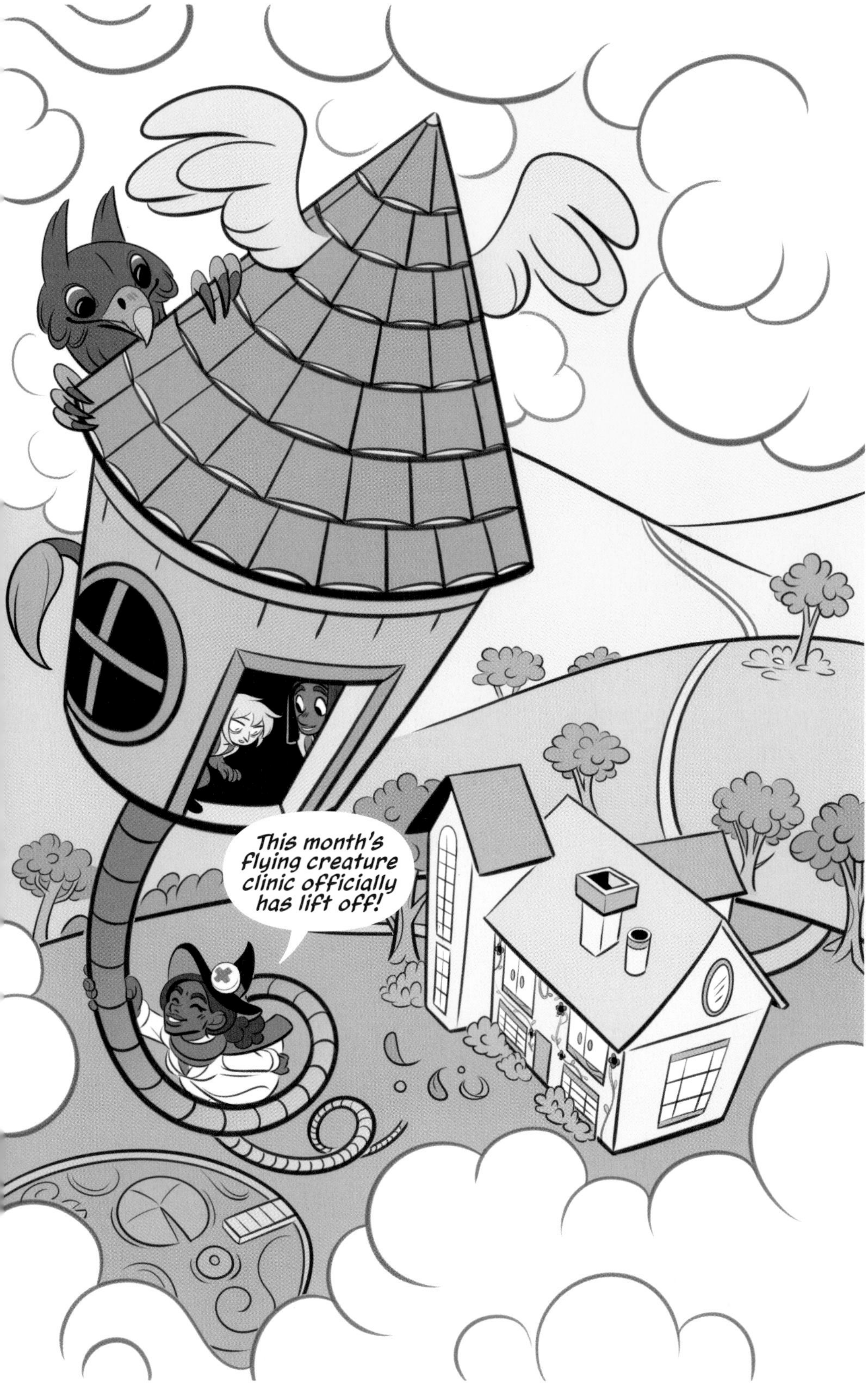
This month's flying creature clinic officially has lift off!

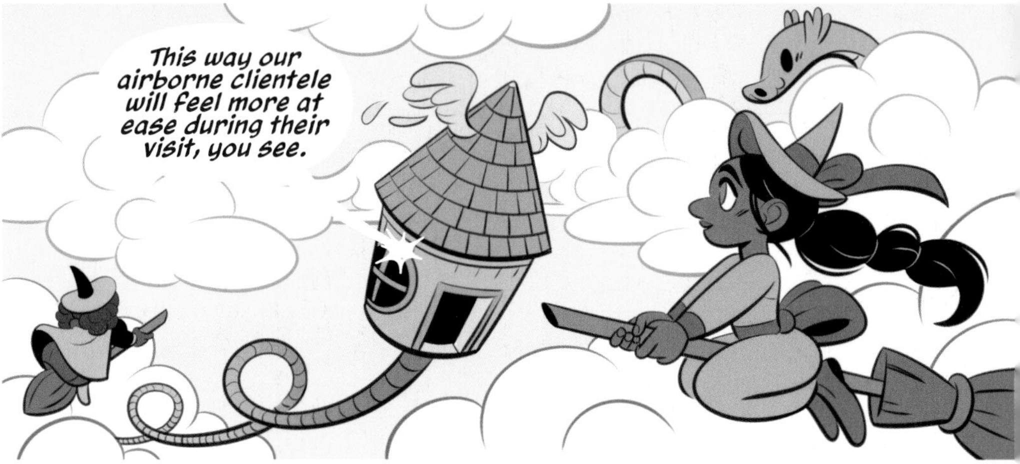
This way our airborne clientele will feel more at ease during their visit, you see.

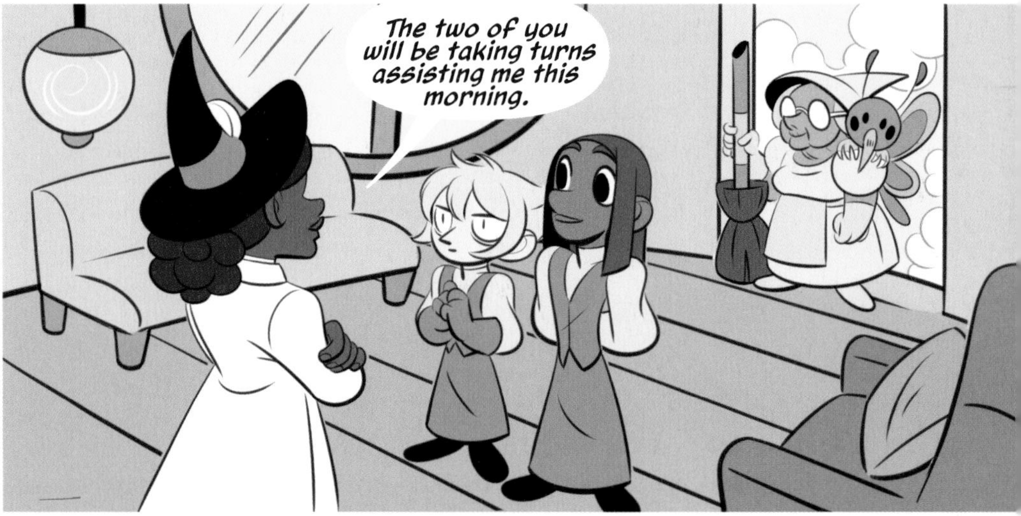
The two of you will be taking turns assisting me this morning.

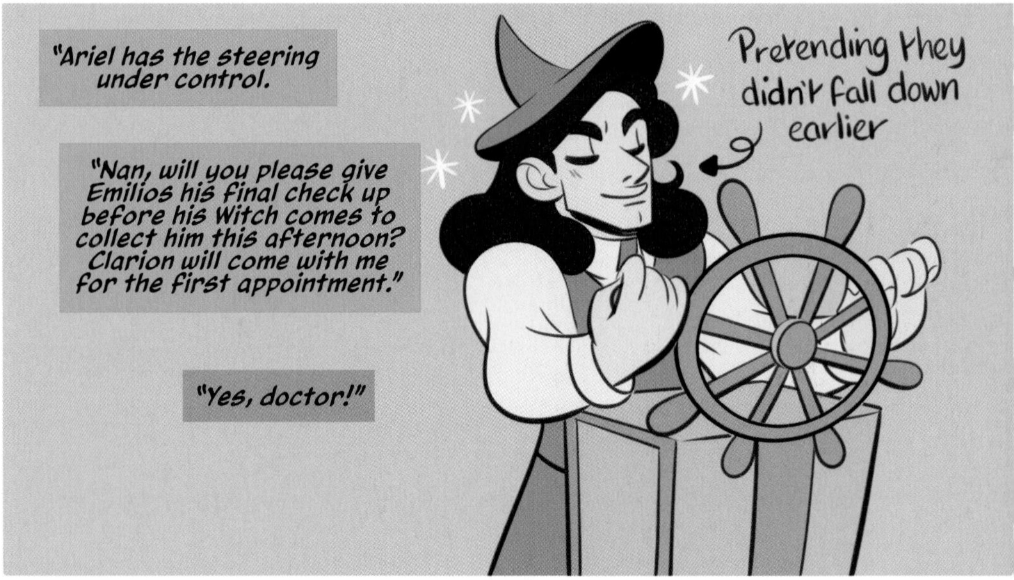
"Ariel has the steering under control.
"Nan, will you please give Emilios his final check up before his Witch comes to collect him this afternoon? Clarion will come with me for the first appointment."
"Yes, doctor!"
Pretending they didn't fall down earlier

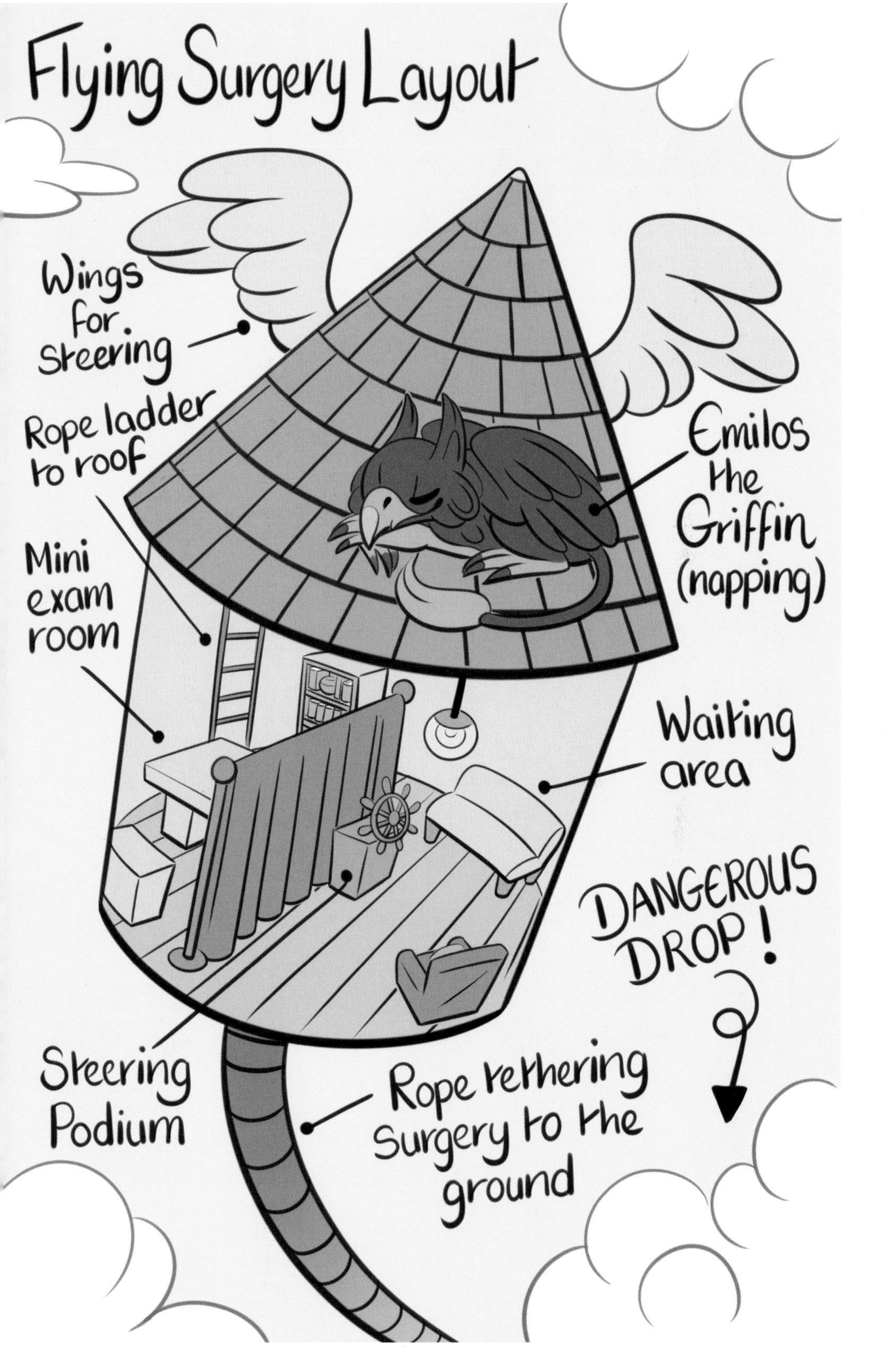
Flying Surgery Layout
Wings for steering
Rope ladder to roof
Mini exam room
Emilos the Griffin (napping)
Waiting area
DANGEROUS DROP!
Steering Podium
Rope tethering Surgery to the ground

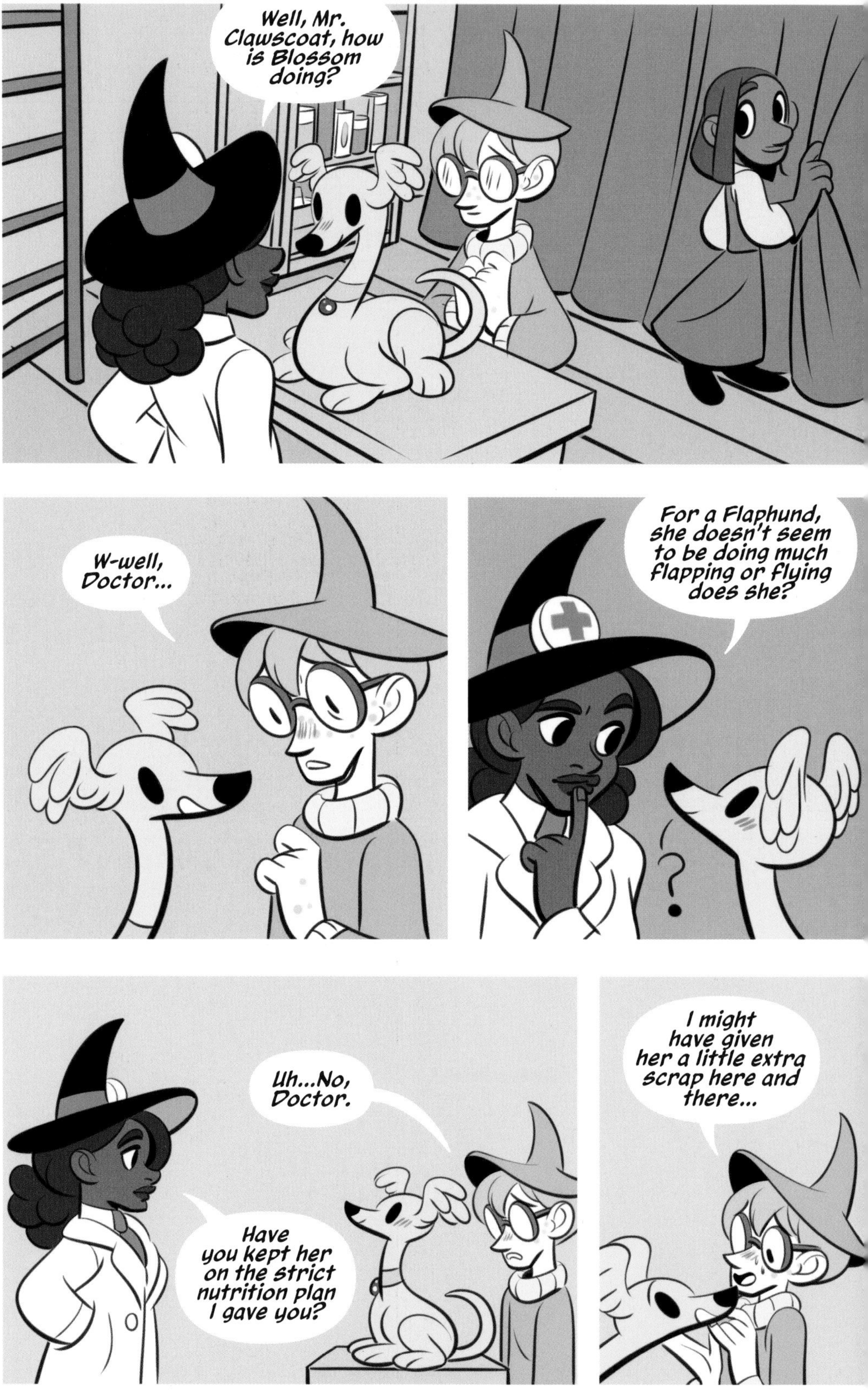
Well, Mr. Clawscoat, how is Blossom doing?
W-well, Doctor...
For a Flaphund, she doesn't seem to be doing much flapping or flying does she?
?
Have you kept her on the strict nutrition plan I gave you?
Uh...No, Doctor.
I might have given her a little extra scrap here and there...

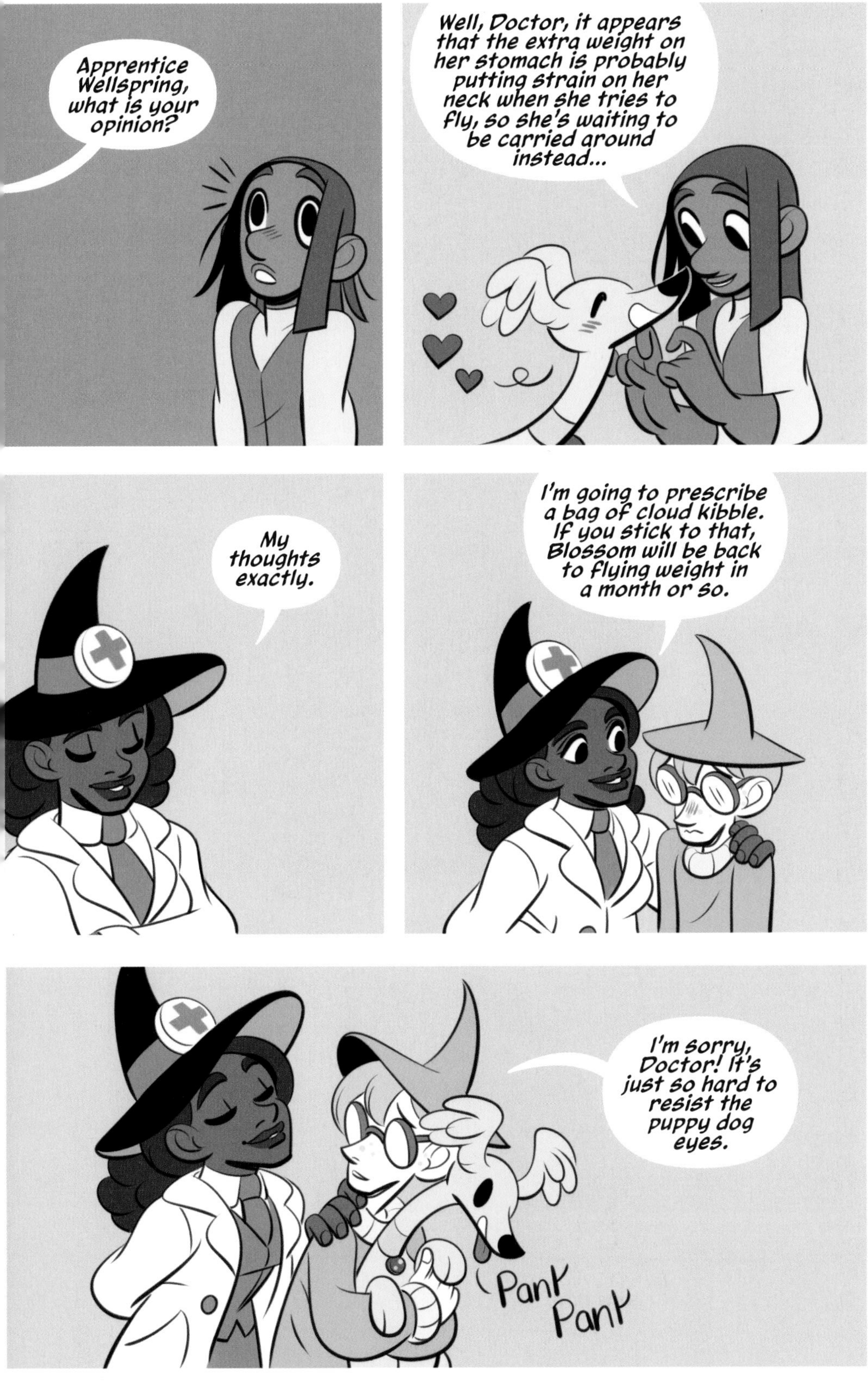
Apprentice Wellspring, what is your opinion?
Well, Doctor, it appears that the extra weight on her stomach is probably putting strain on her neck when she tries to fly, so she's waiting to be carried around instead...
My thoughts exactly.
I'm going to prescribe a bag of cloud kibble. If you stick to that, Blossom will be back to flying weight in a month or so.
I'm sorry, Doctor! It's just so hard to resist the puppy dog eyes.
Pant Pant

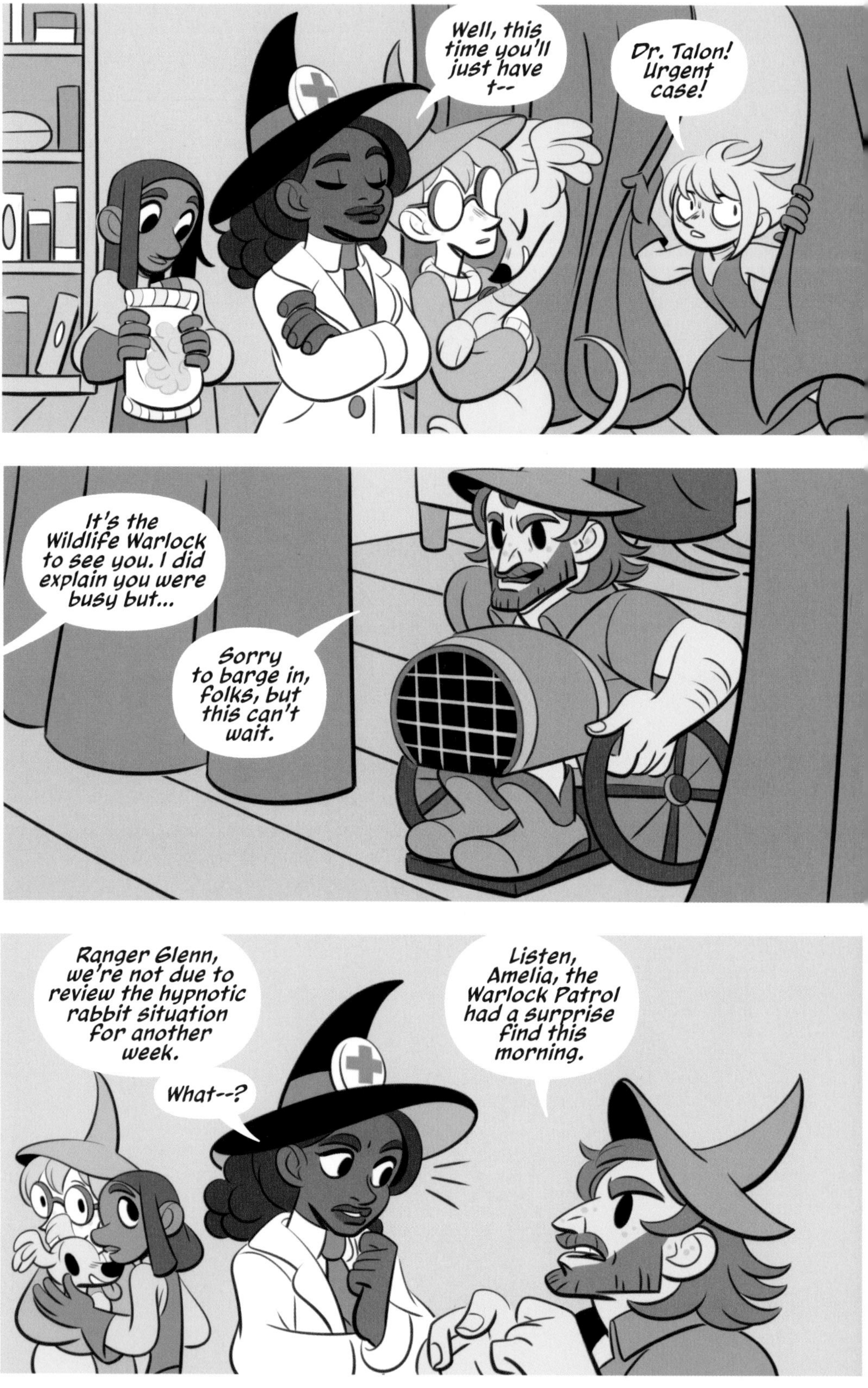
Well, this time you'll just have t--
Dr. Talon! Urgent case!
It's the Wildlife Warlock to see you. I did explain you were busy but...
Sorry to barge in, folks, but this can't wait.
Ranger Glenn, we're not due to review the hypnotic rabbit situation for another week.
What--?
Listen, Amelia, the Warlock Patrol had a surprise find this morning.

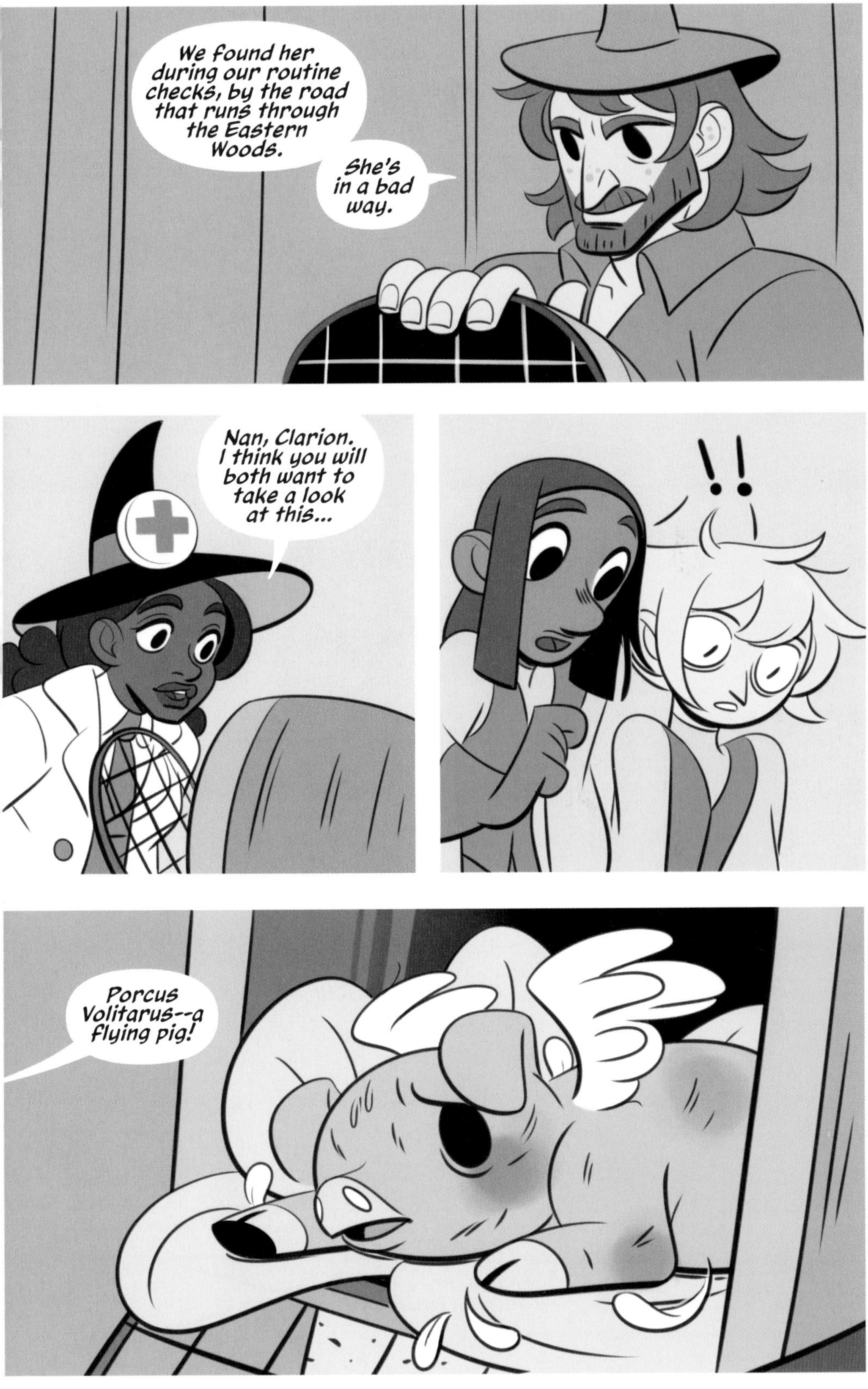

We found her during our routine checks, by the road that runs through the Eastern Woods.
She's in a bad way.
Nan, Clarion. I think you will both want to take a look at this...
!!
Porcus Volitarus--a flying pig!

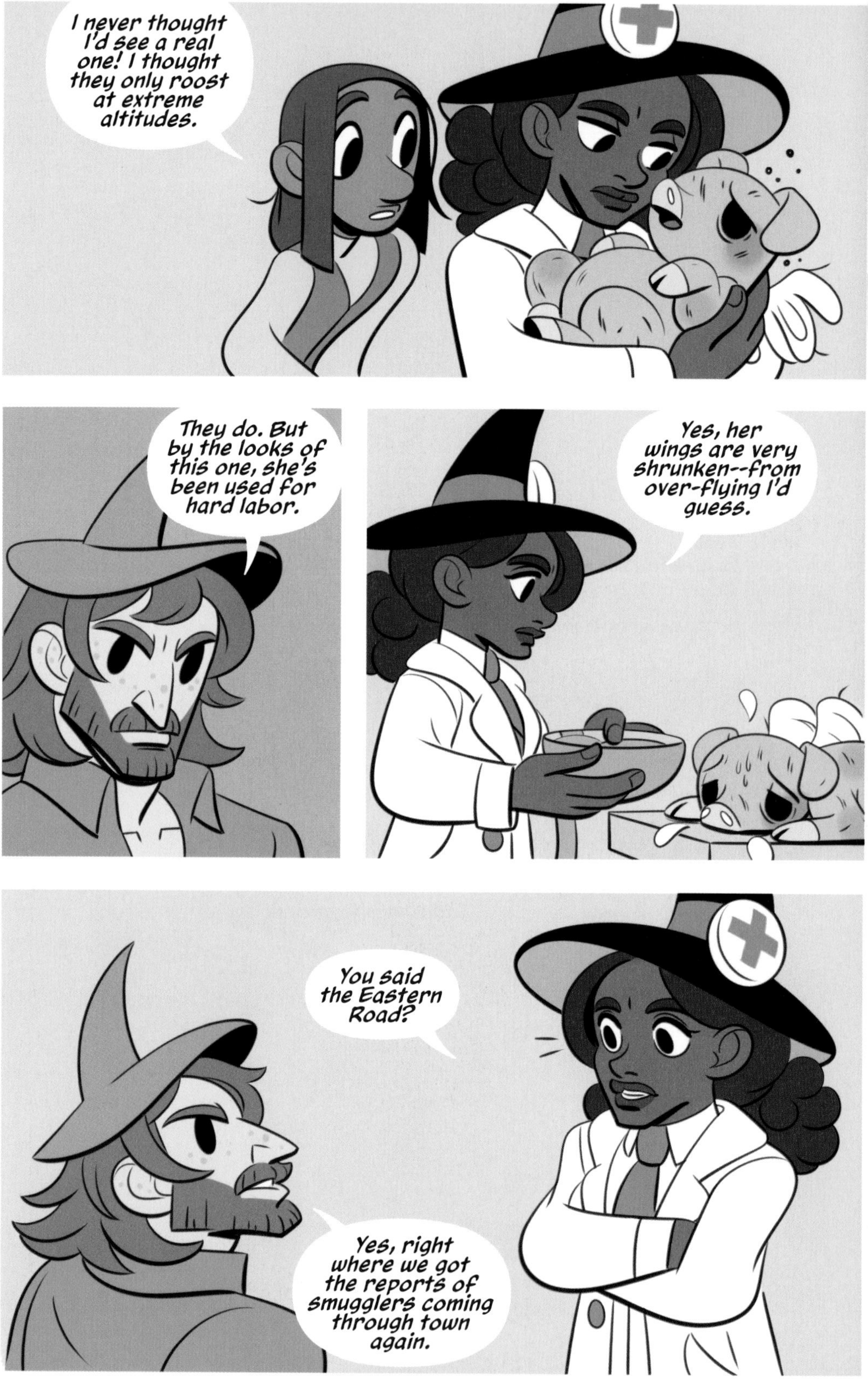
I never thought I'd see a real one! I thought they only roost at extreme altitudes.
They do. But by the looks of this one, she's been used for hard labor.
Yes, her wings are very shrunken--from over-flying I'd guess.
You said the Eastern Road?
Yes, right where we got the reports of smugglers coming through town again.

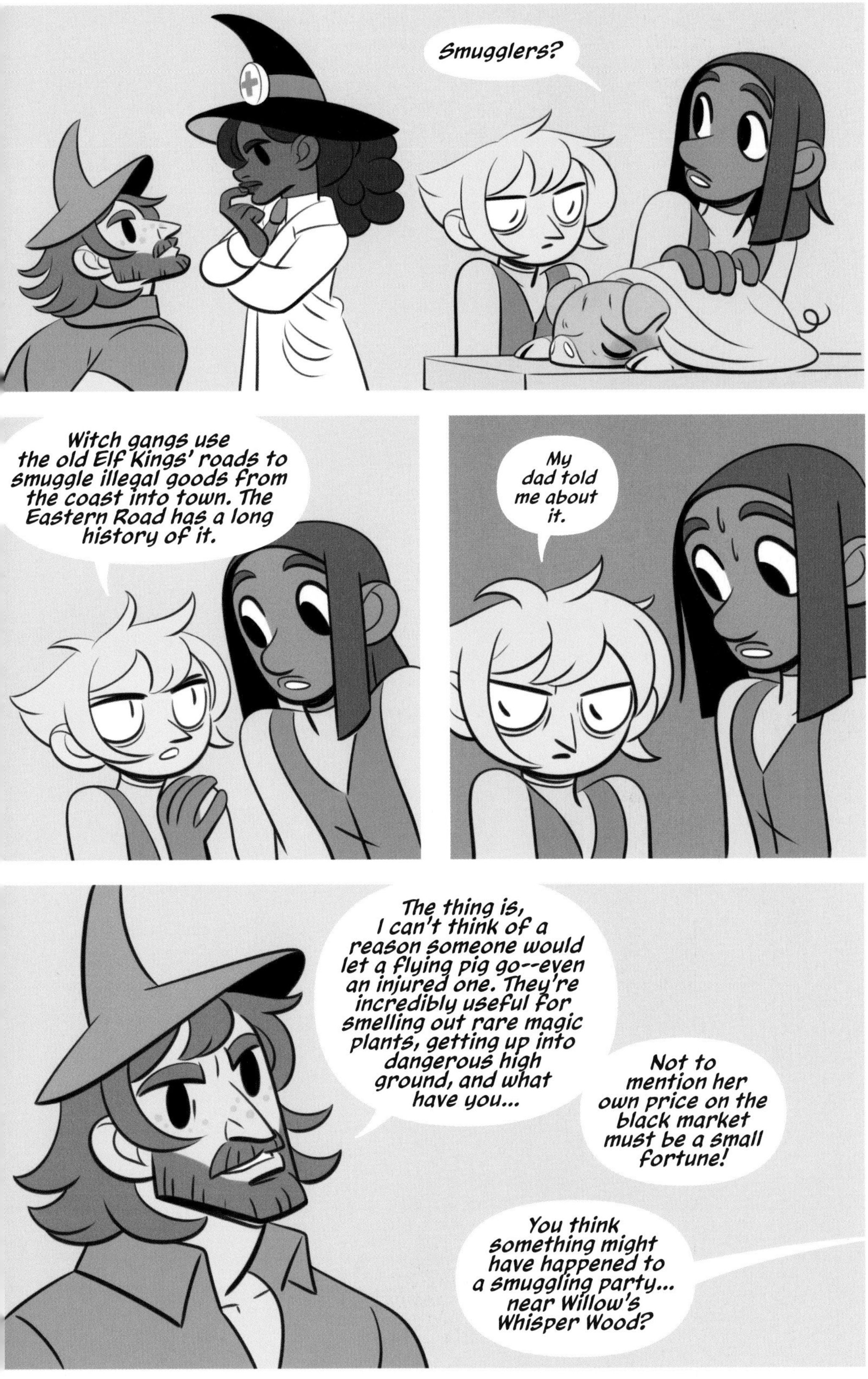
Smugglers?
Witch gangs use the old Elf Kings' roads to smuggle illegal goods from the coast into town. The Eastern Road has a long history of it.
My dad told me about it.
The thing is, I can't think of a reason someone would let a flying pig go--even an injured one. They're incredibly useful for smelling out rare magic plants, getting up into dangerous high ground, and what have you...
Not to mention her own price on the black market must be a small fortune!
You think something might have happened to a smuggling party... near Willow's Whisper Wood?

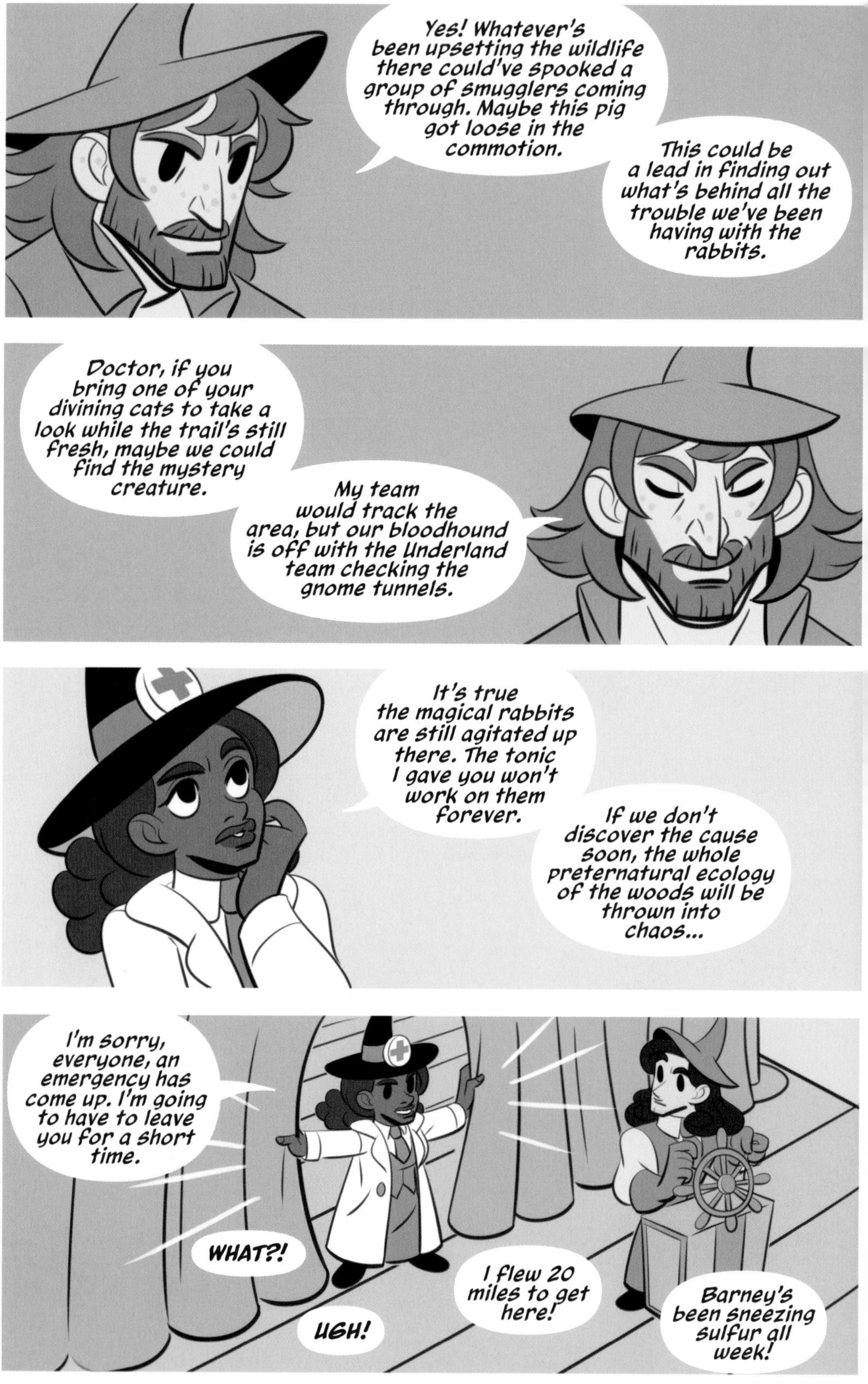
Yes! Whatever's been upsetting the wildlife there could've spooked a group of smugglers coming through. Maybe this pig got loose in the commotion.
This could be a lead in finding out what's behind all the trouble we've been having with the rabbits.
Doctor, if you bring one of your divining cats to take a look while the trail's still fresh, maybe we could find the mystery creature.
My team would track the area, but our bloodhound is off with the Underland team checking the gnome tunnels.
It's true the magical rabbits are still agitated up there. The tonic I gave you won't work on them forever.
If we don't discover the cause soon, the whole preternatural ecology of the woods will be thrown into chaos...
I'm sorry, everyone, an emergency has come up. I'm going to have to leave you for a short time.
WHAT?!
UGH!
I flew 20 miles to get here!
Barney's been sneezing sulfur all week!

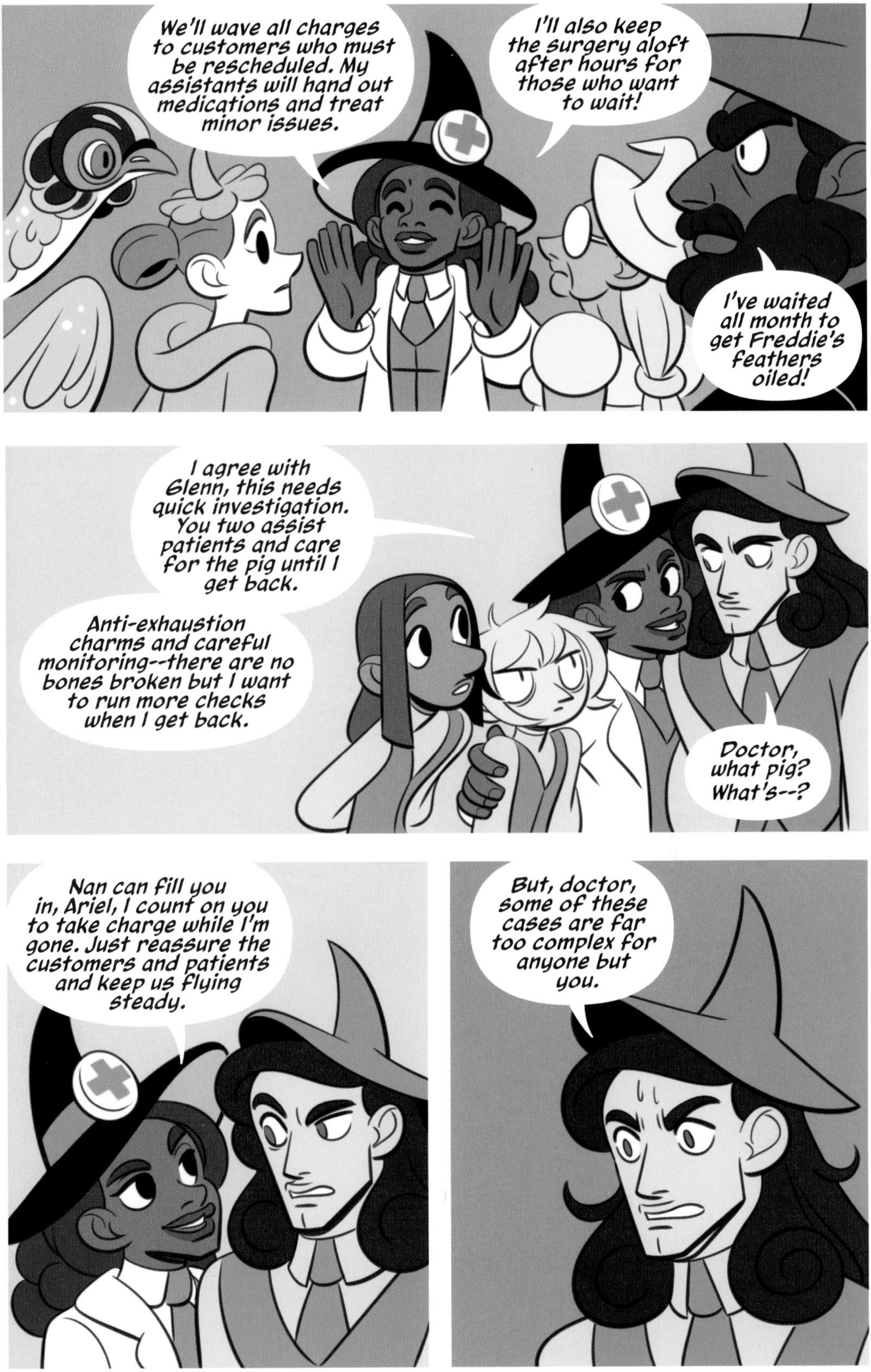
We'll wave all charges to customers who must be rescheduled. My assistants will hand out medications and treat minor issues.
I'll also keep the surgery aloft after hours for those who want to wait!
I've waited all month to get Freddie's feathers oiled!
I agree with Glenn, this needs quick investigation. You two assist patients and care for the pig until I get back.
Anti-exhaustion charms and careful monitoring--there are no bones broken but I want to run more checks when I get back.
Doctor, what pig? What's--?
Nan can fill you in, Ariel, I count on you to take charge while I'm gone. Just reassure the customers and patients and keep us flying steady.
But, doctor, some of these cases are far too complex for anyone but you.

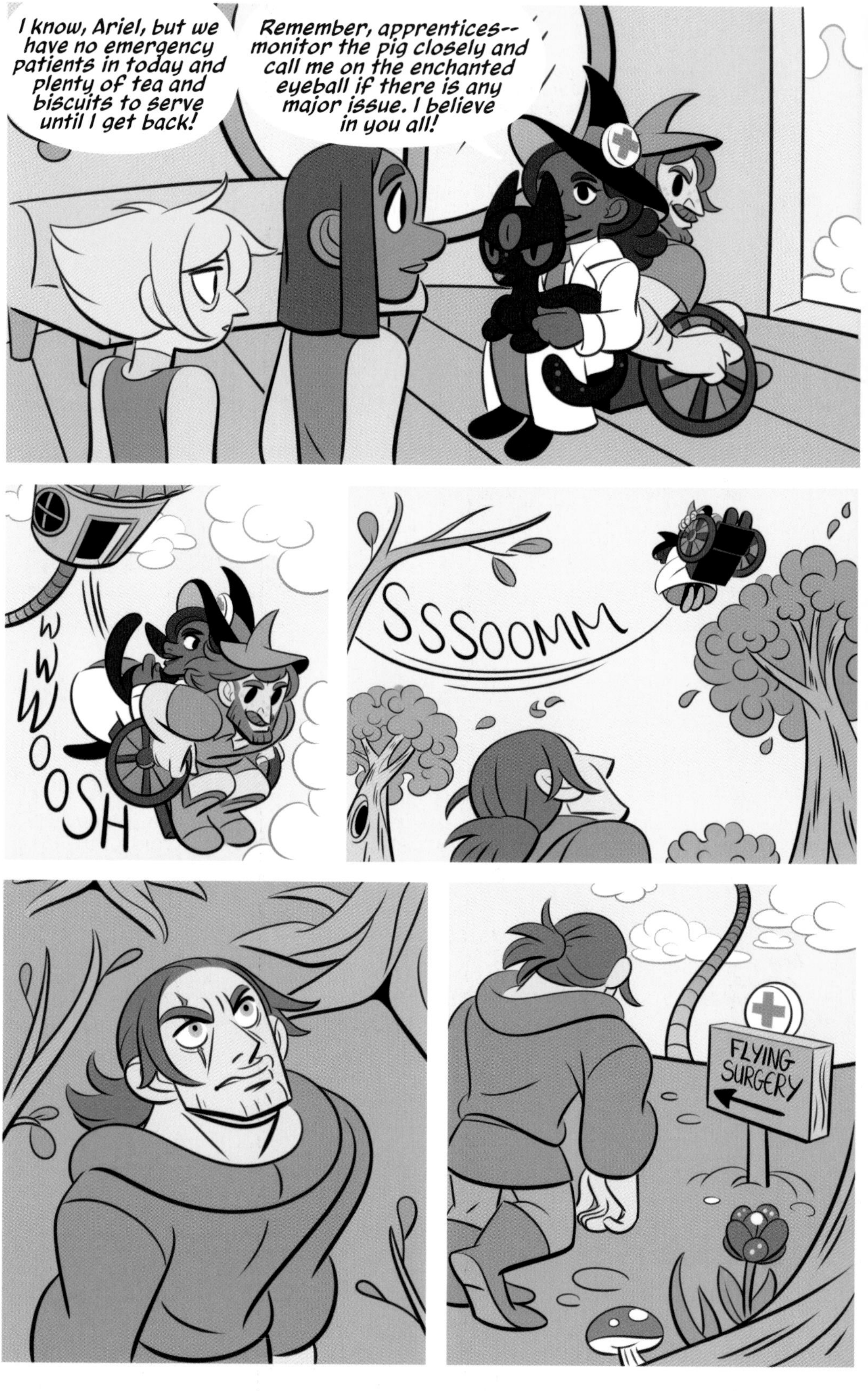
I know, Ariel, but we have no emergency patients in today and plenty of tea and biscuits to serve until I get back!
Remember, apprentices-- monitor the pig closely and call me on the enchanted eyeball if there is any major issue. I believe in you all!
WWWWOOOSH
SSSOOMM
FLYING SURGERY

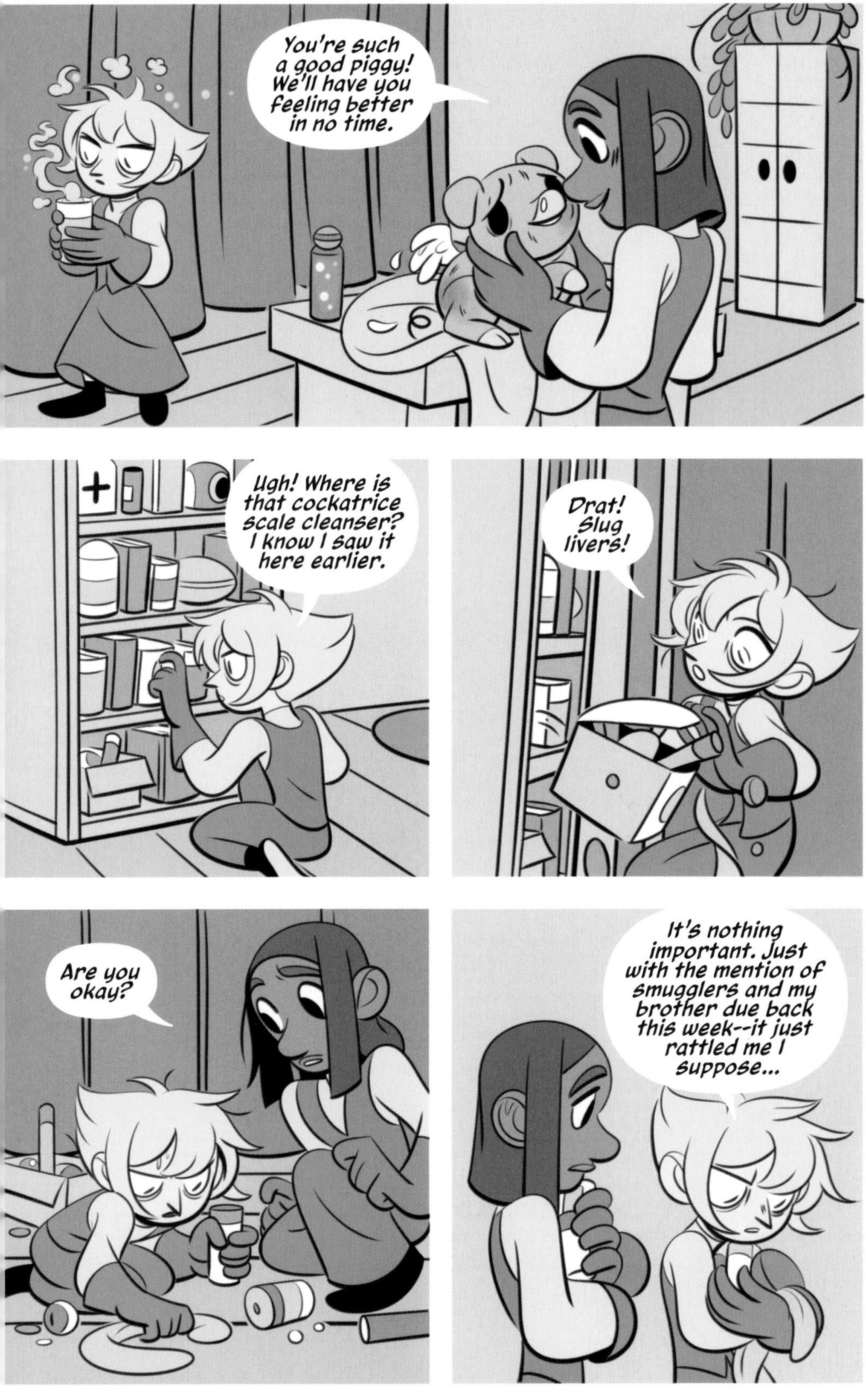
You're such a good piggy! We'll have you feeling better in no time.
Ugh! Where is that cockatrice scale cleanser? I know I saw it here earlier.
Drat! Slug livers!
Are you okay?
It's nothing important. Just with the mention of smugglers and my brother due back this week--it just rattled me I suppose...

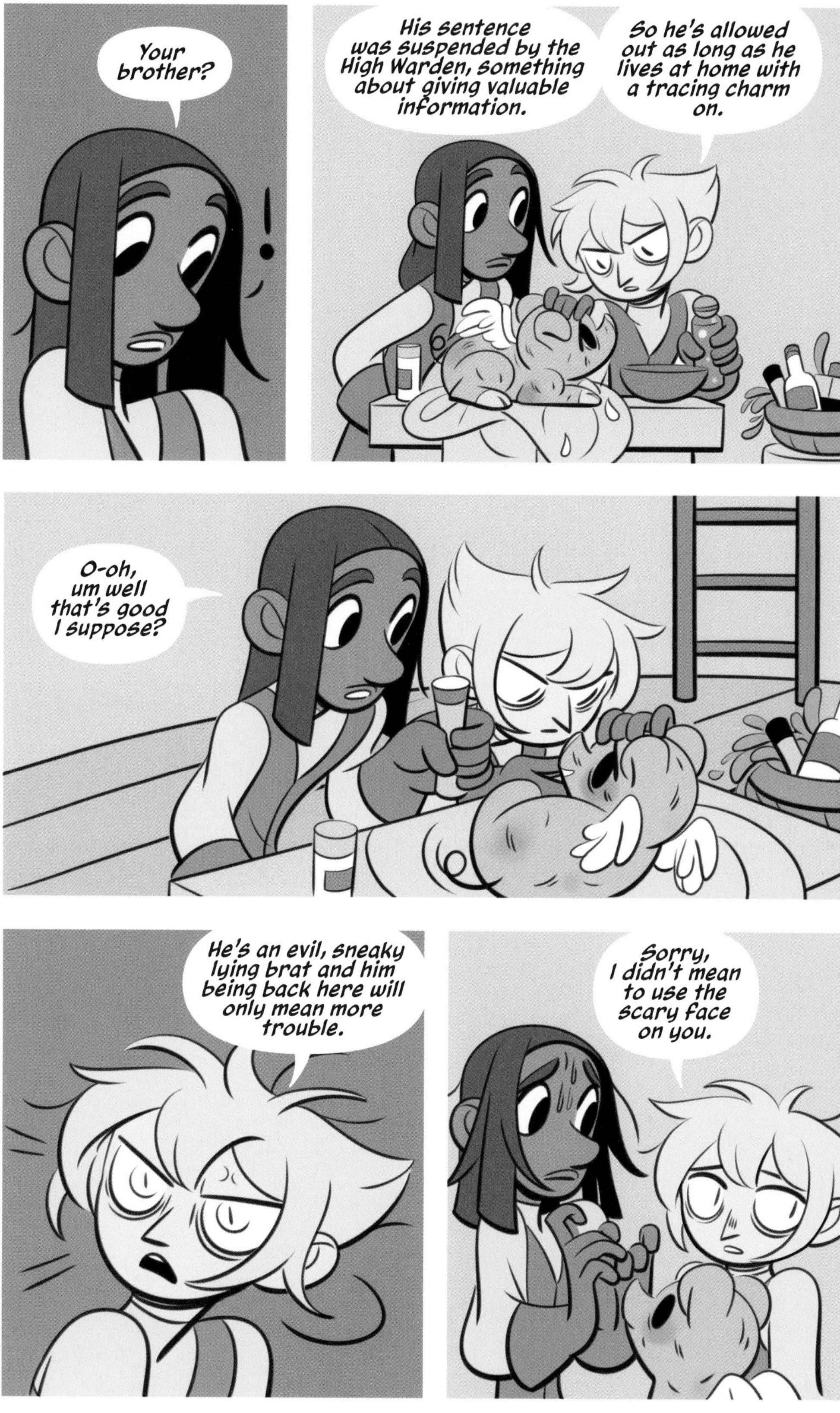
Your brother?
His sentence was suspended by the High Warden, something about giving valuable information.
So he's allowed out as long as he lives at home with a tracing charm on.
O-oh, um well that's good I suppose?
He's an evil, sneaky lying brat and him being back here will only mean more trouble.
Sorry, I didn't mean to use the scary face on you.

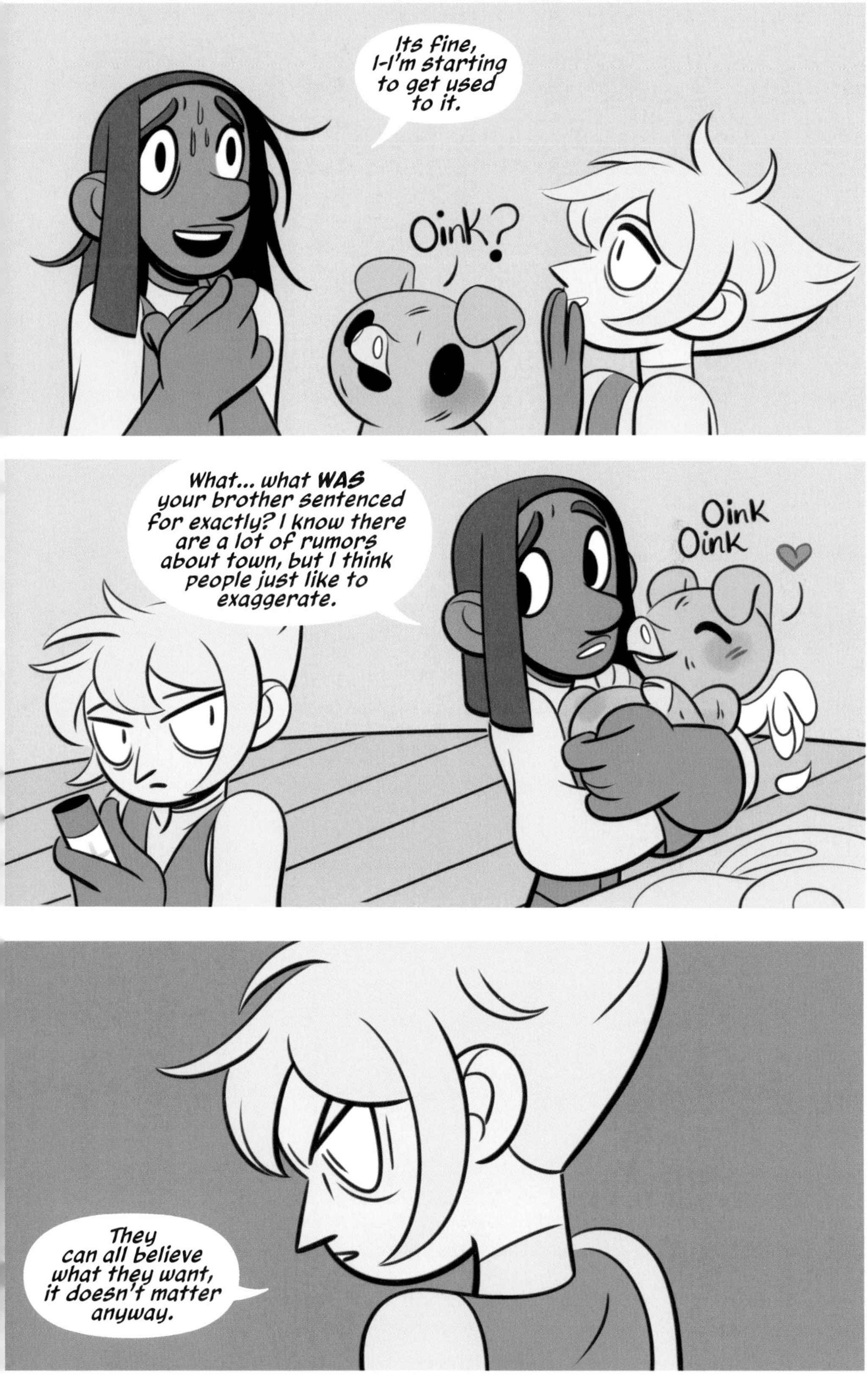
Its fine, I-I'm starting to get used to it.
Oink?
What... what WAS your brother sentenced for exactly? I know there are a lot of rumors about town, but I think people just like to exaggerate.
Oink Oink
They can all believe what they want, it doesn't matter anyway.

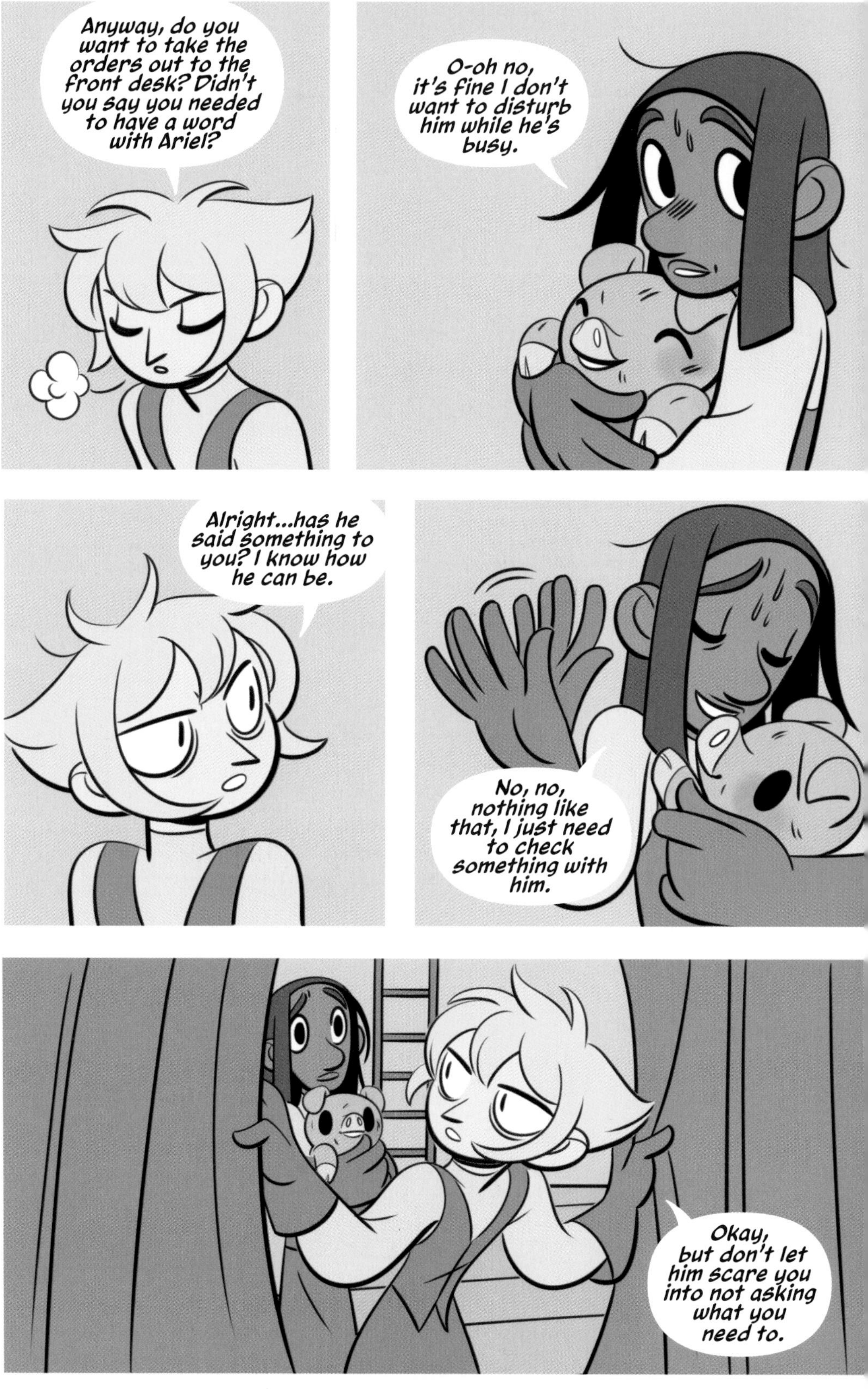
Anyway, do you want to take the orders out to the front desk? Didn't you say you needed to have a word with Ariel?
O-oh no, it's fine I don't want to disturb him while he's busy.
Alright...has he said something to you? I know how he can be.
No, no, nothing like that, I just need to check something with him.
Okay, but don't let him scare you into not asking what you need to.

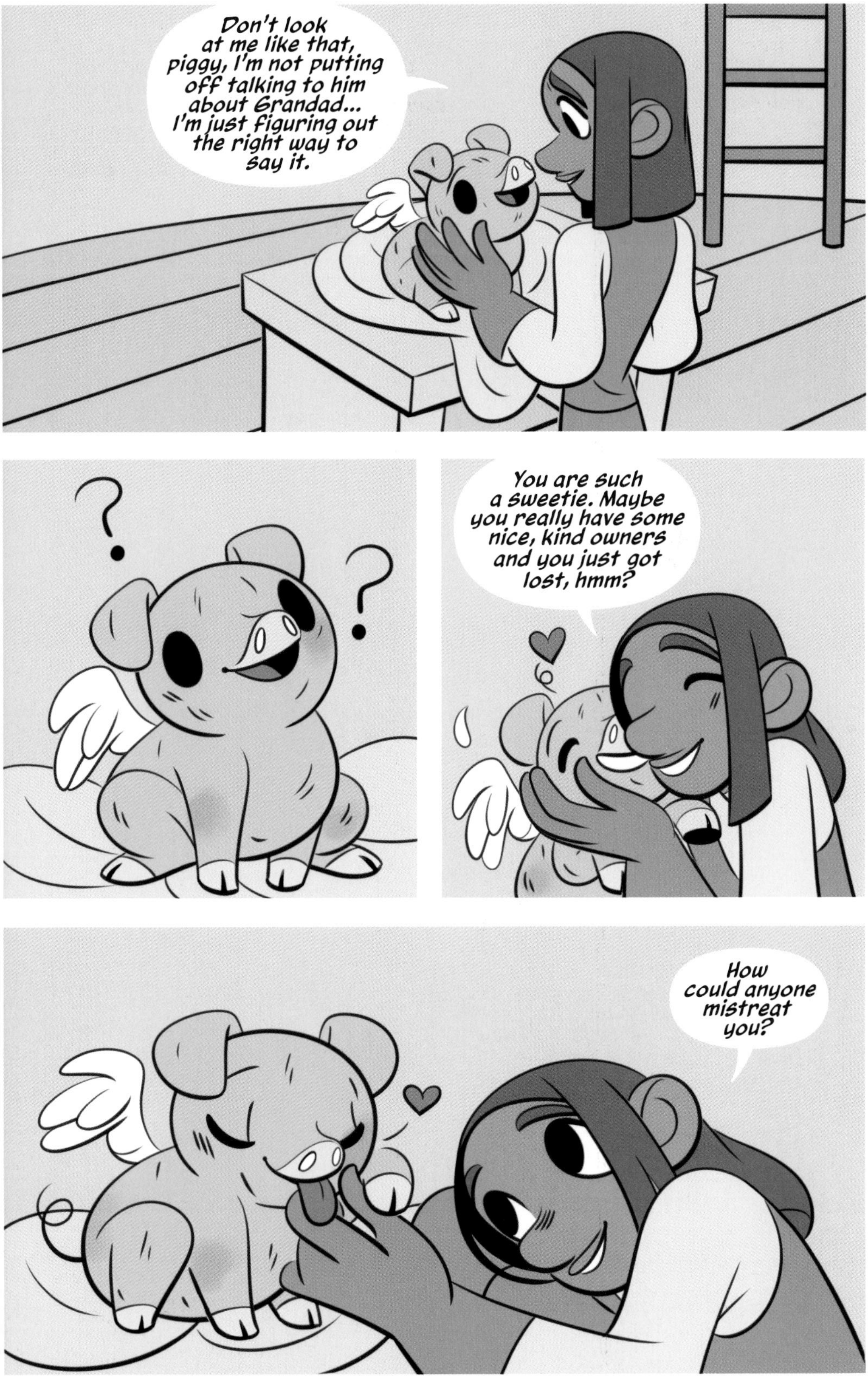
Don't look at me like that, piggy, I'm not putting off talking to him about Grandad... I'm just figuring out the right way to say it.
You are such a sweetie. Maybe you really have some nice, kind owners and you just got lost, hmm?
How could anyone mistreat you?

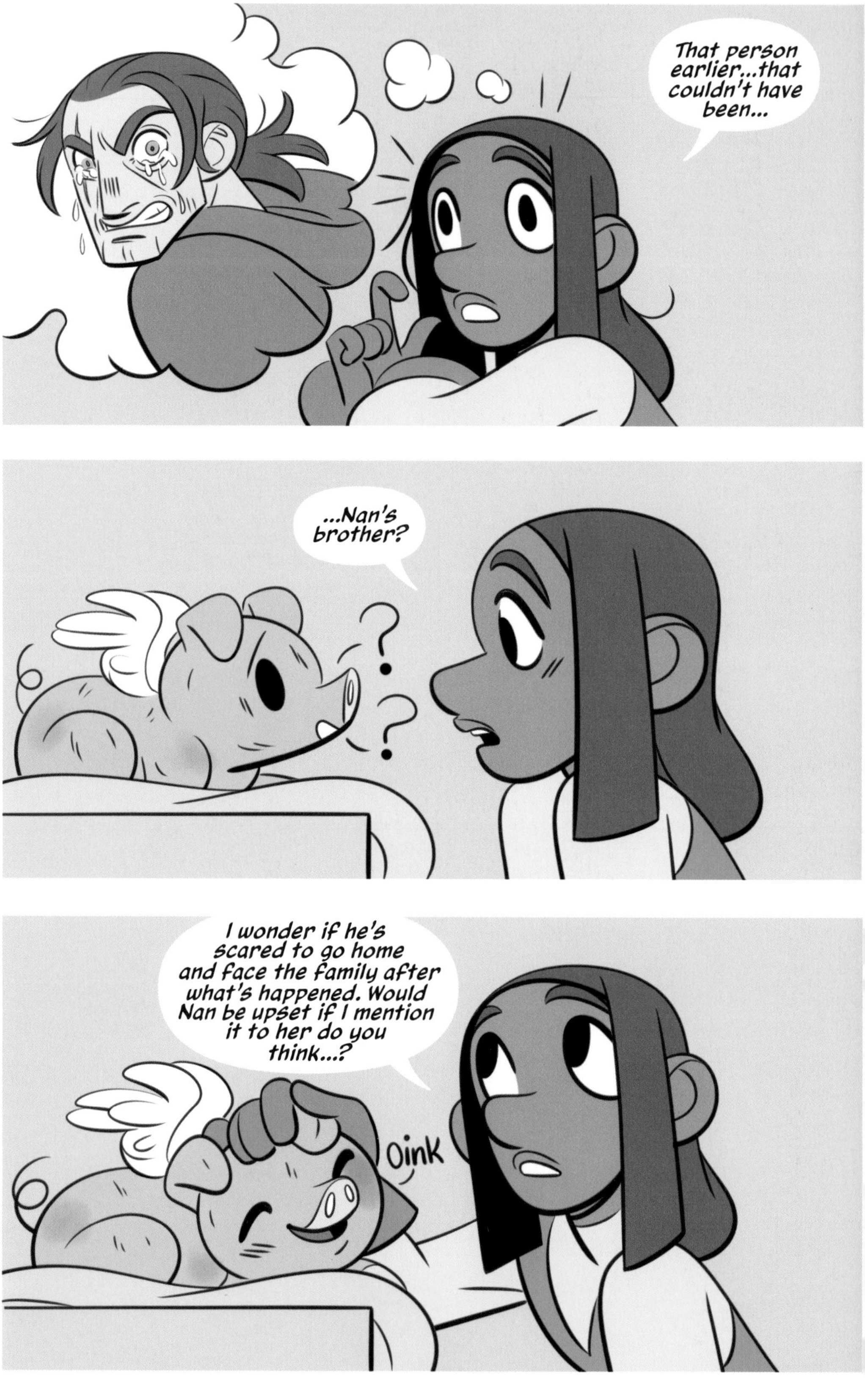
That person earlier...that couldn't have been...
...Nan's brother?
I wonder if he's scared to go home and face the family after what's happened. Would Nan be upset if I mention it to her do you think...?
Oink

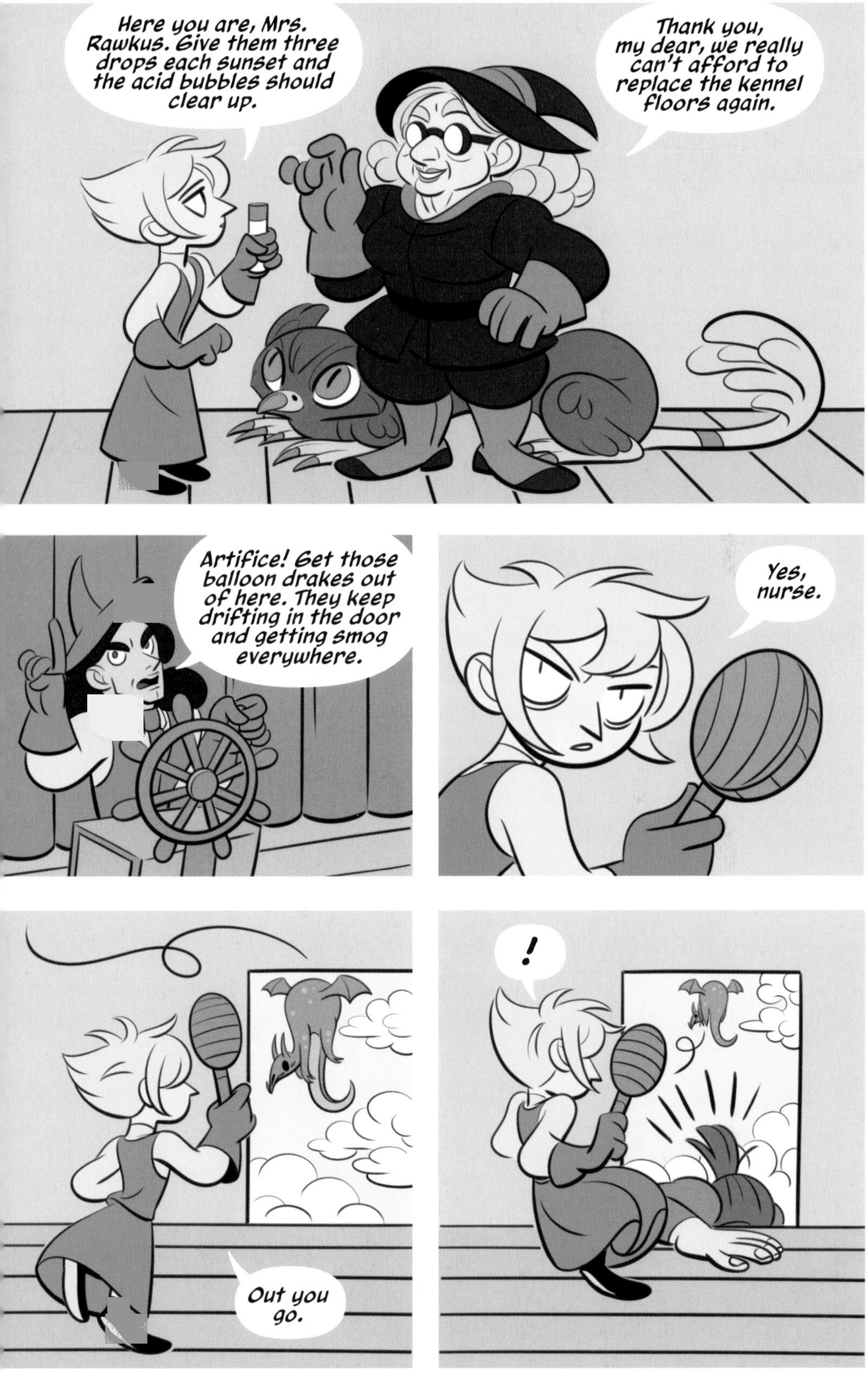
Here you are, Mrs. Rawkus. Give them three drops each sunset and the acid bubbles should clear up.
Thank you, my dear, we really can't afford to replace the kennel floors again.
Artifice! Get those balloon drakes out of here. They keep drifting in the door and getting smog everywhere.
Yes, nurse.
Out you go.
!

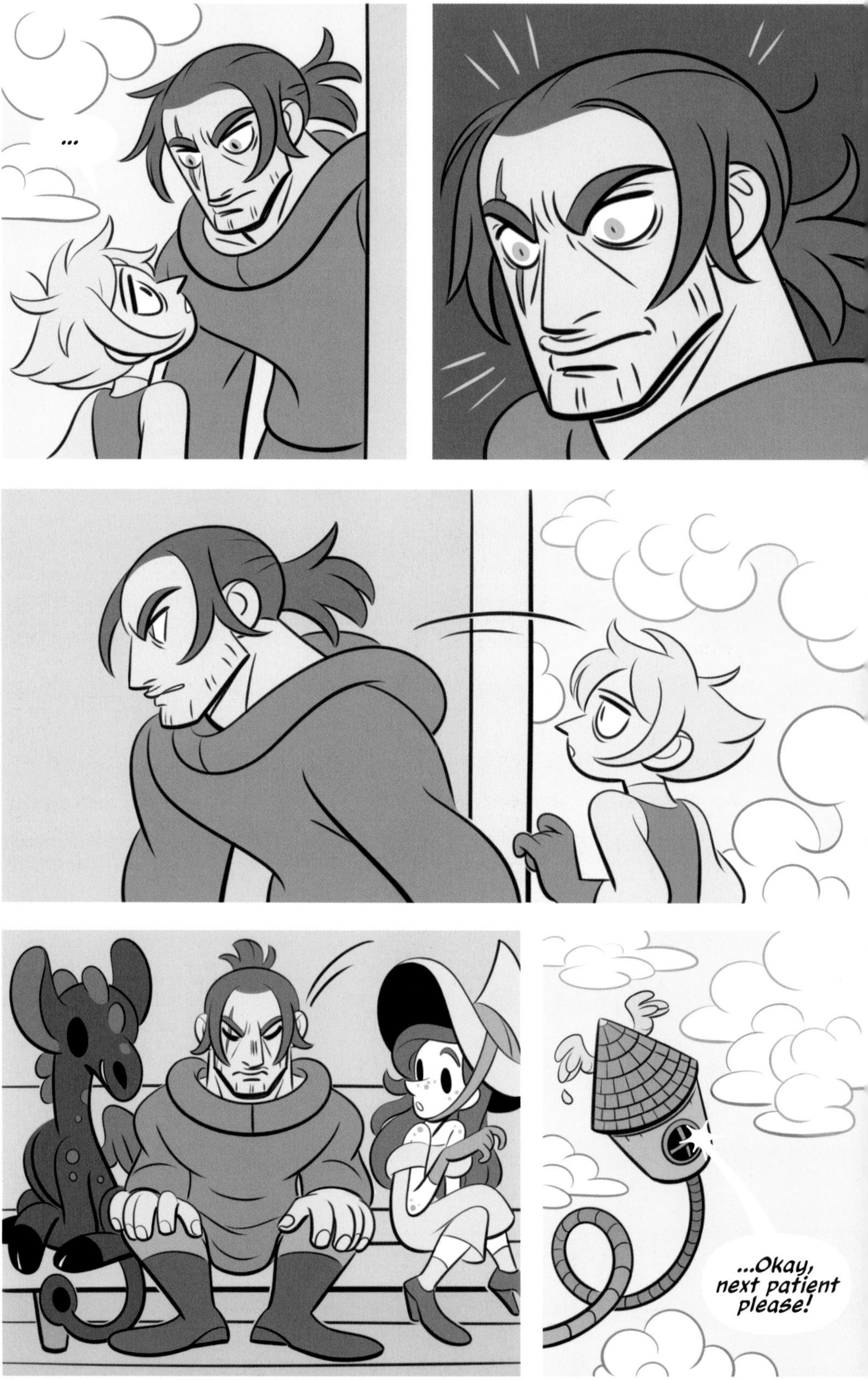
...
...Okay, next patient please!

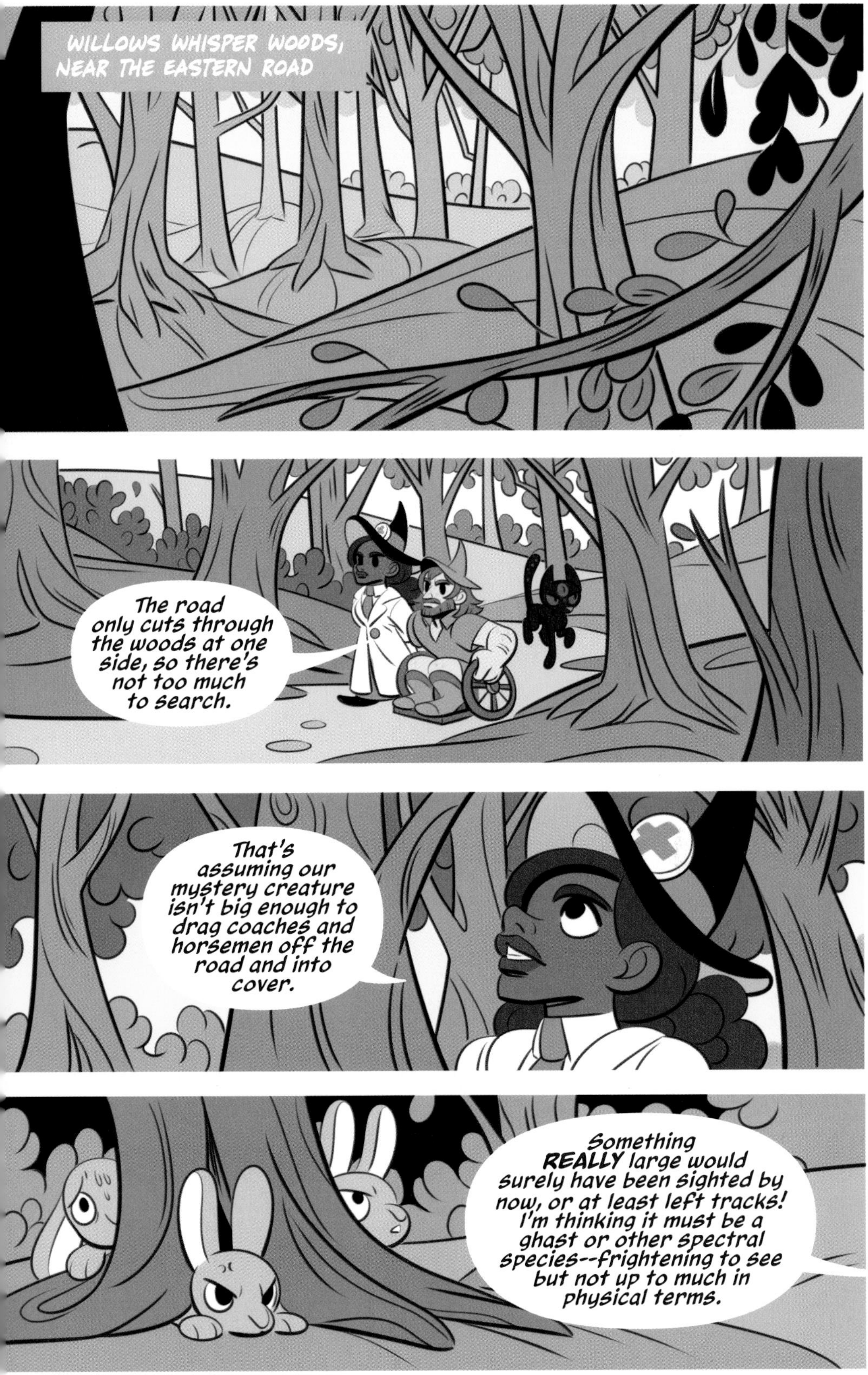
WILLOWS WHISPER WOODS, NEAR THE EASTERN ROAD
The road only cuts through the woods at one side, so there's not too much to search.
That's assuming our mystery creature isn't big enough to drag coaches and horsemen off the road and into cover.
Something REALLY large would surely have been sighted by now, or at least left tracks! I'm thinking it must be a ghast or other spectral species--frightening to see but not up to much in physical terms.

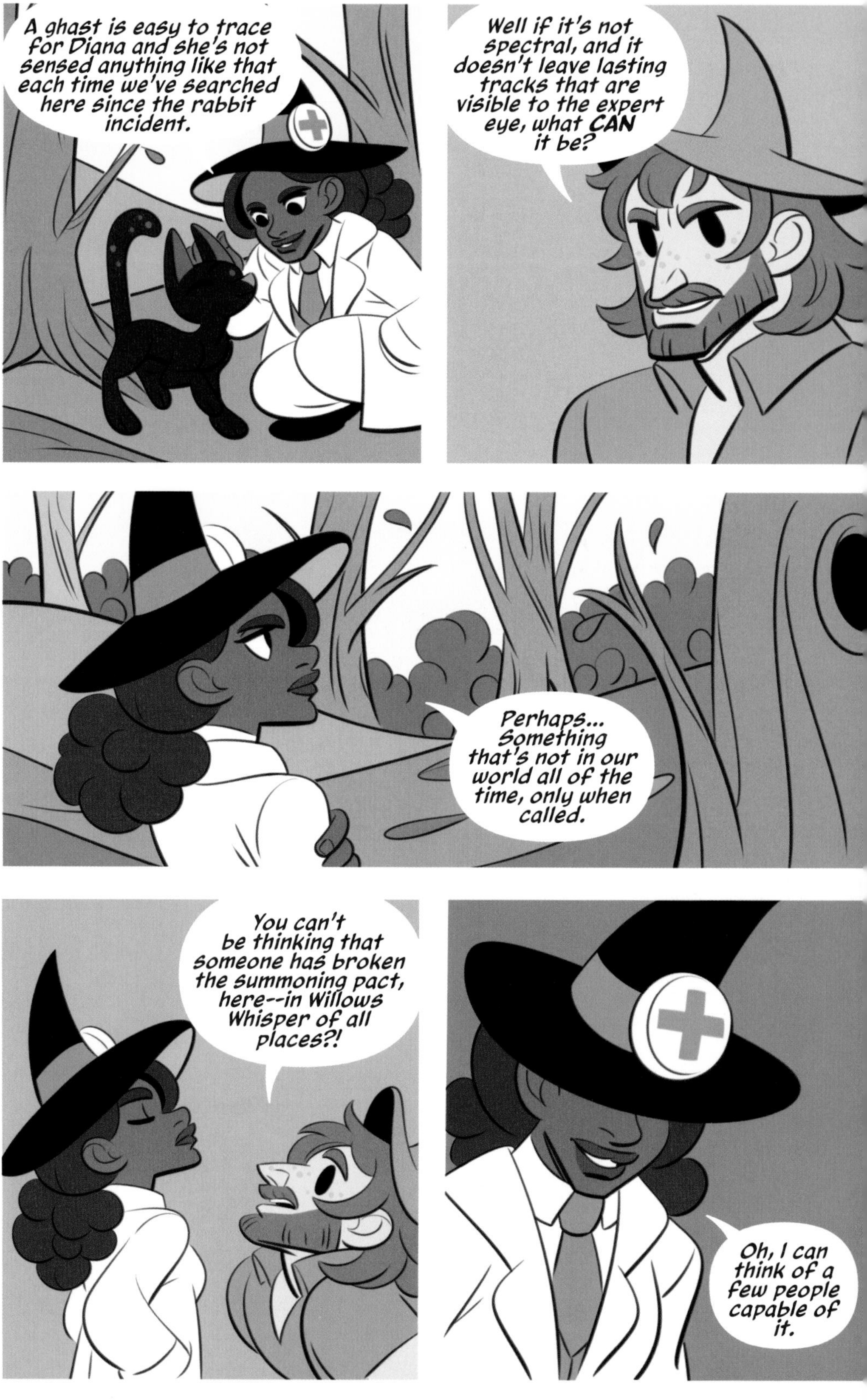
A ghast is easy to trace for Diana and she's not sensed anything like that each time we've searched here since the rabbit incident.
Well if it's not spectral, and it doesn't leave lasting tracks that are visible to the expert eye, what **CAN** it be?
Perhaps... Something that's not in our world all of the time, only when called.
You can't be thinking that someone has broken the summoning pact, here--in Willows Whisper of all places?!
Oh, I can think of a few people capable of it.

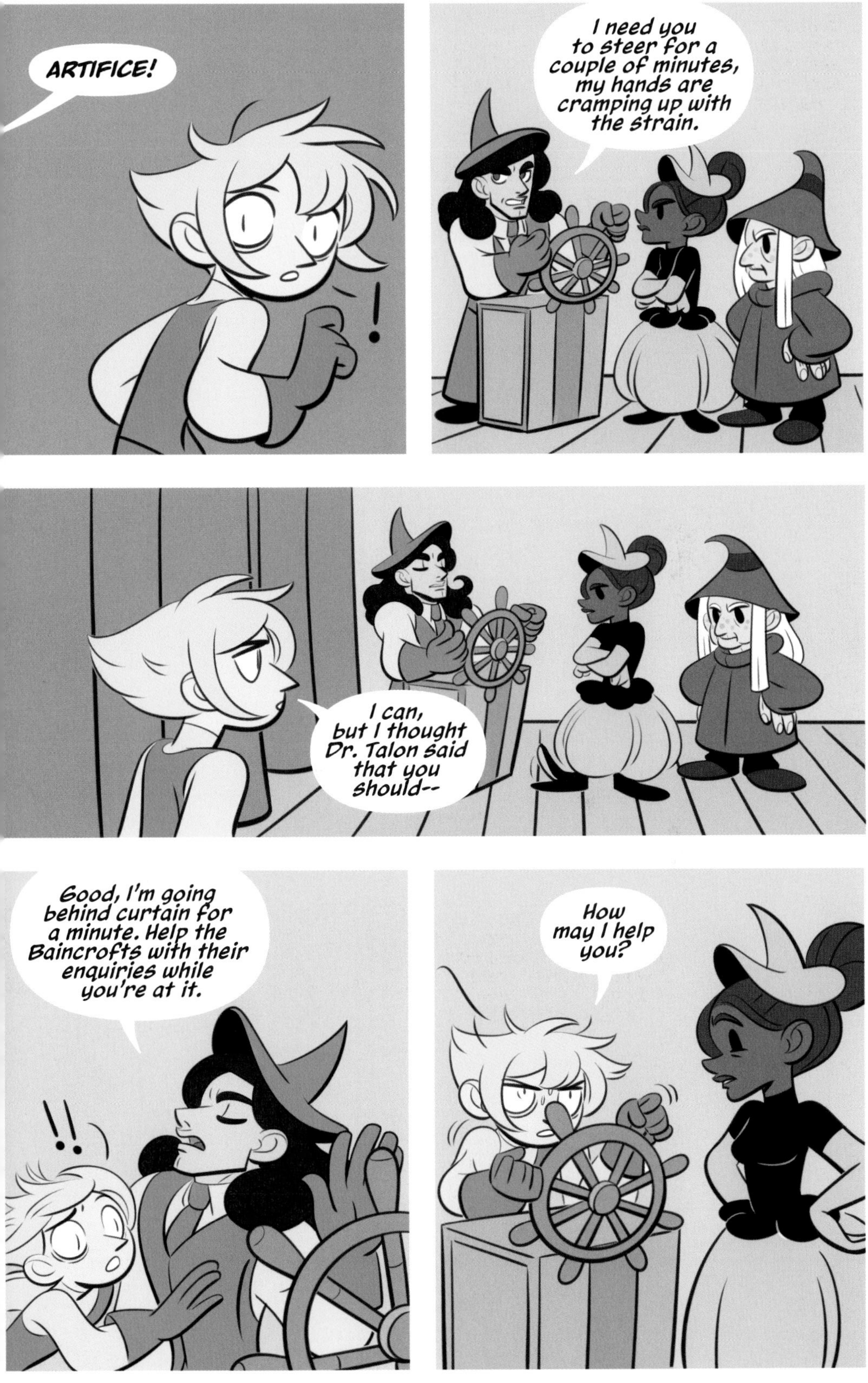
ARTIFICE!
I need you to steer for a couple of minutes, my hands are cramping up with the strain.
I can, but I thought Dr. Talon said that you should--
Good, I'm going behind curtain for a minute. Help the Baincrofts with their enquiries while you're at it.
!!
How may I help you?

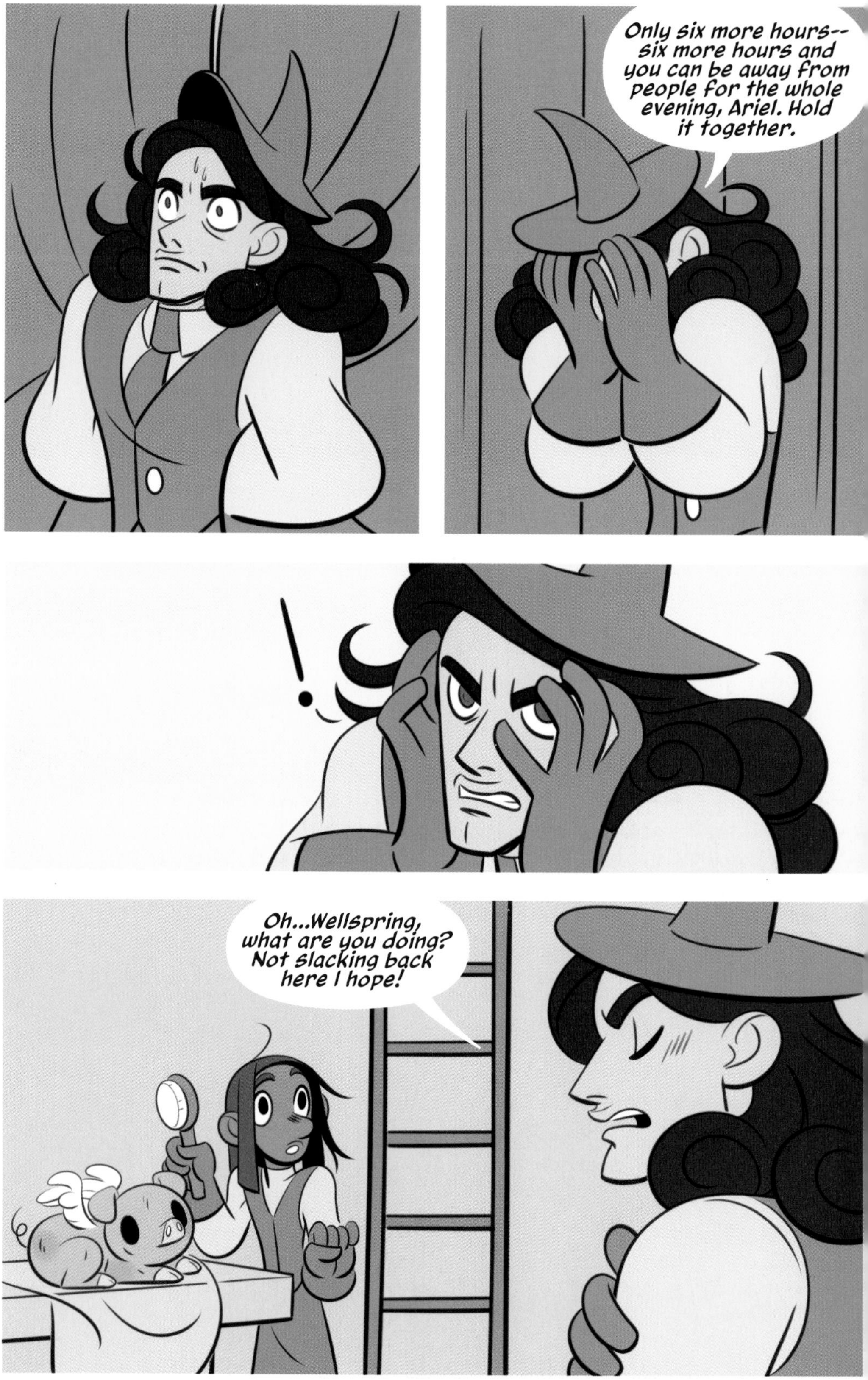
Only six more hours--six more hours and you can be away from people for the whole evening, Ariel. Hold it together.
!
Oh...Wellspring, what are you doing? Not slacking back here I hope!

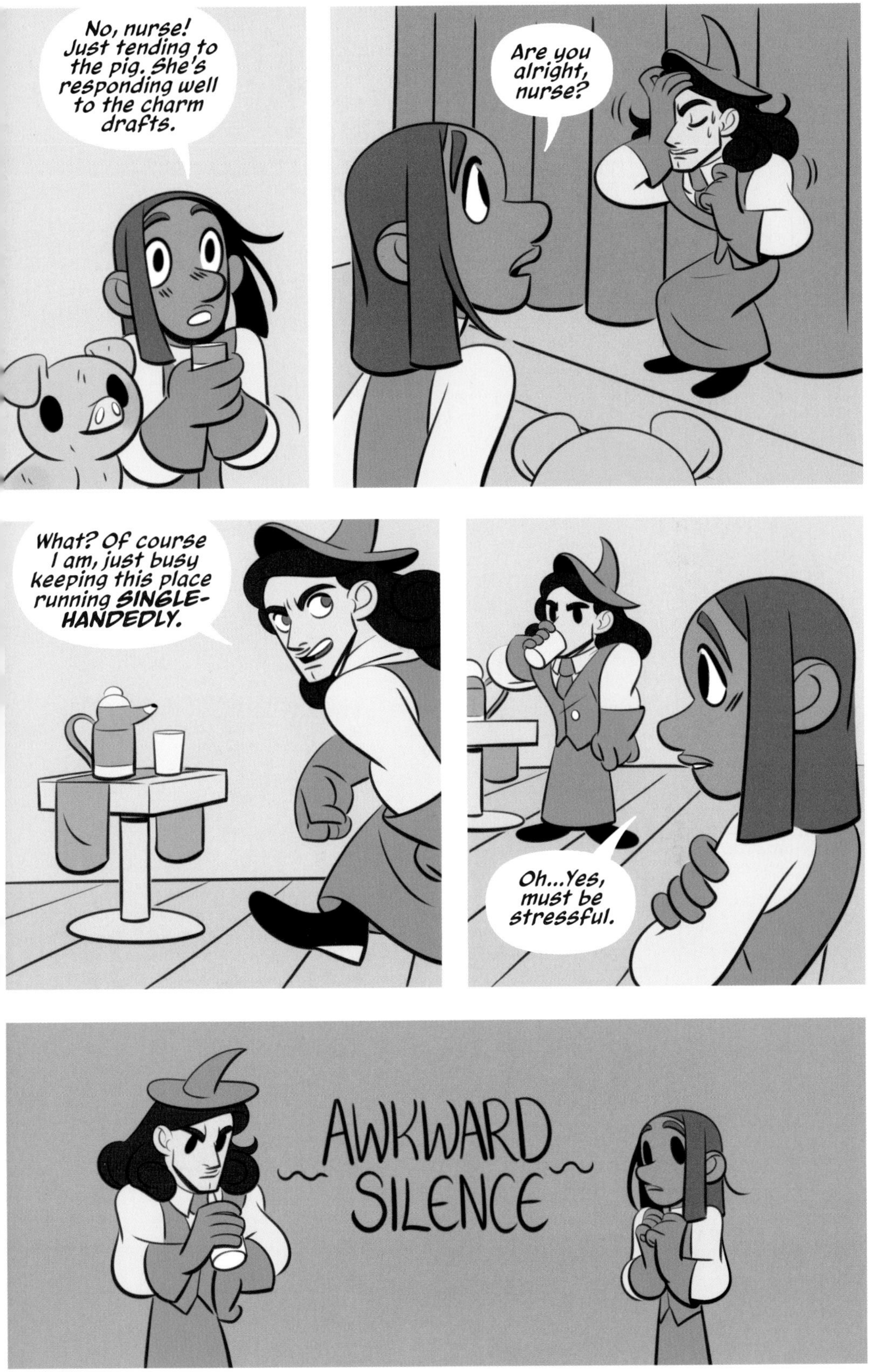
No, nurse! Just tending to the pig. She's responding well to the charm drafts.
Are you alright, nurse?
What? Of course I am, just busy keeping this place running **SINGLE-HANDEDLY.**
Oh...Yes, must be stressful.
~AWKWARD SILENCE~

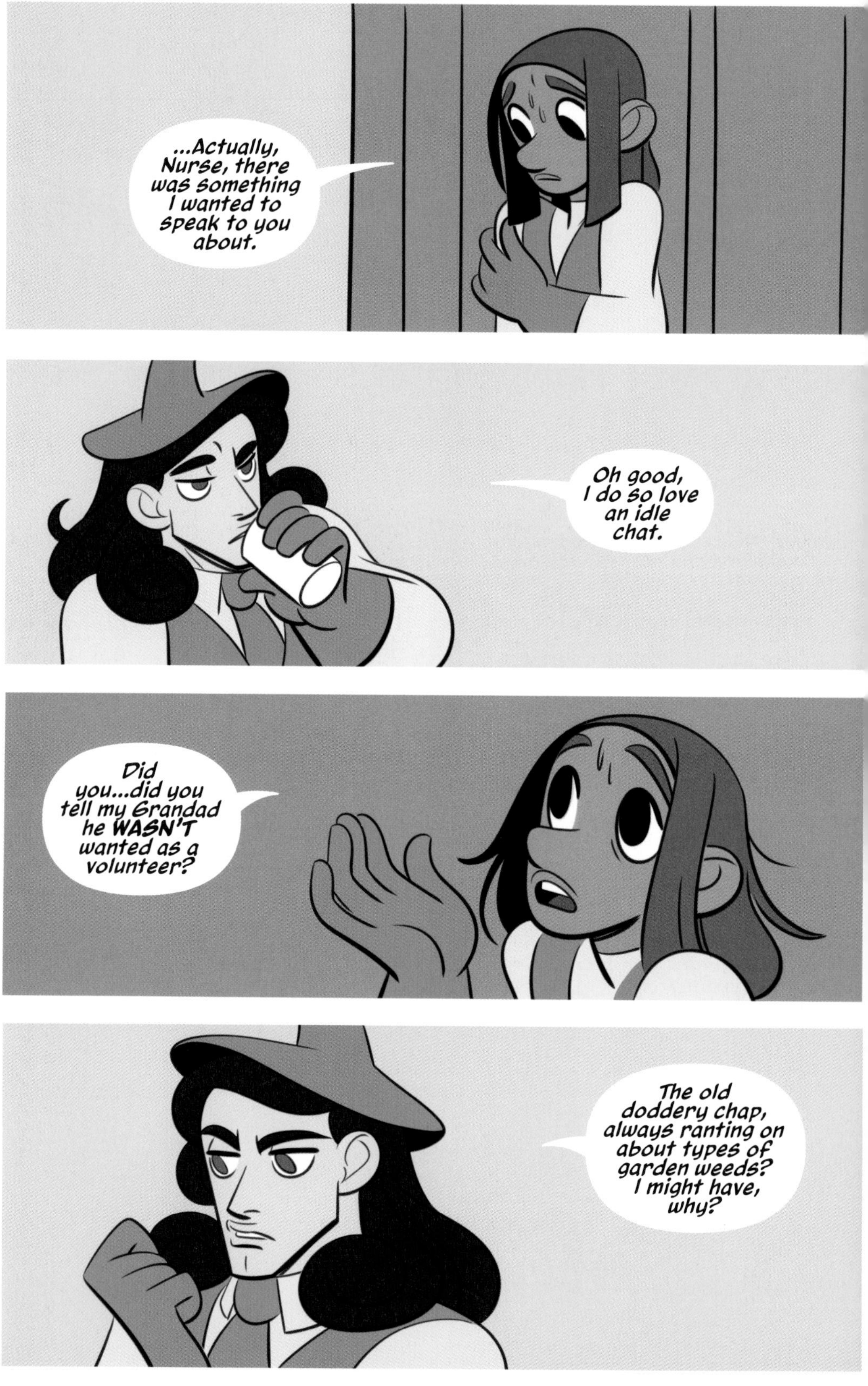
...Actually, Nurse, there was something I wanted to speak to you about.
Oh good, I do so love an idle chat.
Did you...did you tell my Grandad he WASN'T wanted as a volunteer?
The old doddery chap, always ranting on about types of garden weeds? I might have, why?

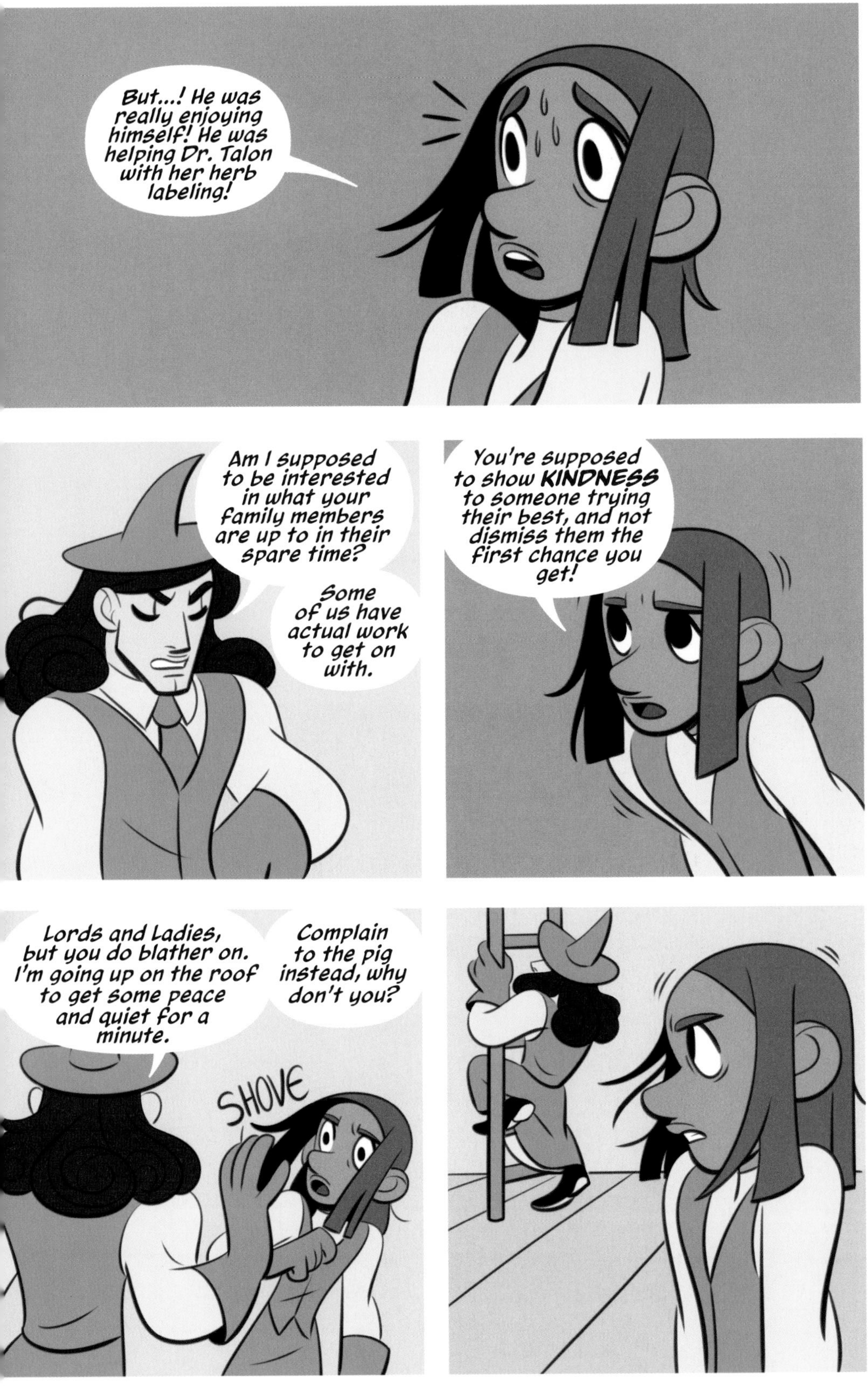
But...! He was really enjoying himself! He was helping Dr. Talon with her herb labeling!
Am I supposed to be interested in what your family members are up to in their spare time?
Some of us have actual work to get on with.
You're supposed to show KINDNESS to someone trying their best, and not dismiss them the first chance you get!
Lords and Ladies, but you do blather on. I'm going up on the roof to get some peace and quiet for a minute.
Complain to the pig instead, why don't you?
SHOVE

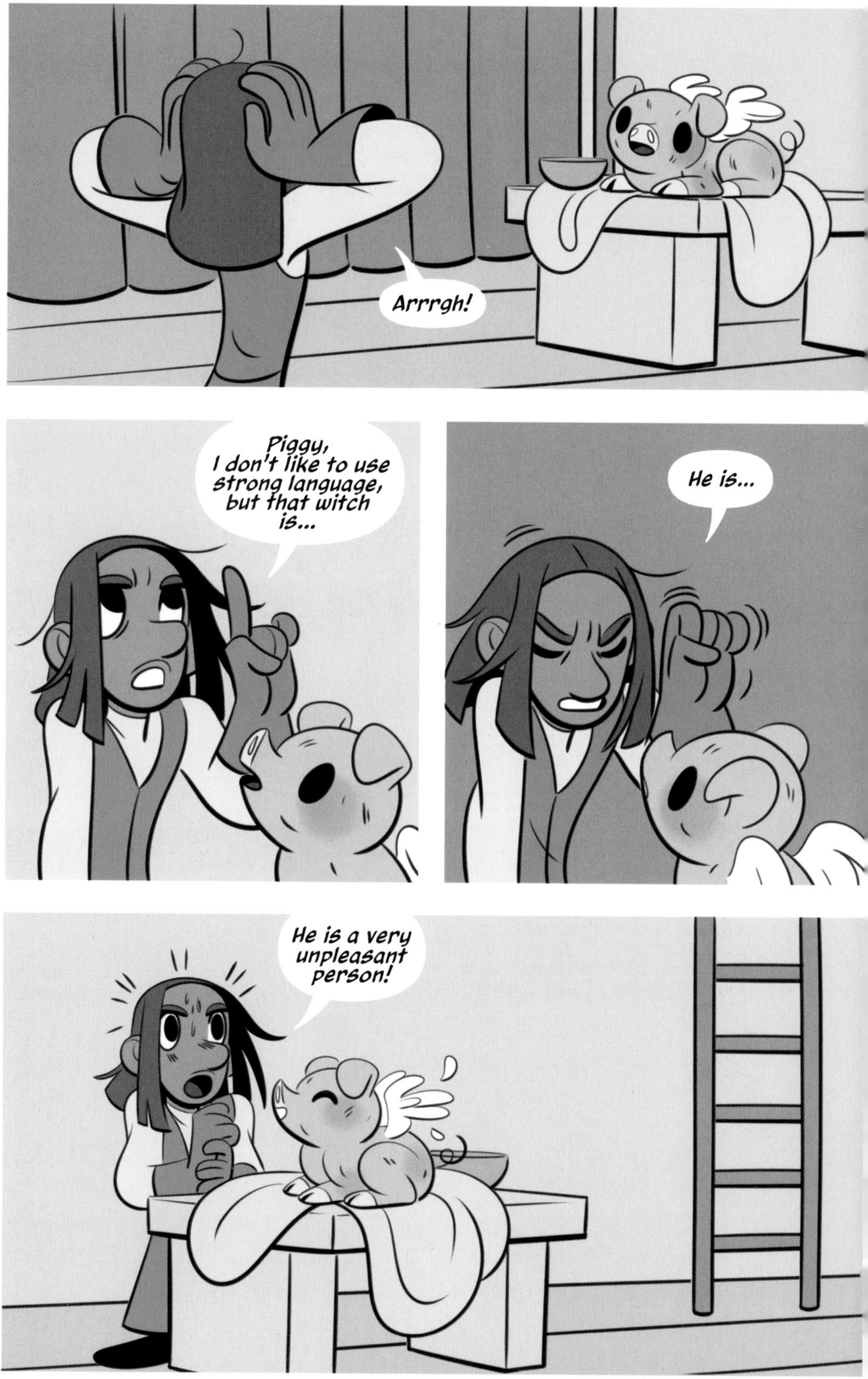
Arrrgh!
Piggy, I don't like to use strong language, but that witch is...
He is...
He is a very unpleasant person!

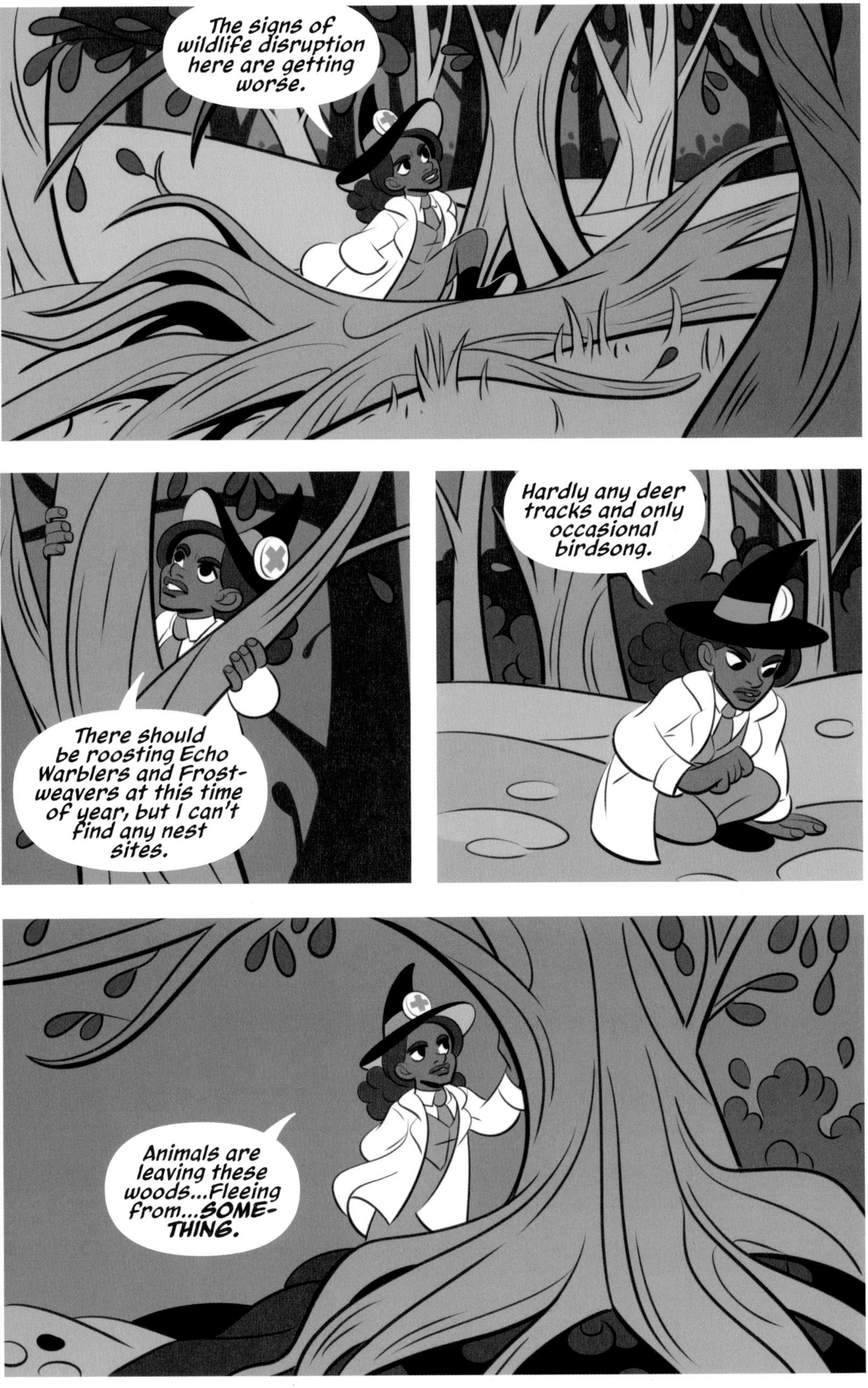
The signs of wildlife disruption here are getting worse.
There should be roosting Echo Warblers and Frost-weavers at this time of year, but I can't find any nest sites.
Hardly any deer tracks and only occasional birdsong.
Animals are leaving these woods...Fleeing from...SOME-THING.

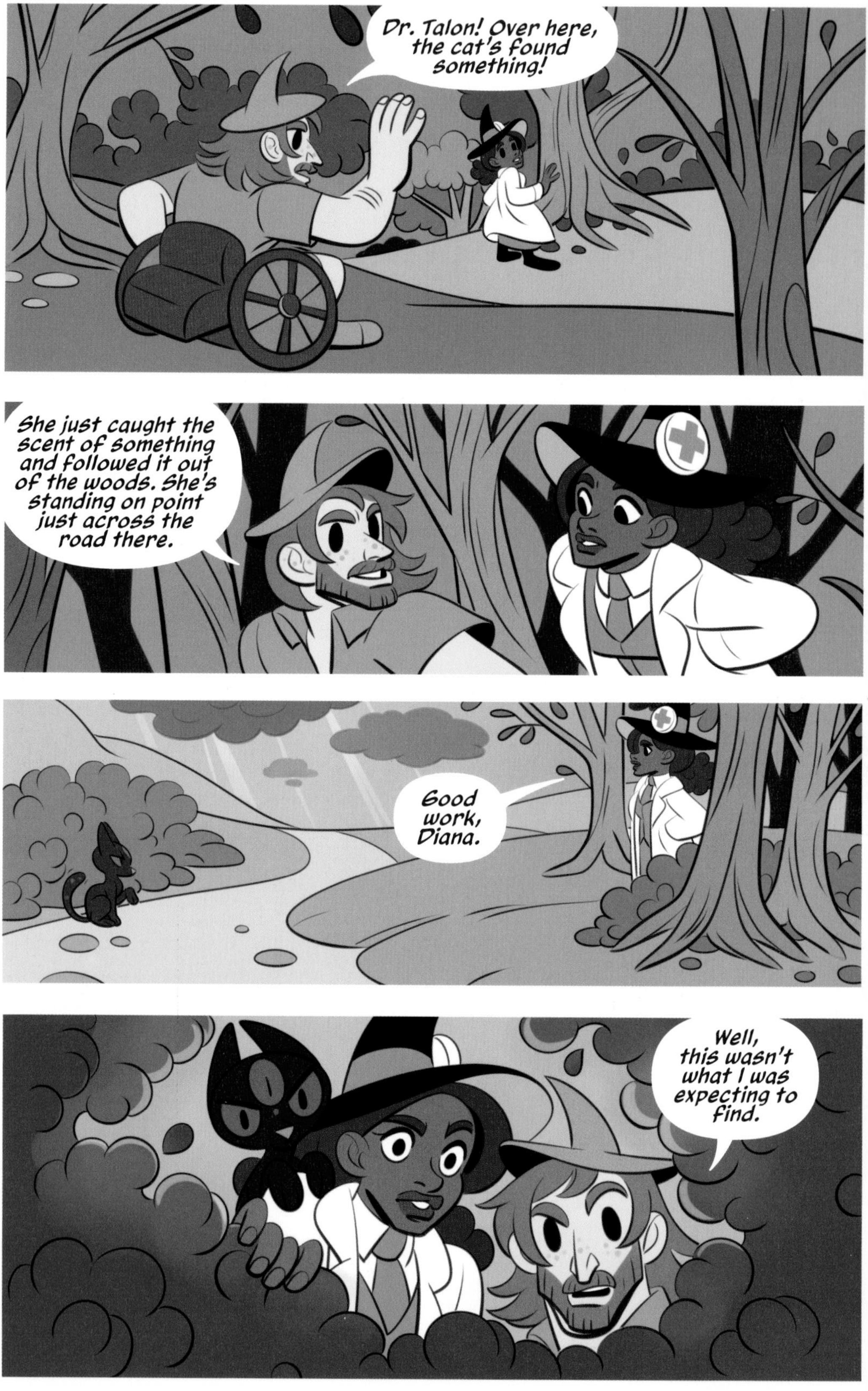
Dr. Talon! Over here, the cat's found something!
She just caught the scent of something and followed it out of the woods. She's standing on point just across the road there.
Good work, Diana.
Well, this wasn't what I was expecting to find.

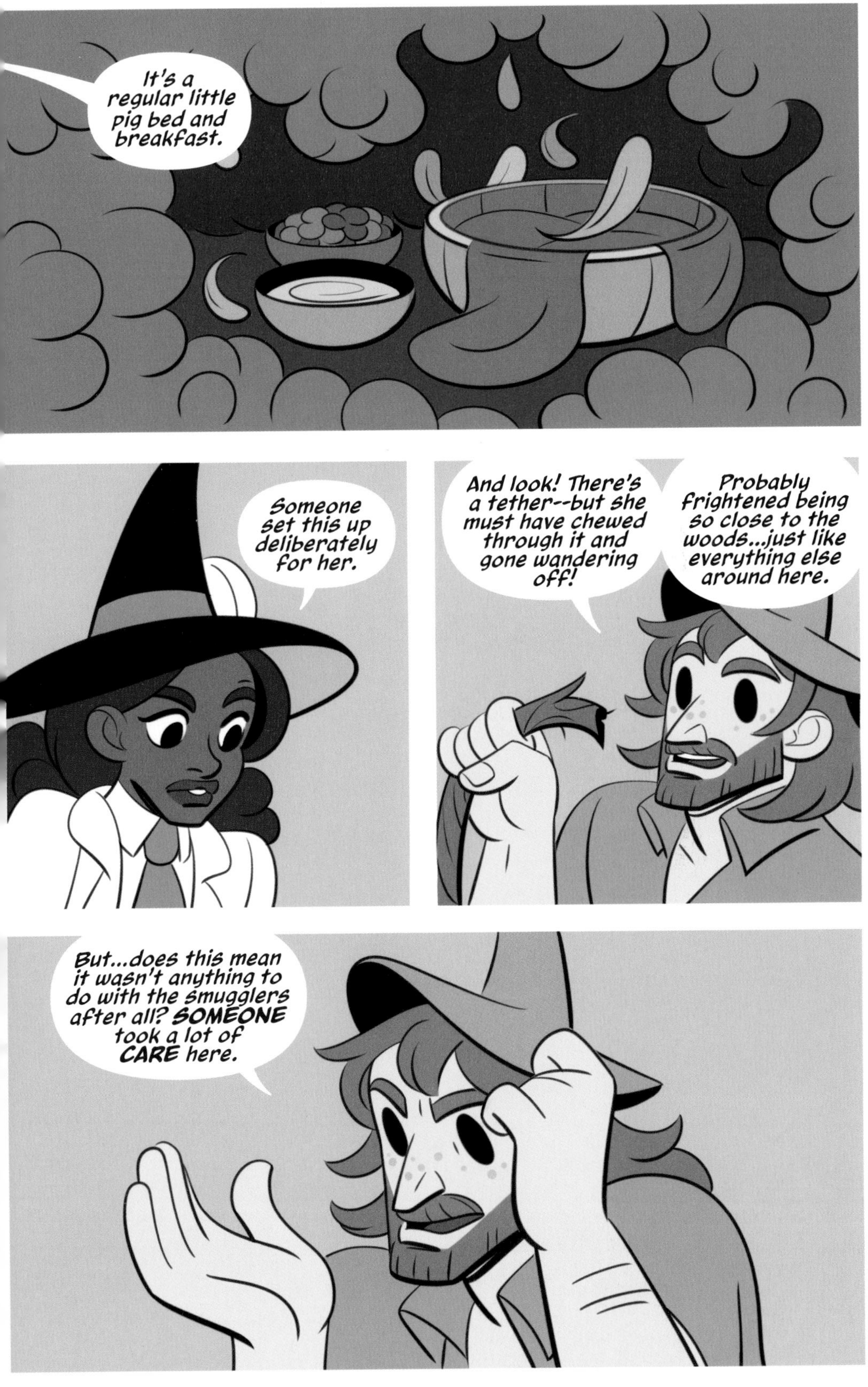
It's a regular little pig bed and breakfast.
Someone set this up deliberately for her.
And look! There's a tether--but she must have chewed through it and gone wandering off!
Probably frightened being so close to the woods...just like everything else around here.
But...does this mean it wasn't anything to do with the smugglers after all? SOMEONE took a lot of CARE here.

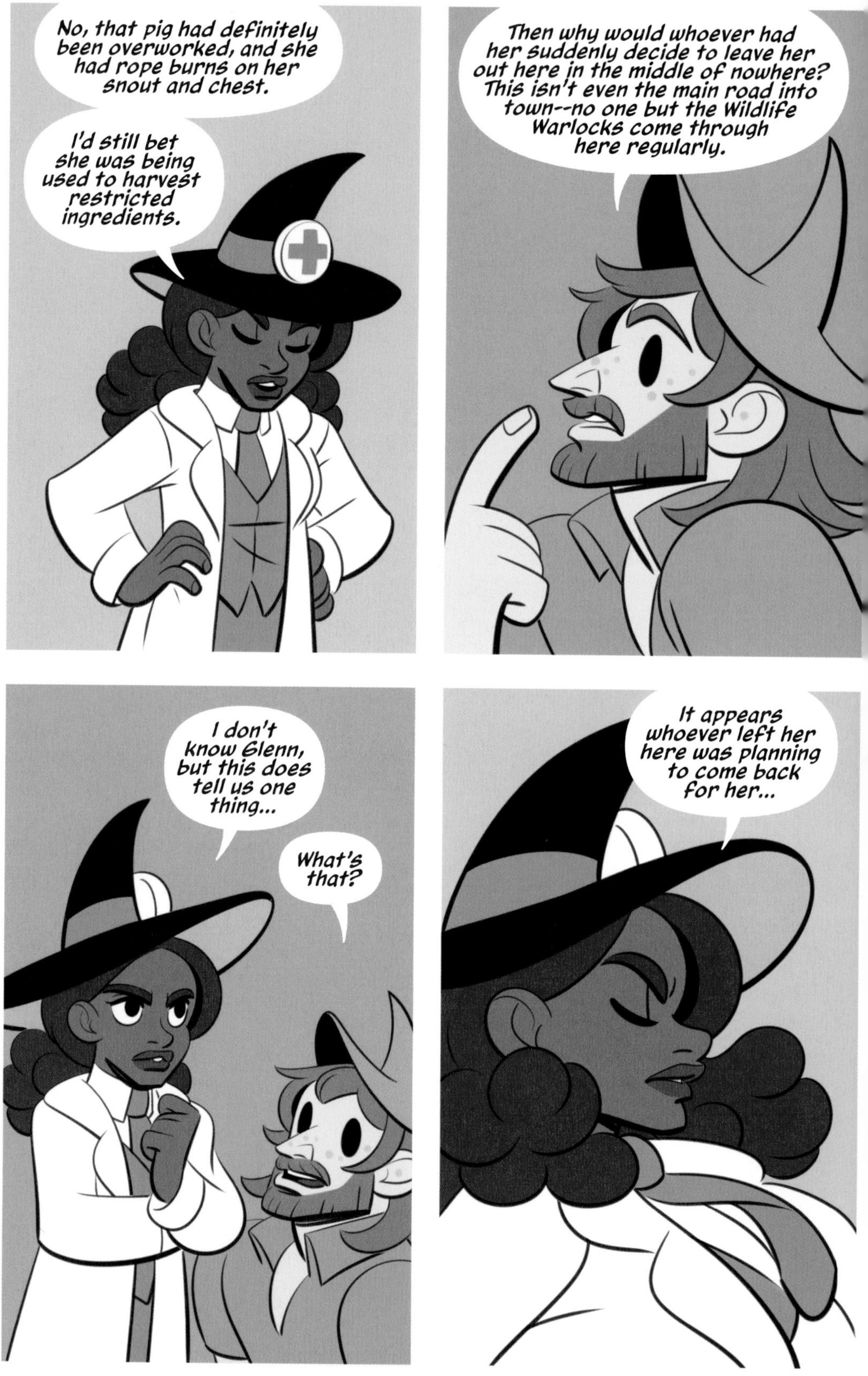
No, that pig had definitely been overworked, and she had rope burns on her snout and chest.
I'd still bet she was being used to harvest restricted ingredients.
Then why would whoever had her suddenly decide to leave her out here in the middle of nowhere? This isn't even the main road into town--no one but the Wildlife Warlocks come through here regularly.
I don't know Glenn, but this does tell us one thing...
What's that?
It appears whoever left her here was planning to come back for her...

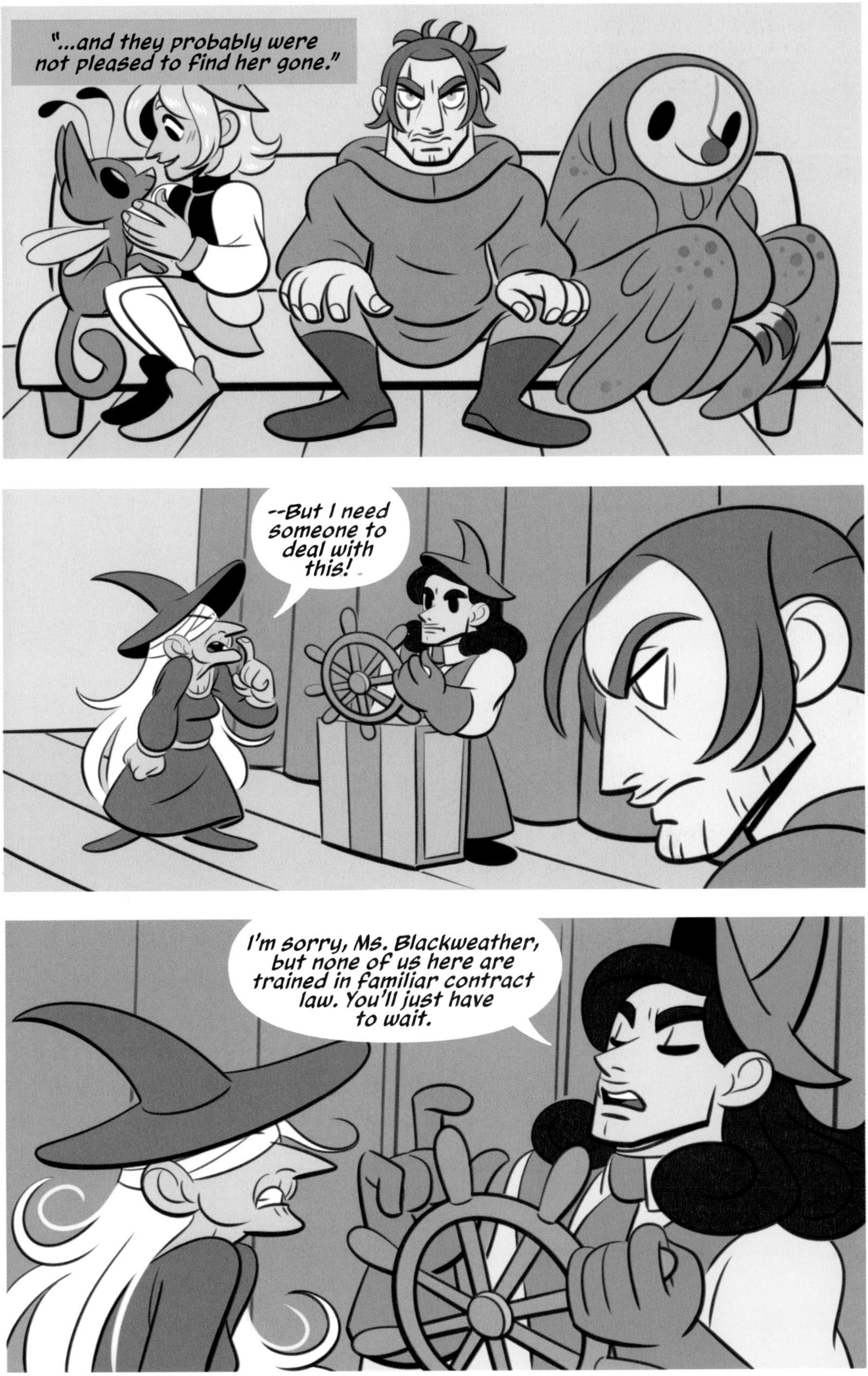
"...and they probably were not pleased to find her gone."
--But I need someone to deal with this!
I'm sorry, Ms. Blackweather, but none of us here are trained in familiar contract law. You'll just have to wait.

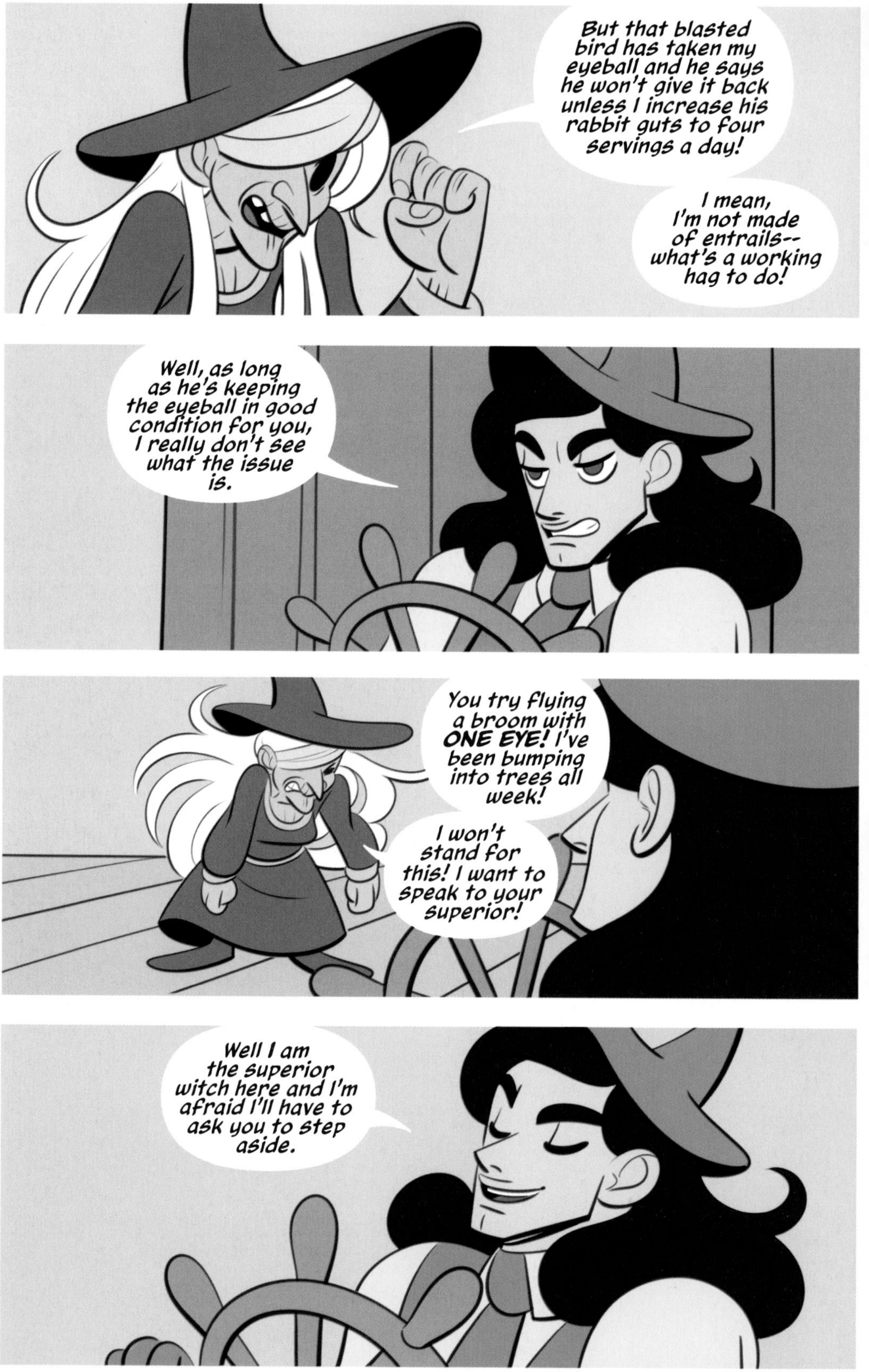
But that blasted bird has taken my eyeball and he says he won't give it back unless I increase his rabbit guts to four servings a day!
I mean, I'm not made of entrails-- what's a working hag to do!
Well, as long as he's keeping the eyeball in good condition for you, I really don't see what the issue is.
You try flying a broom with ONE EYE! I've been bumping into trees all week!
I won't stand for this! I want to speak to your superior!
Well I am the superior witch here and I'm afraid I'll have to ask you to step aside.

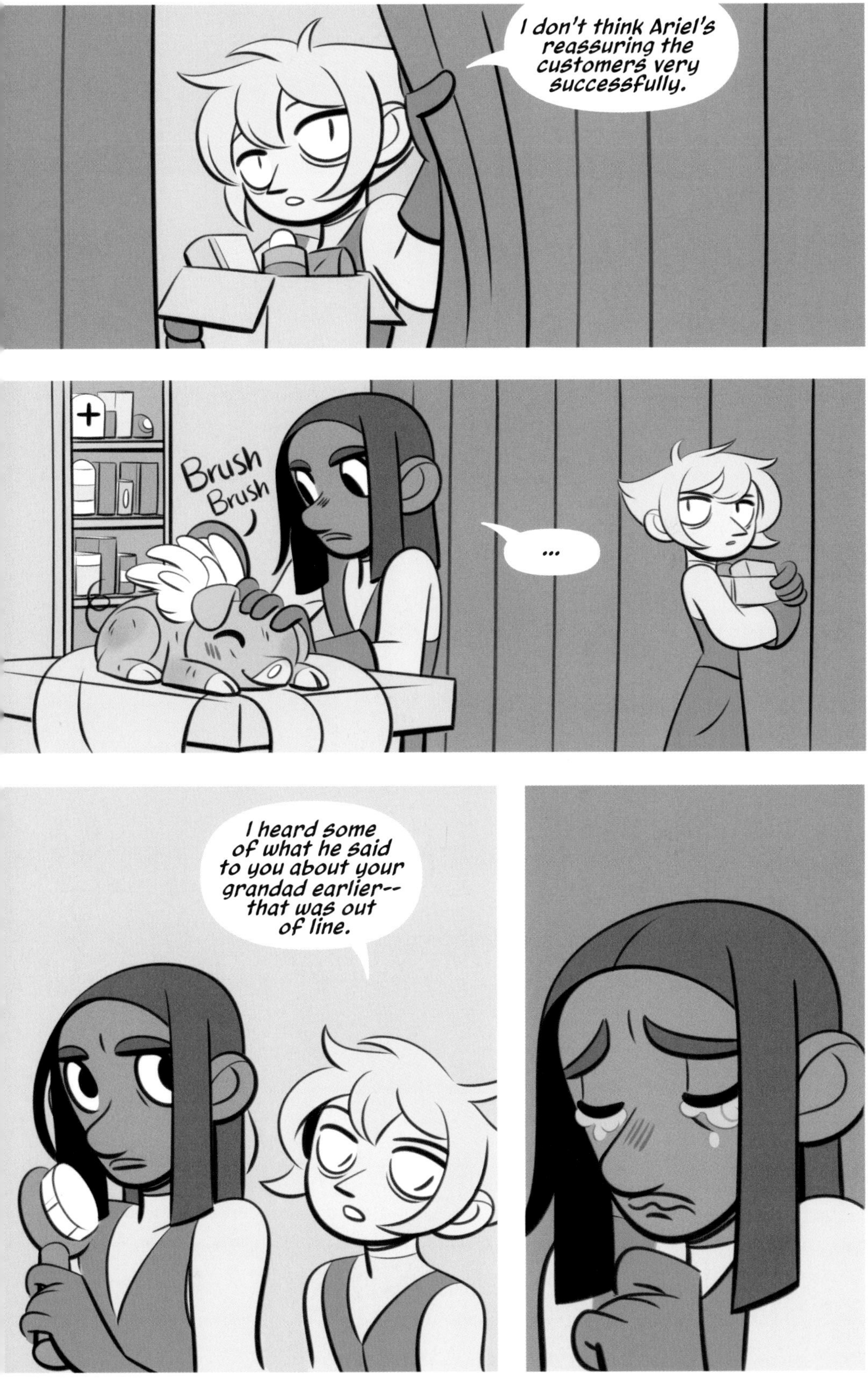
I don't think Ariel's reassuring the customers very successfully.
Brush Brush
...
I heard some of what he said to you about your grandad earlier-- that was out of line.

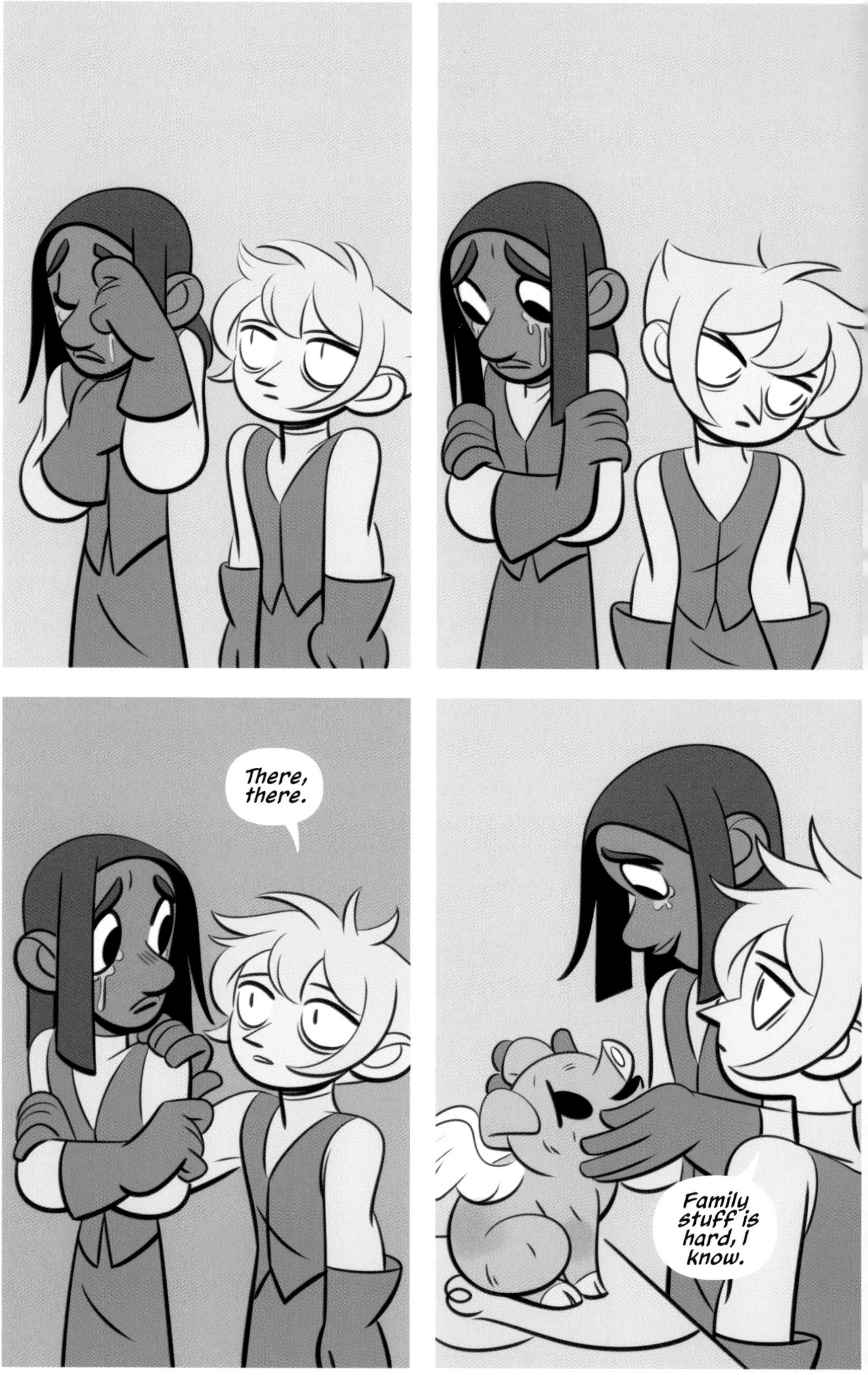
There, there.
Family stuff is hard, I know.

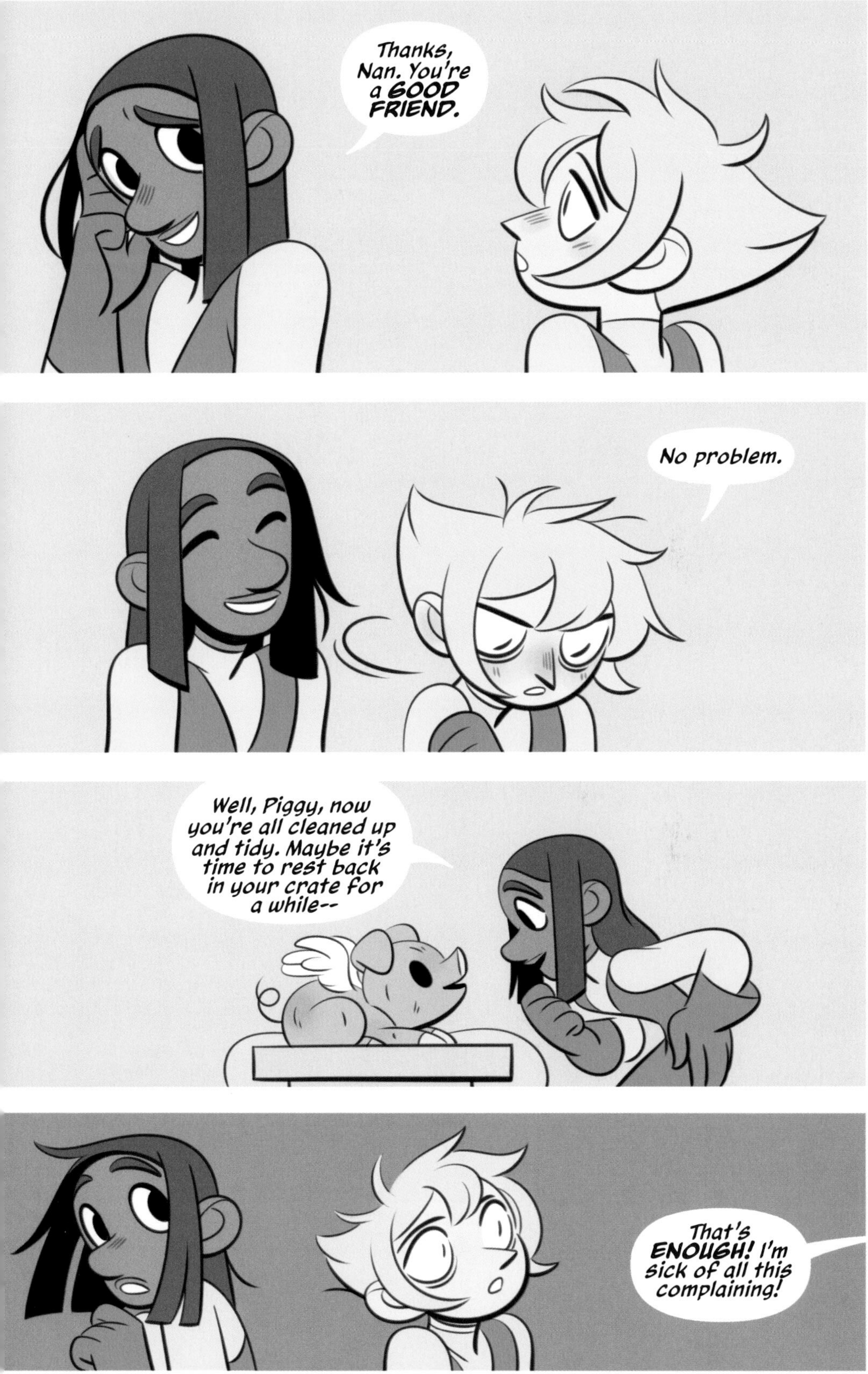

Thanks, Nan. You're a GOOD FRIEND.
No problem.
Well, Piggy, now you're all cleaned up and tidy. Maybe it's time to rest back in your crate for a while--
That's ENOUGH! I'm sick of all this complaining!

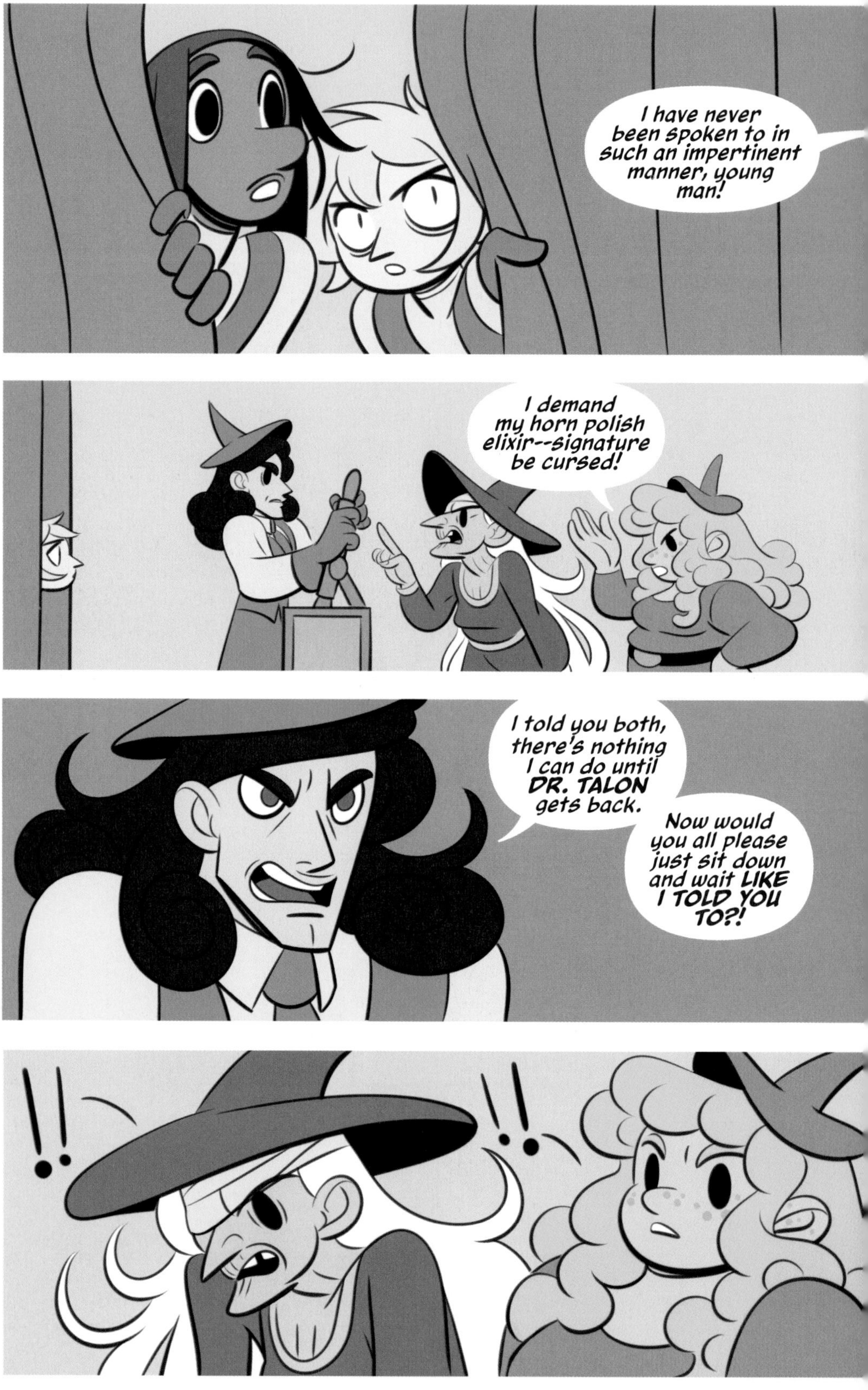
I have never been spoken to in such an impertinent manner, young man!
I demand my horn polish elixir--signature be cursed!
I told you both, there's nothing I can do until DR. TALON gets back.
Now would you all please just sit down and wait LIKE I TOLD YOU TO?!
!!
!!

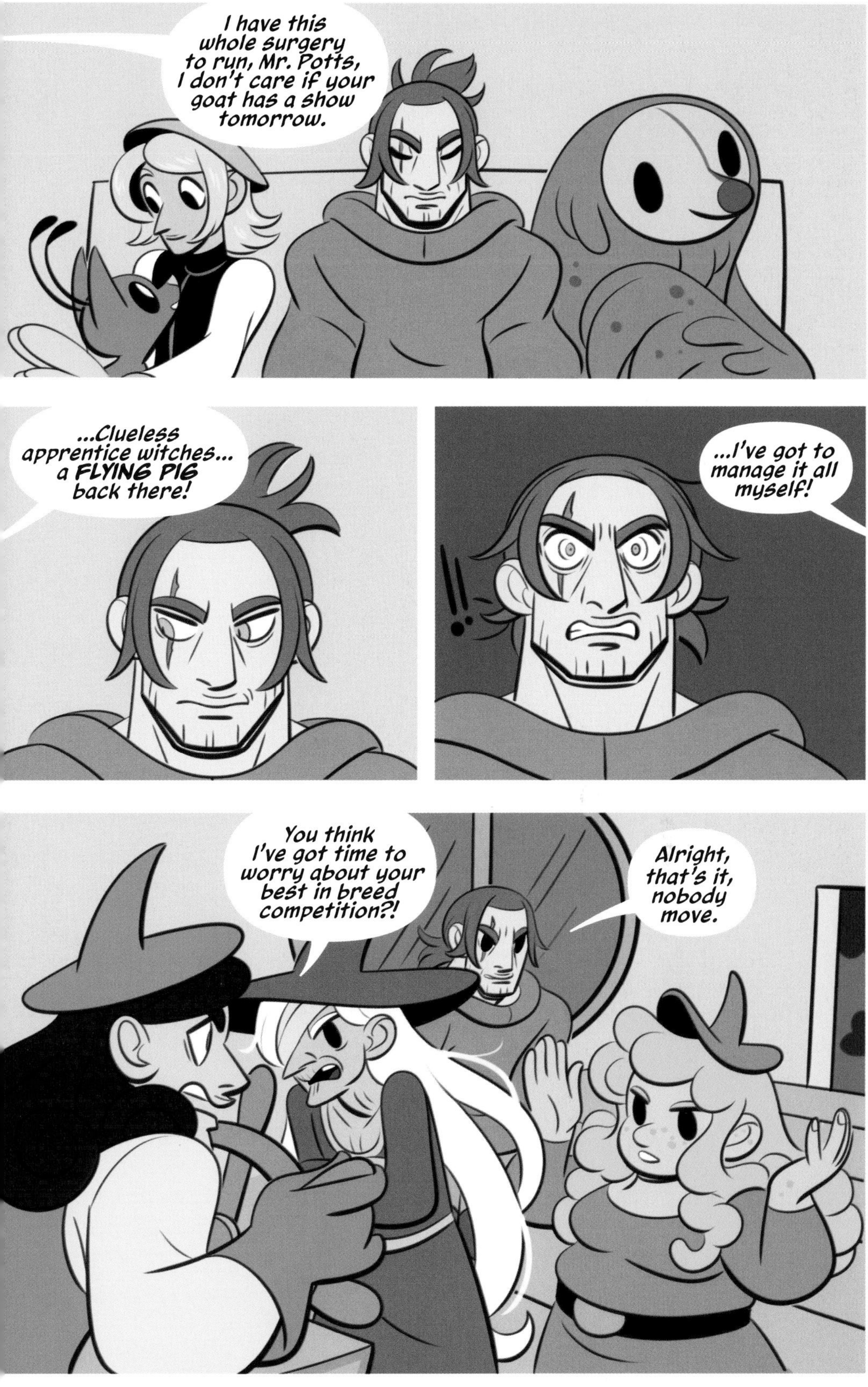
I have this whole surgery to run, Mr. Potts, I don't care if your goat has a show tomorrow.
...Clueless apprentice witches... a FLYING PIG back there!
...I've got to manage it all myself!
!!
You think I've got time to worry about your best in breed competition?!
Alright, that's it, nobody move.

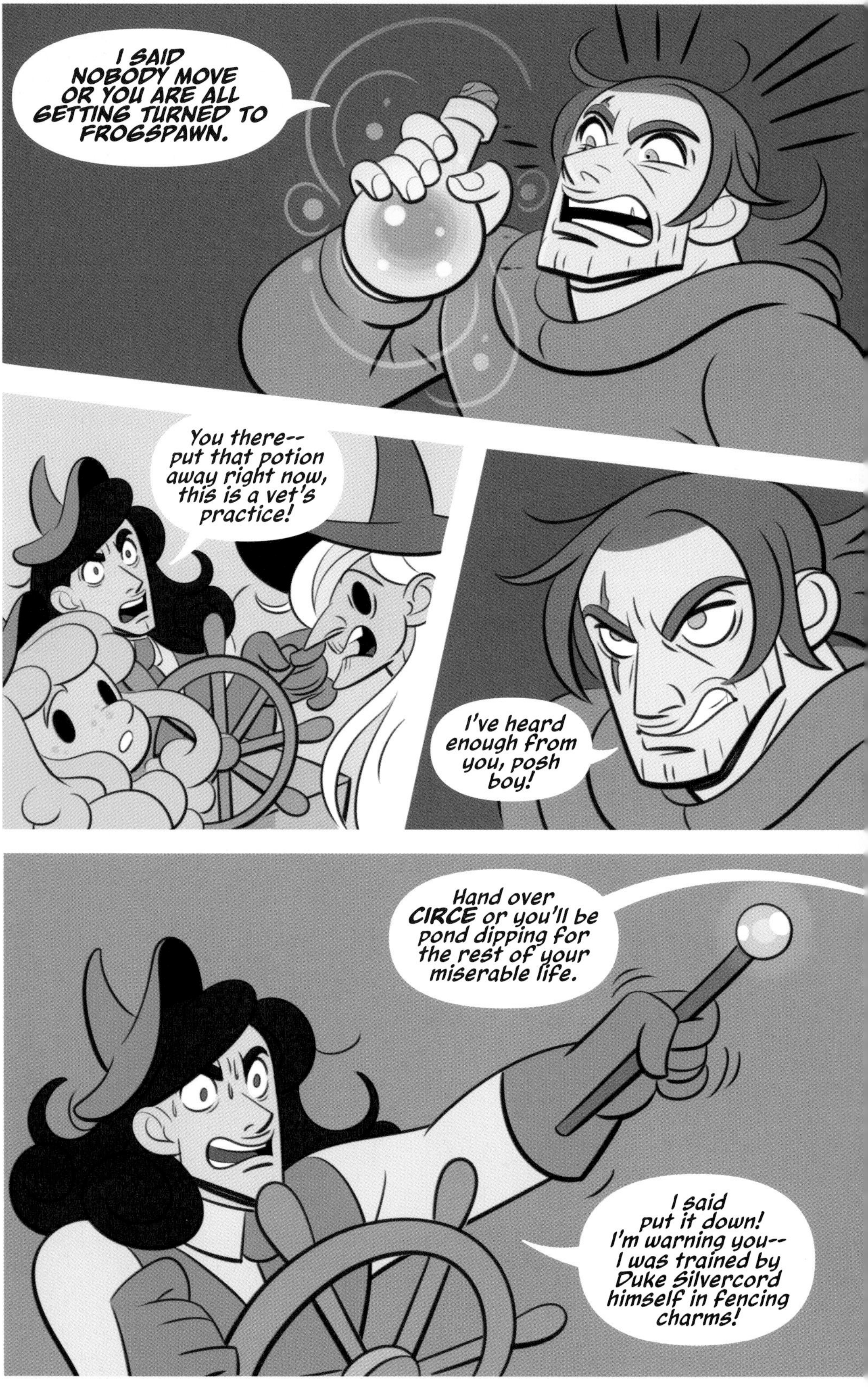
I SAID NOBODY MOVE OR YOU ARE ALL GETTING TURNED TO FROGSPAWN.
You there-- put that potion away right now, this is a vet's practice!
I've heard enough from you, posh boy!
Hand over CIRCE or you'll be pond dipping for the rest of your miserable life.
I said put it down! I'm warning you-- I was trained by Duke Silvercord himself in fencing charms!

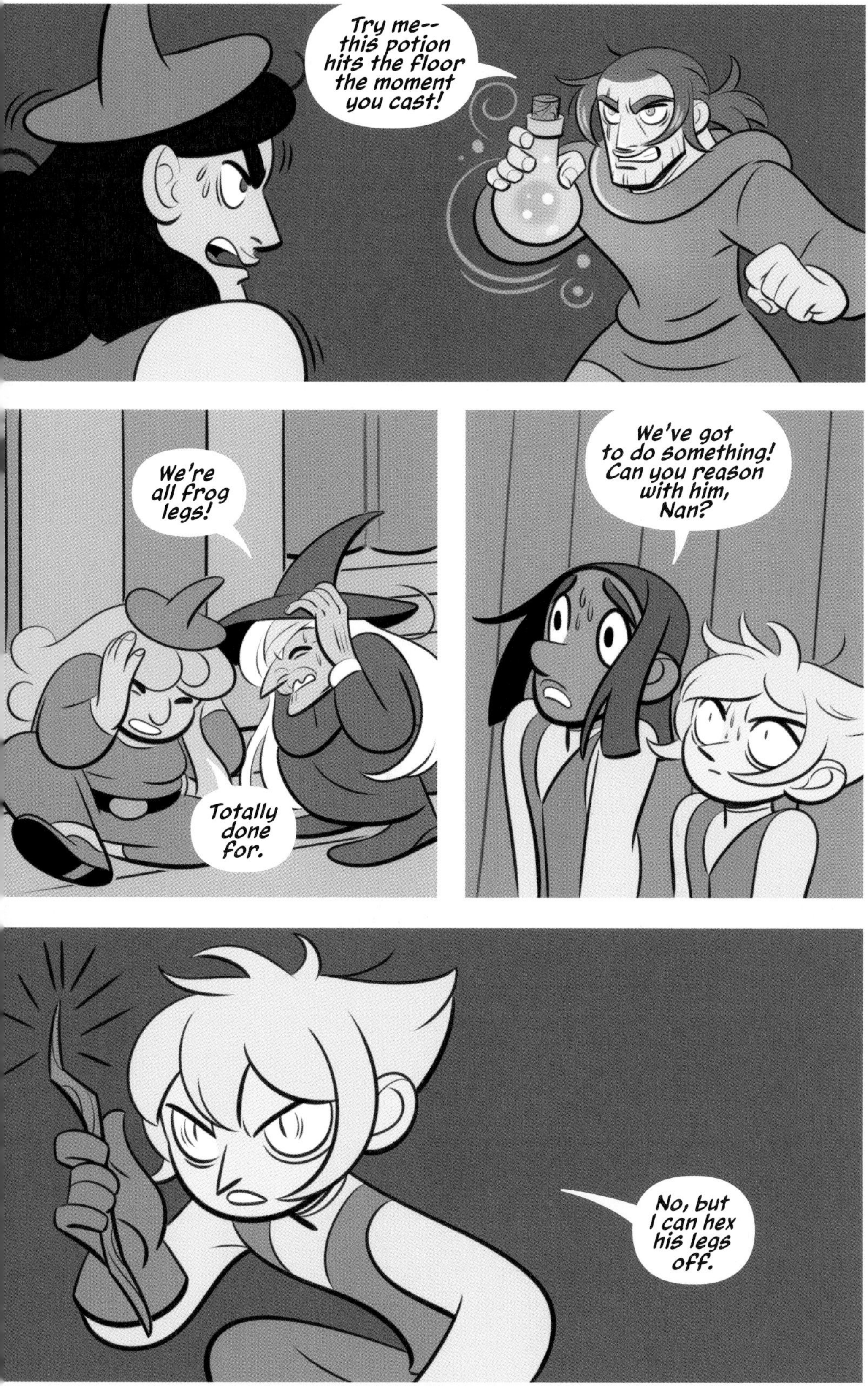
Try me--
this potion
hits the floor
the moment
you cast!
We're all frog legs!
Totally done for.
We've got to do something! Can you reason with him, Nan?
No, but I can hex his legs off.

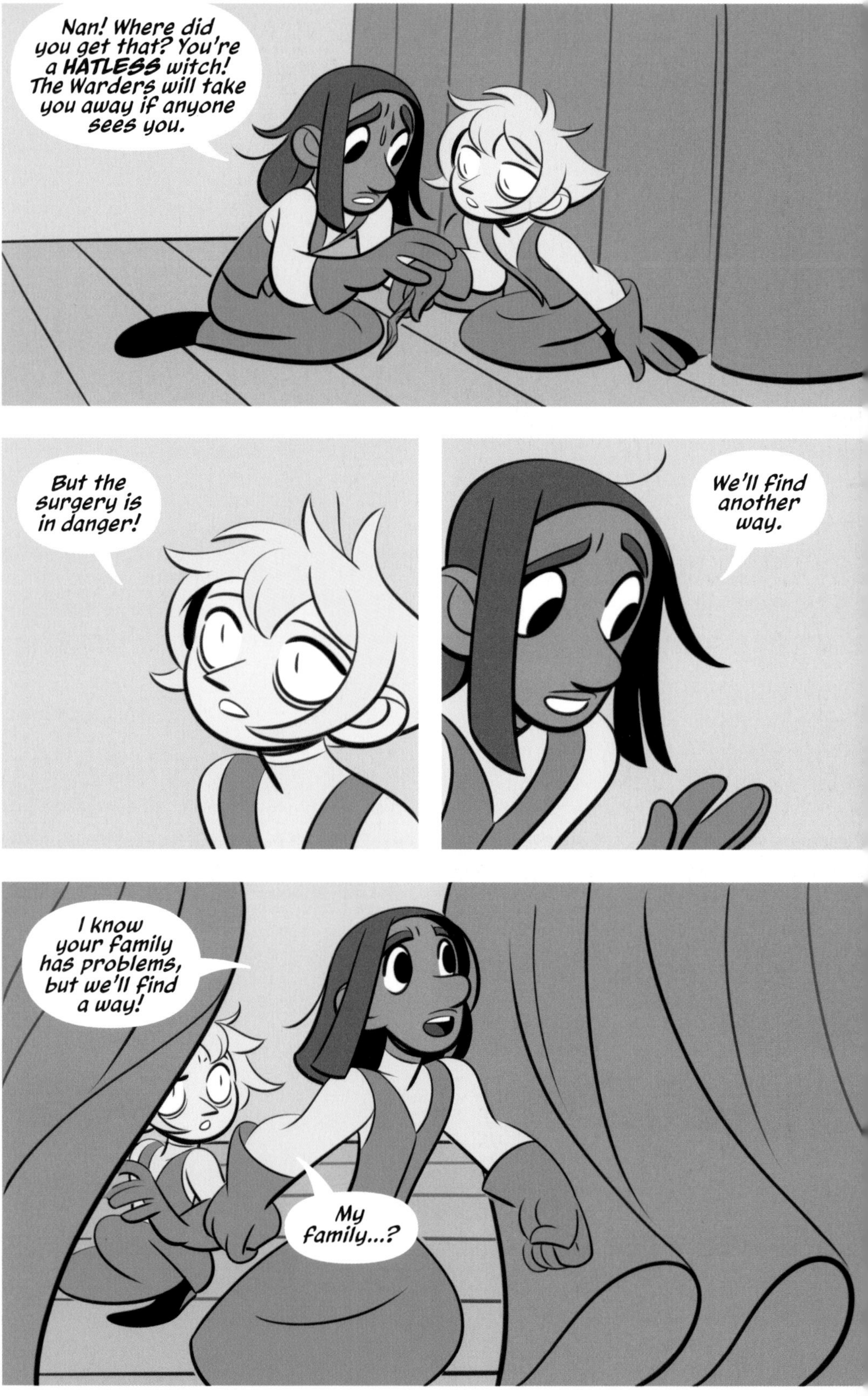
Nan! Where did you get that? You're a HATLESS witch! The Warders will take you away if anyone sees you.
But the surgery is in danger!
We'll find another way.
I know your family has problems, but we'll find a way!
My family...?

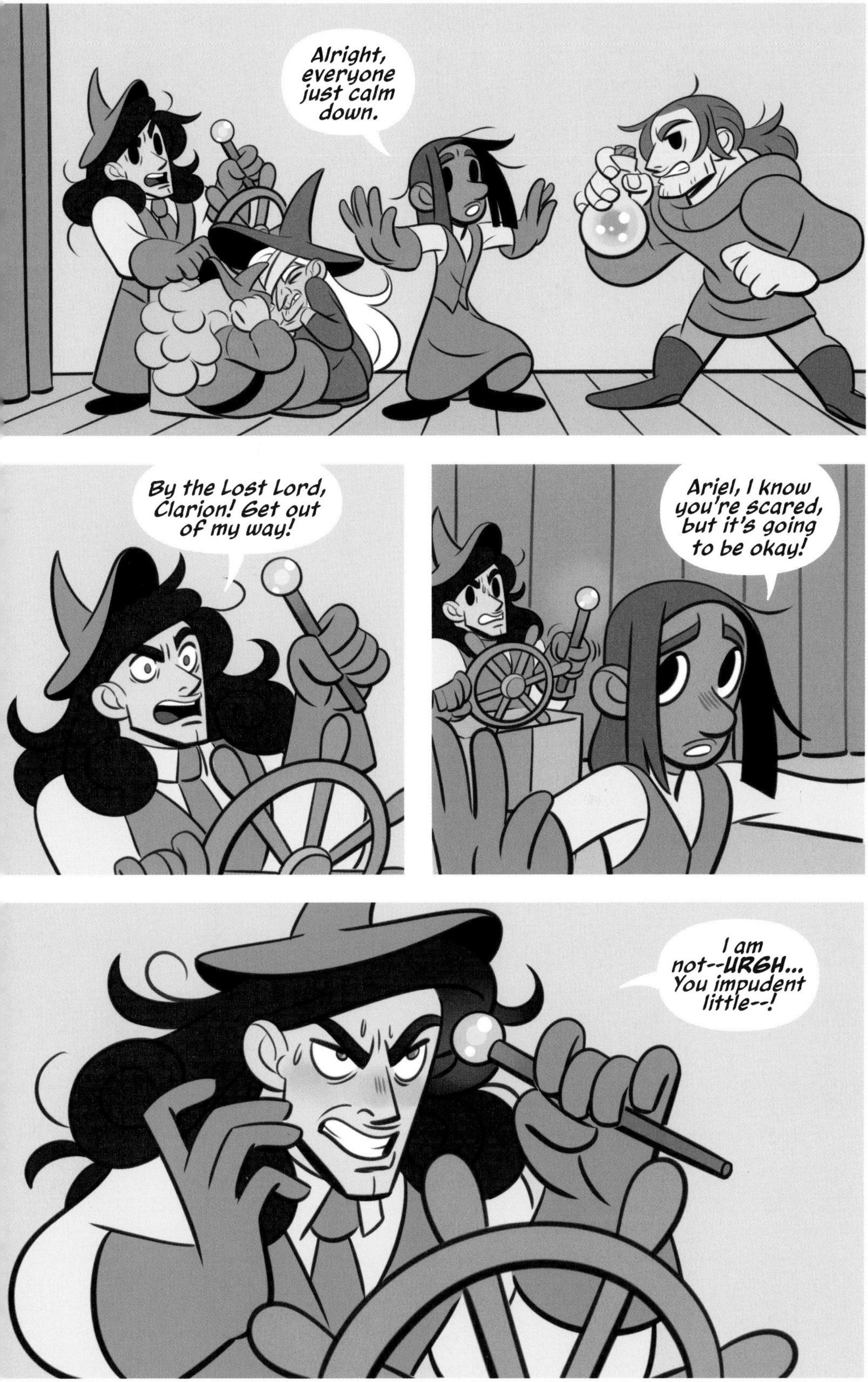
Alright, everyone just calm down.
By the Lost Lord, Clarion! Get out of my way!
Ariel, I know you're scared, but it's going to be okay!
I am not--URGH... You impudent little--!

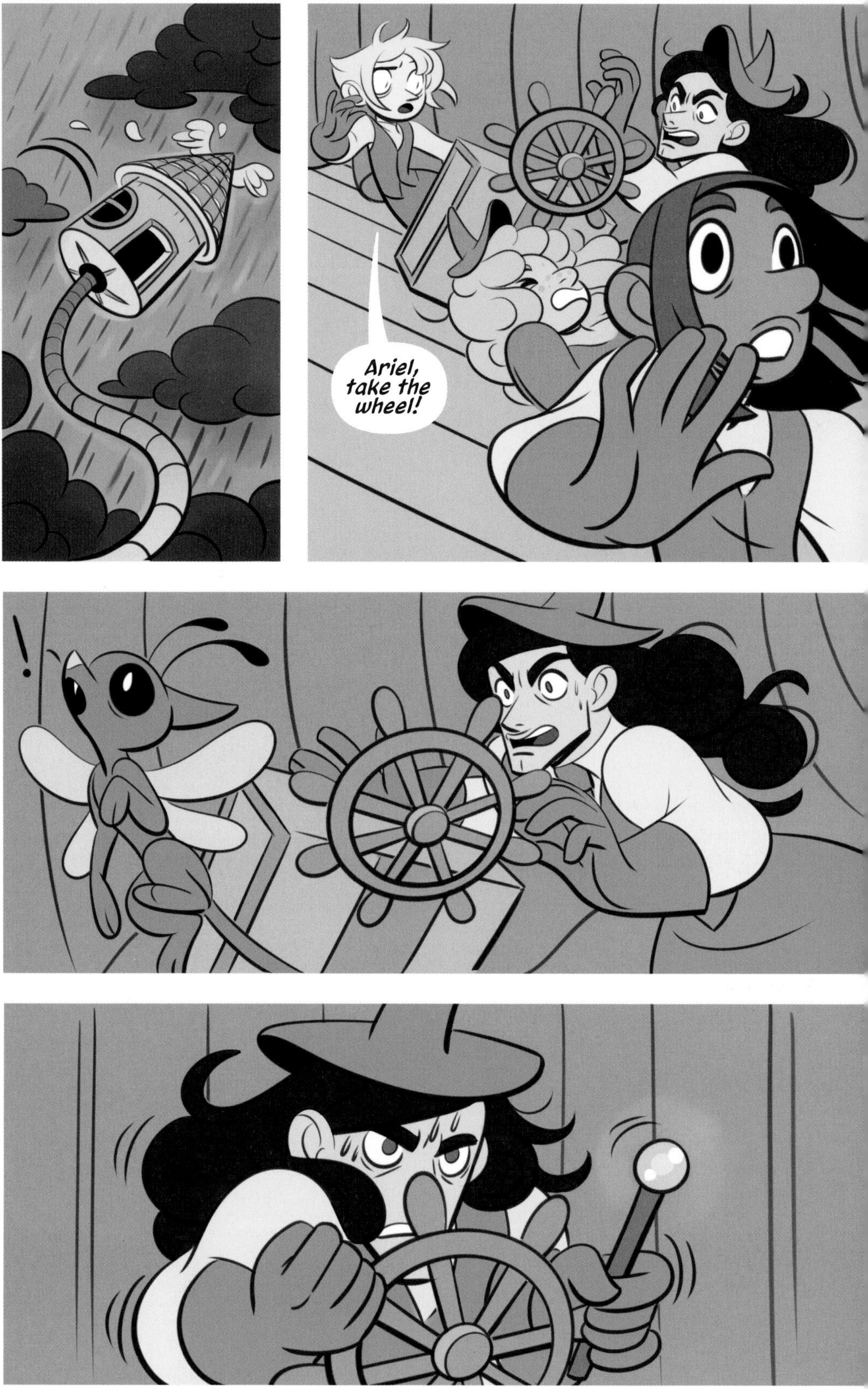
Ariel, take the wheel!
!

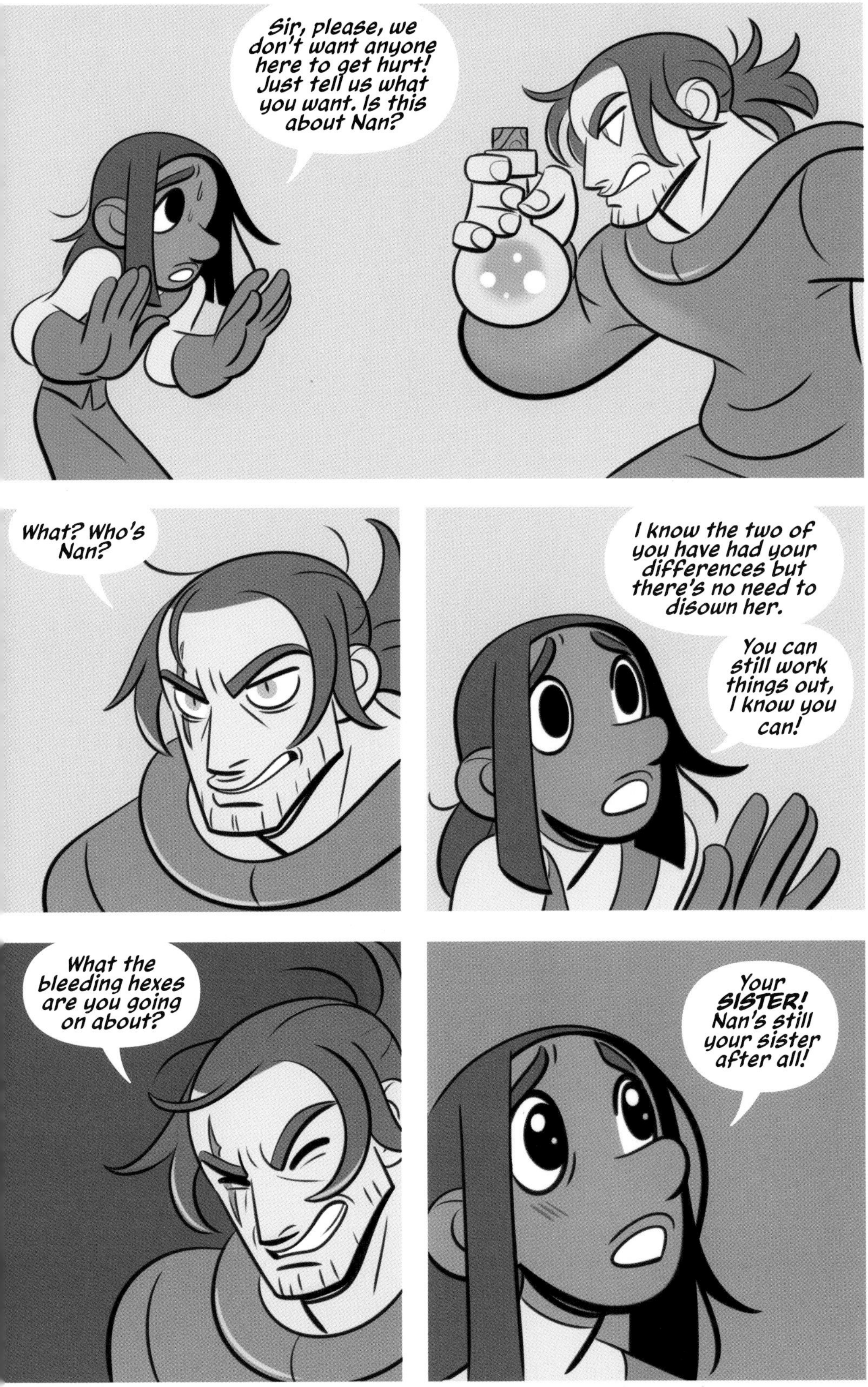
Sir, please, we don't want anyone here to get hurt! Just tell us what you want. Is this about Nan?
What? Who's Nan?
I know the two of you have had your differences but there's no need to disown her.
You can still work things out, I know you can!
What the bleeding hexes are you going on about?
Your SISTER! Nan's still your sister after all!

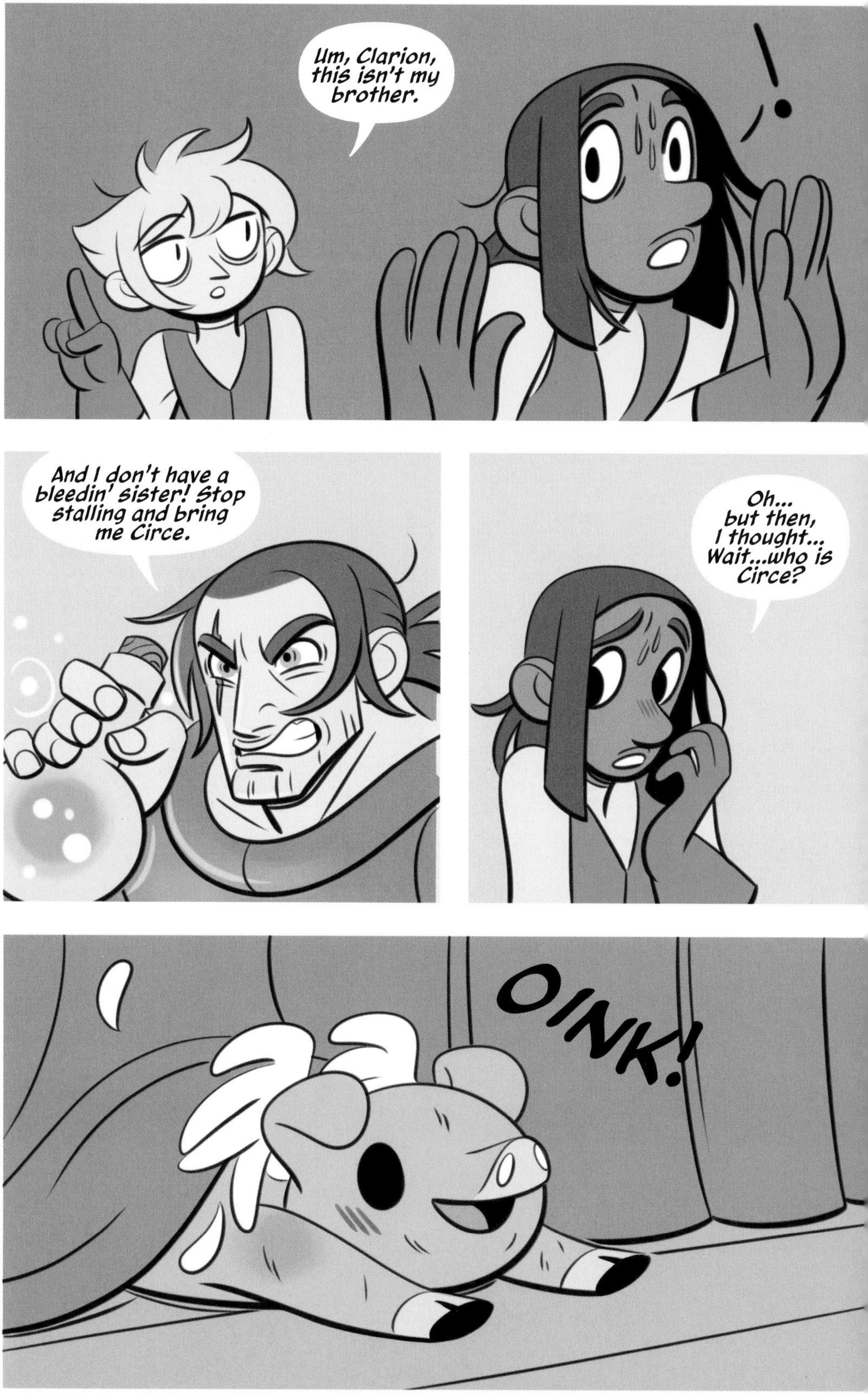
Um, Clarion, this isn't my brother.
!
And I don't have a bleedin' sister! Stop stalling and bring me Circe.
Oh... but then, I thought... Wait...who is Circe?
OINK!

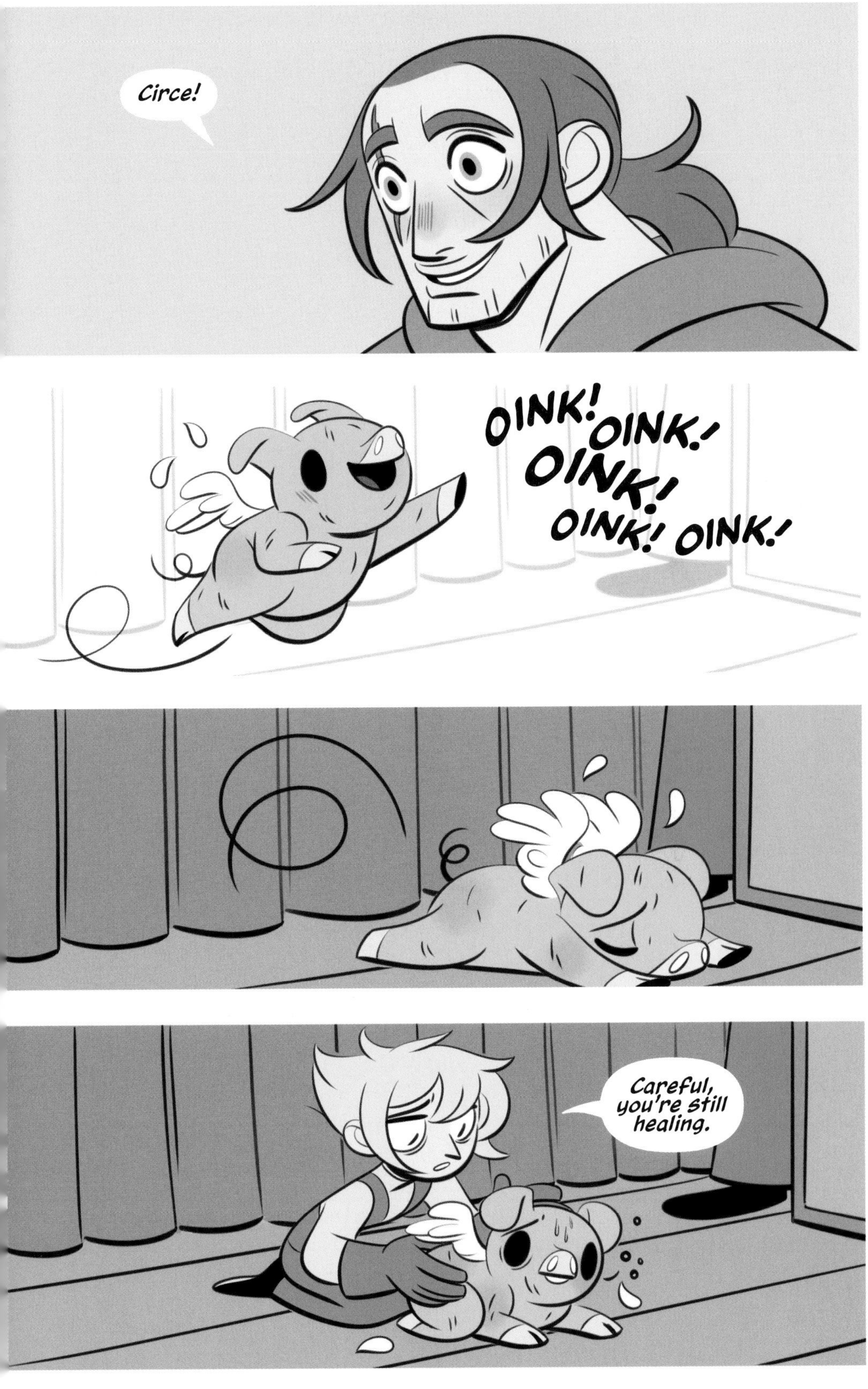
Circe!
OINK! OINK! OINK! OINK! OINK!
Careful, you're still healing.

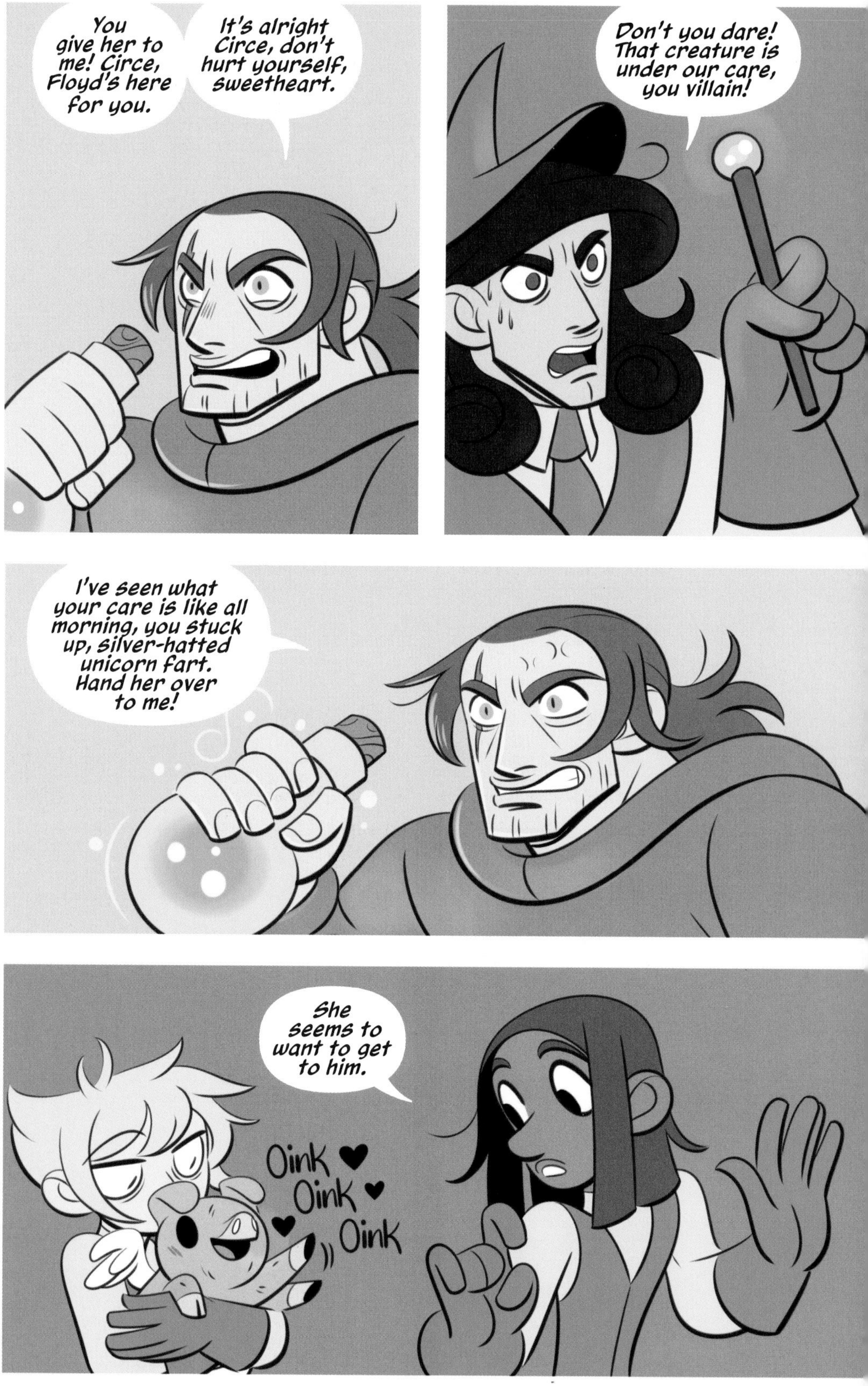
You give her to me! Circe, Floyd's here for you.
It's alright Circe, don't hurt yourself, sweetheart.
Don't you dare! That creature is under our care, you villain!
I've seen what your care is like all morning, you stuck up, silver-hatted unicorn fart. Hand her over to me!
She seems to want to get to him.
Oink
Oink
Oink

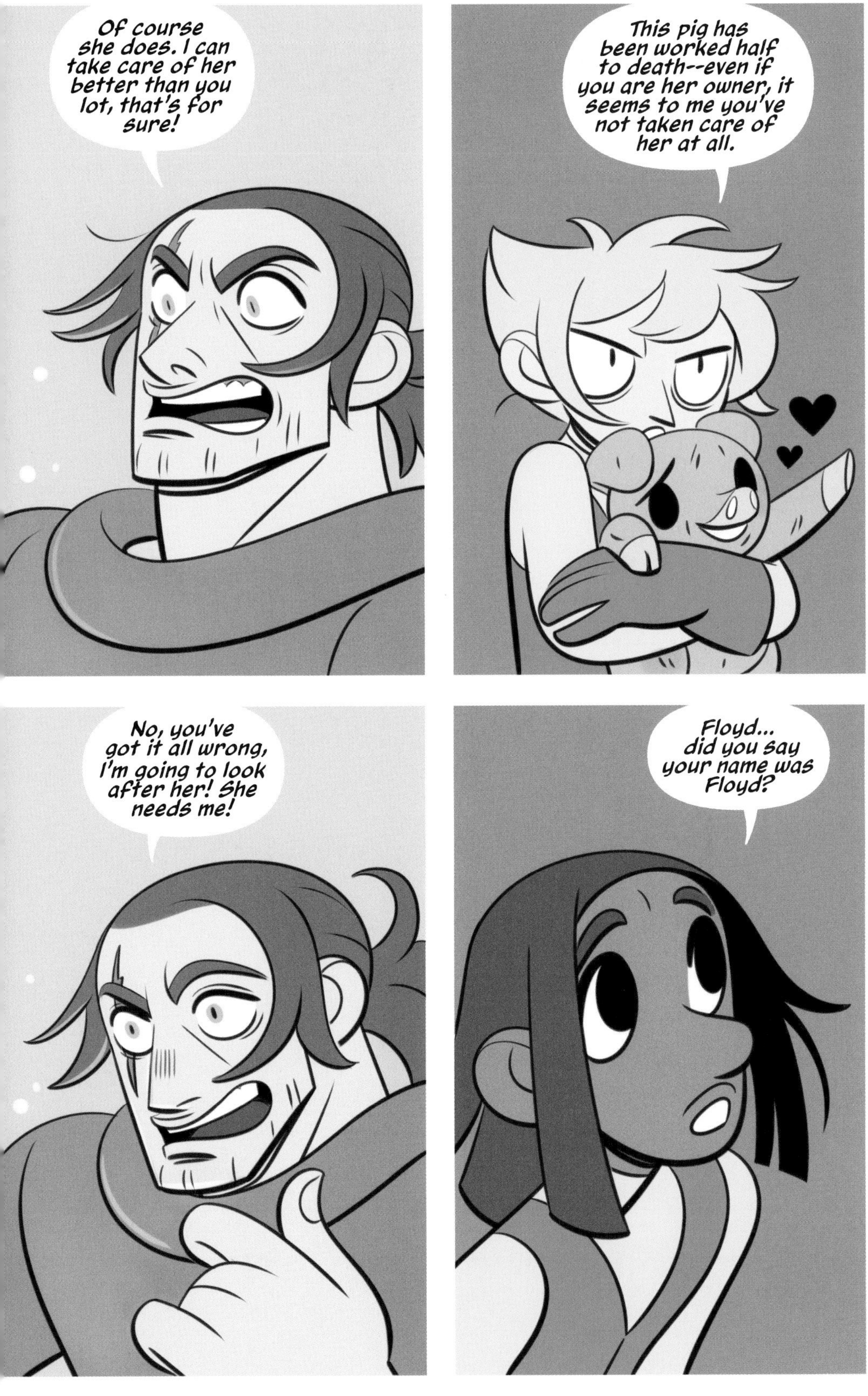
Of course she does. I can take care of her better than you lot, that's for sure!
This pig has been worked half to death--even if you are her owner, it seems to me you've not taken care of her at all.
No, you've got it all wrong, I'm going to look after her! She needs me!
Floyd... did you say your name was Floyd?

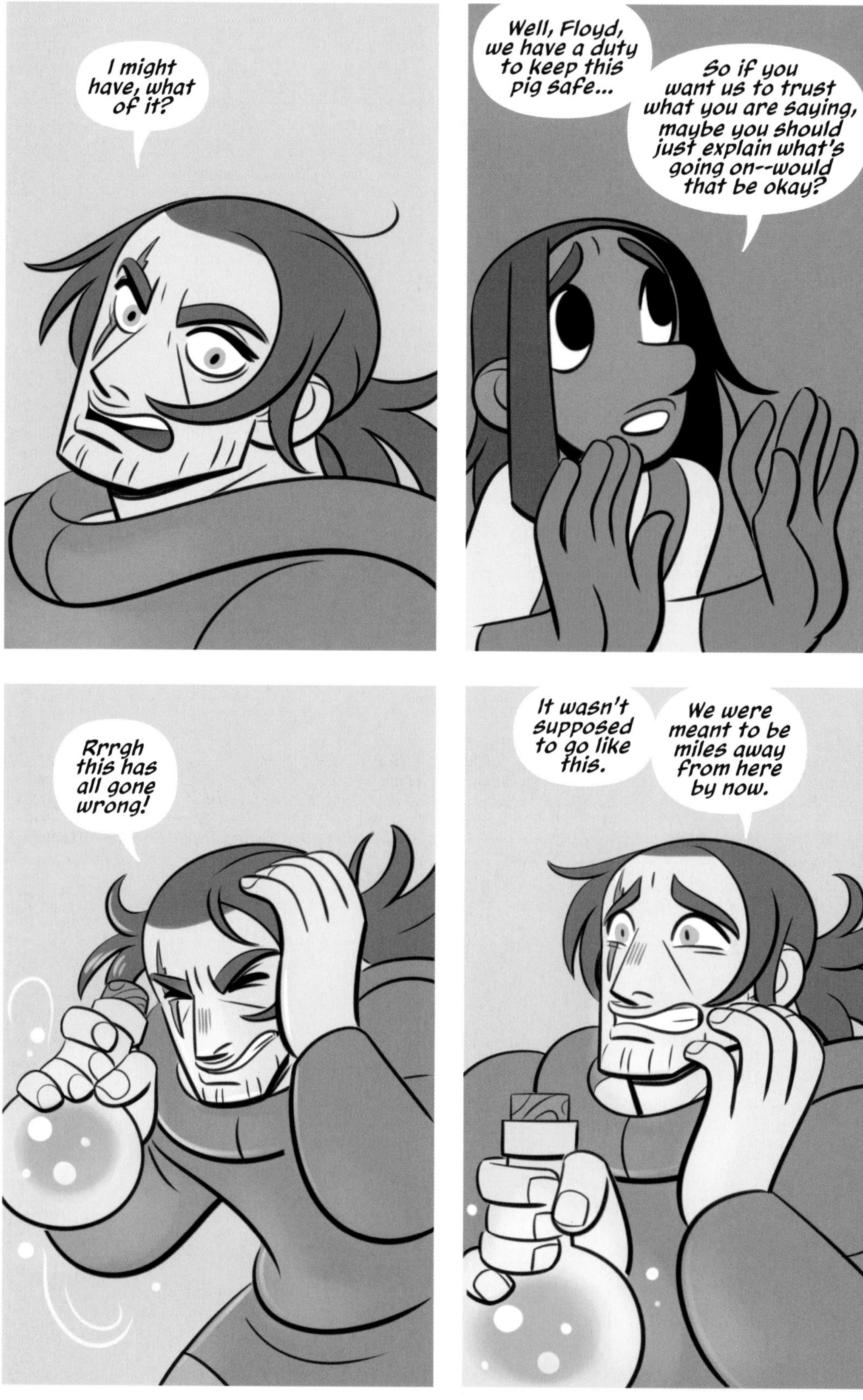
I might have, what of it?
Well, Floyd, we have a duty to keep this pig safe...
So if you want us to trust what you are saying, maybe you should just explain what's going on--would that be okay?
Rrrgh this has all gone wrong!
It wasn't supposed to go like this.
We were meant to be miles away from here by now.

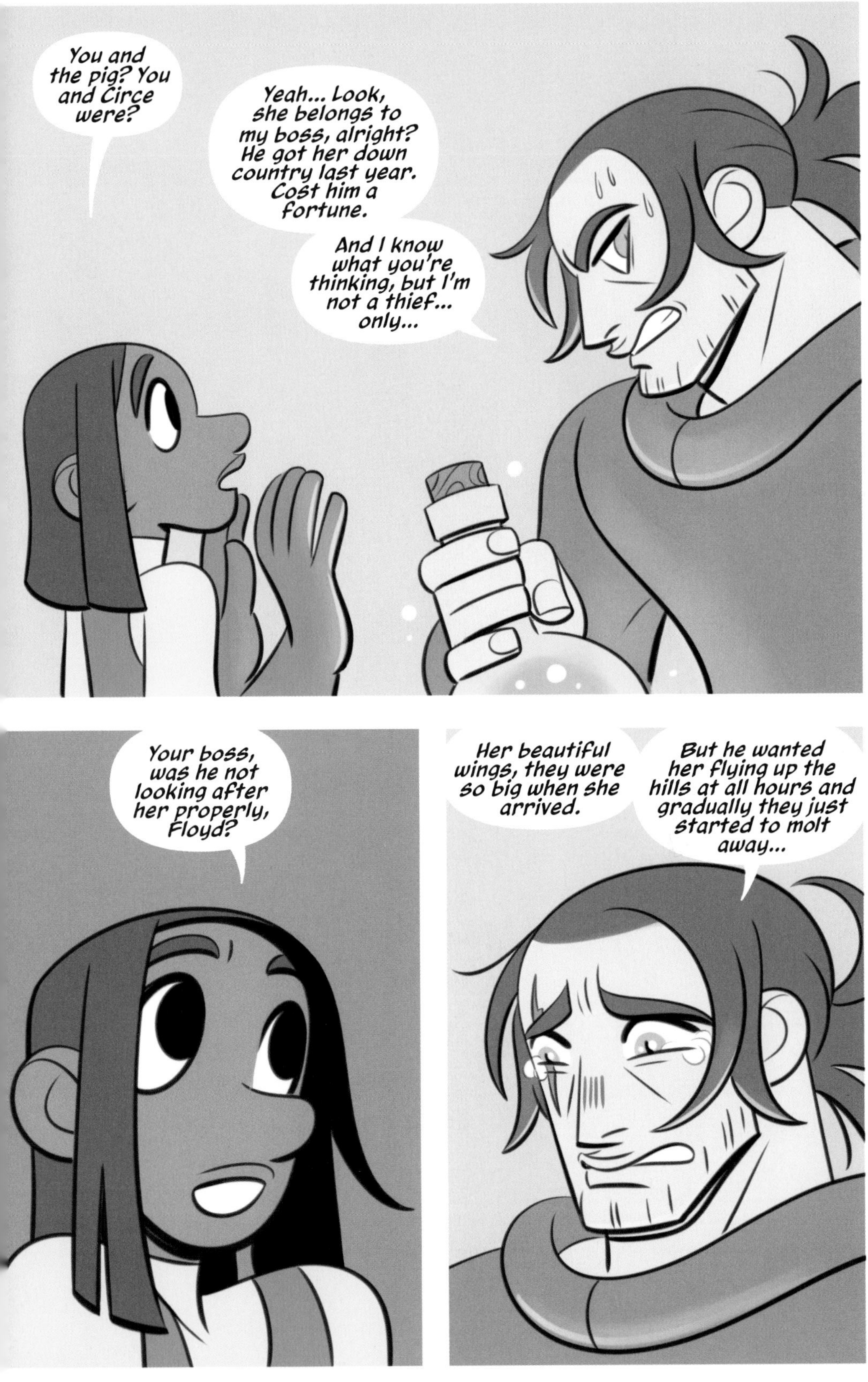
You and the pig? You and Circe were?
Yeah... Look, she belongs to my boss, alright? He got her down country last year. Cost him a fortune.
And I know what you're thinking, but I'm not a thief... only...
Your boss, was he not looking after her properly, Floyd?
Her beautiful wings, they were so big when she arrived.
But he wanted her flying up the hills at all hours and gradually they just started to molt away...

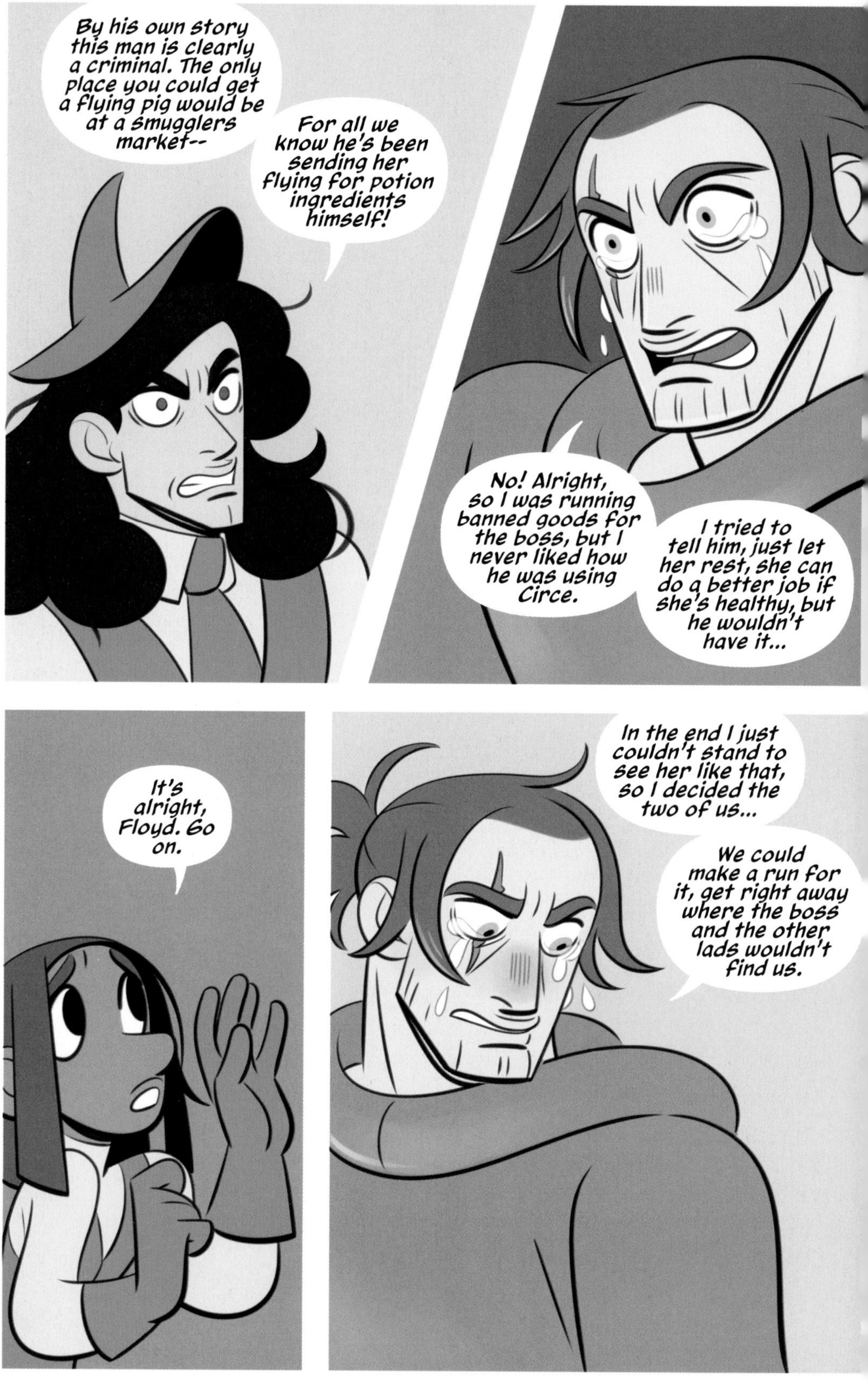
By his own story this man is clearly a criminal. The only place you could get a flying pig would be at a smugglers market--
For all we know he's been sending her flying for potion ingredients himself!
No! Alright, so I was running banned goods for the boss, but I never liked how he was using Circe.
I tried to tell him, just let her rest, she can do a better job if she's healthy, but he wouldn't have it...
It's alright, Floyd. Go on.
In the end I just couldn't stand to see her like that, so I decided the two of us...
We could make a run for it, get right away where the boss and the other lads wouldn't find us.

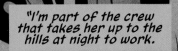

"I'm part of the crew that takes her up to the hills at night to work.

"The other guards in the back of the coach have a habit of taking a nap on the way back, so I jumped out with her while no one was looking.

"I hid her away as best I could and promised I'd come back, then I caught back up to the coach and snuck on board with the empty crate, that way no one back at the storehouse would suspect me straight away.

"They all had to agree with me that she must have snuck away on her own--none of them could admit to the boss they were asleep, see.

"I managed to get away just before dawn. The boss was still screaming and ordering the whole road from The High Hills to Bracken Town searched. I thought everyone would be distracted for hours looking and by then we'd have caught the early post cart into the city...only...only..."

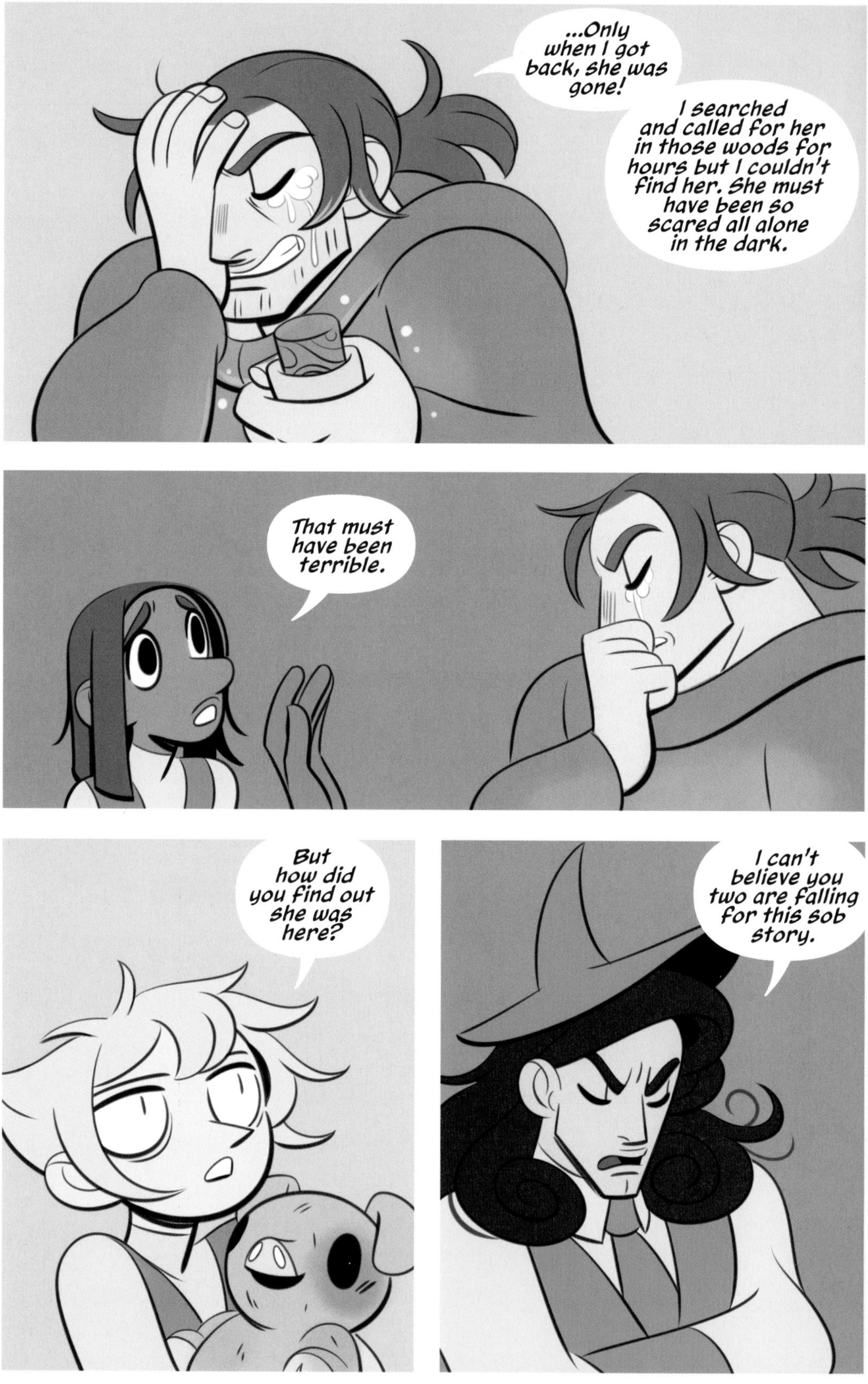
...Only when I got back, she was gone!
I searched and called for her in those woods for hours but I couldn't find her. She must have been so scared all alone in the dark.
That must have been terrible.
But how did you find out she was here?
I can't believe you two are falling for this sob story.

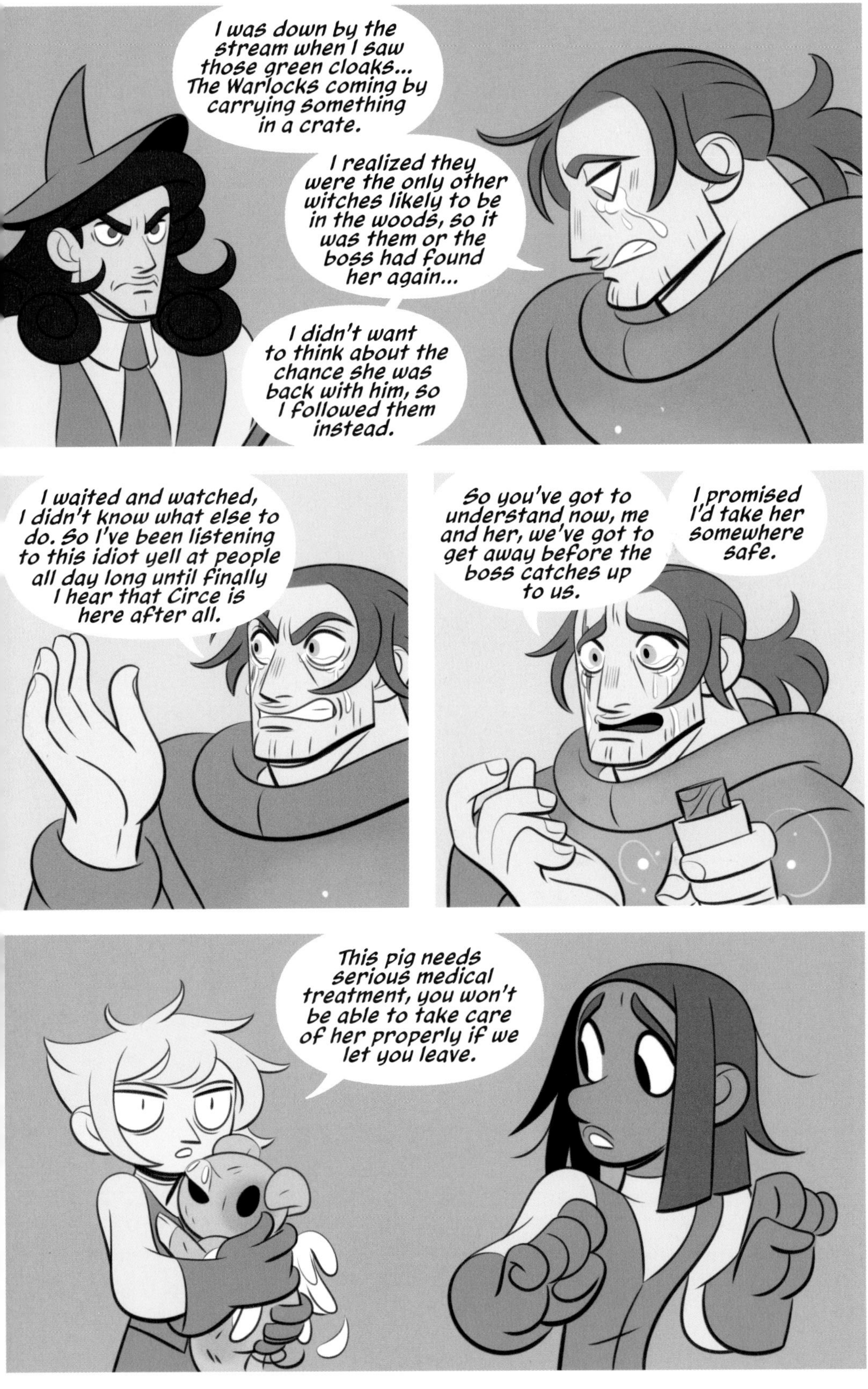
I was down by the stream when I saw those green cloaks... The Warlocks coming by carrying something in a crate.
I realized they were the only other witches likely to be in the woods, so it was them or the boss had found her again...
I didn't want to think about the chance she was back with him, so I followed them instead.
I waited and watched, I didn't know what else to do. So I've been listening to this idiot yell at people all day long until finally I hear that Circe is here after all.
So you've got to understand now, me and her, we've got to get away before the boss catches up to us.
I promised I'd take her somewhere safe.
This pig needs serious medical treatment, you won't be able to take care of her properly if we let you leave.

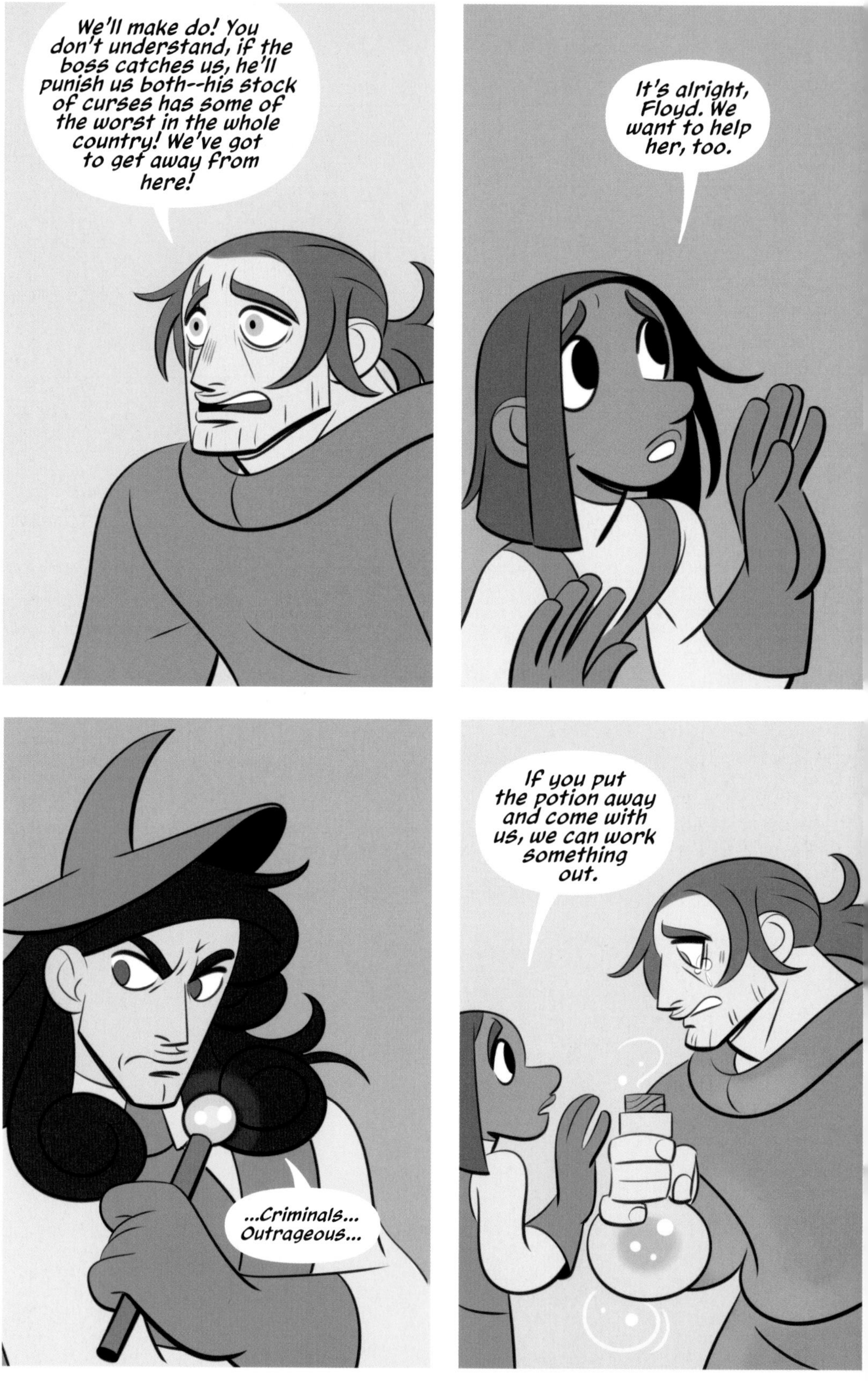
We'll make do! You don't understand, if the boss catches us, he'll punish us both--his stock of curses has some of the worst in the whole country! We've got to get away from here!
It's alright, Floyd. We want to help her, too.
...Criminals... Outrageous...
If you put the potion away and come with us, we can work something out.

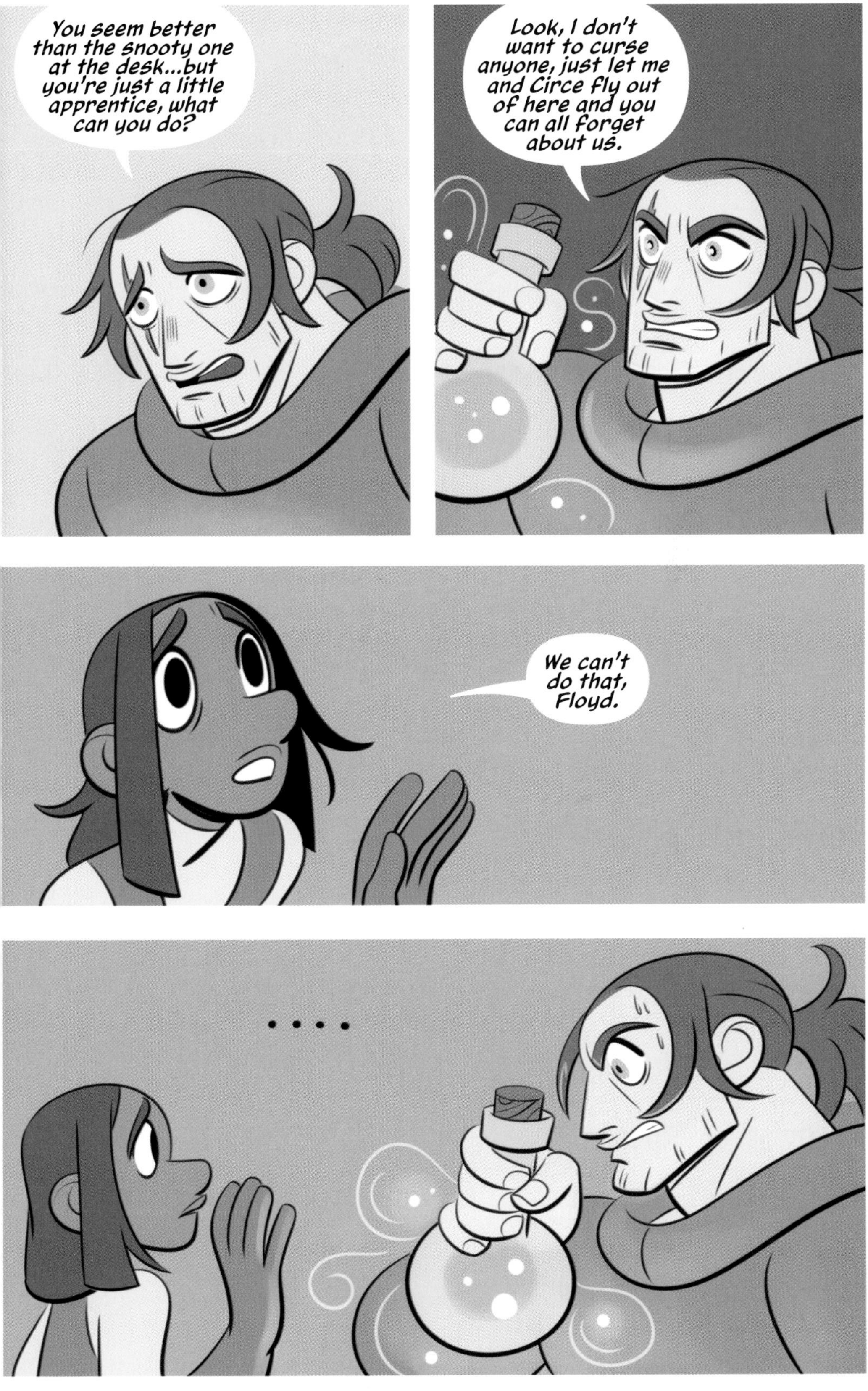
You seem better than the snooty one at the desk...but you're just a little apprentice, what can you do?
Look, I don't want to curse anyone, just let me and Circe fly out of here and you can all forget about us.
We can't do that, Floyd.
....

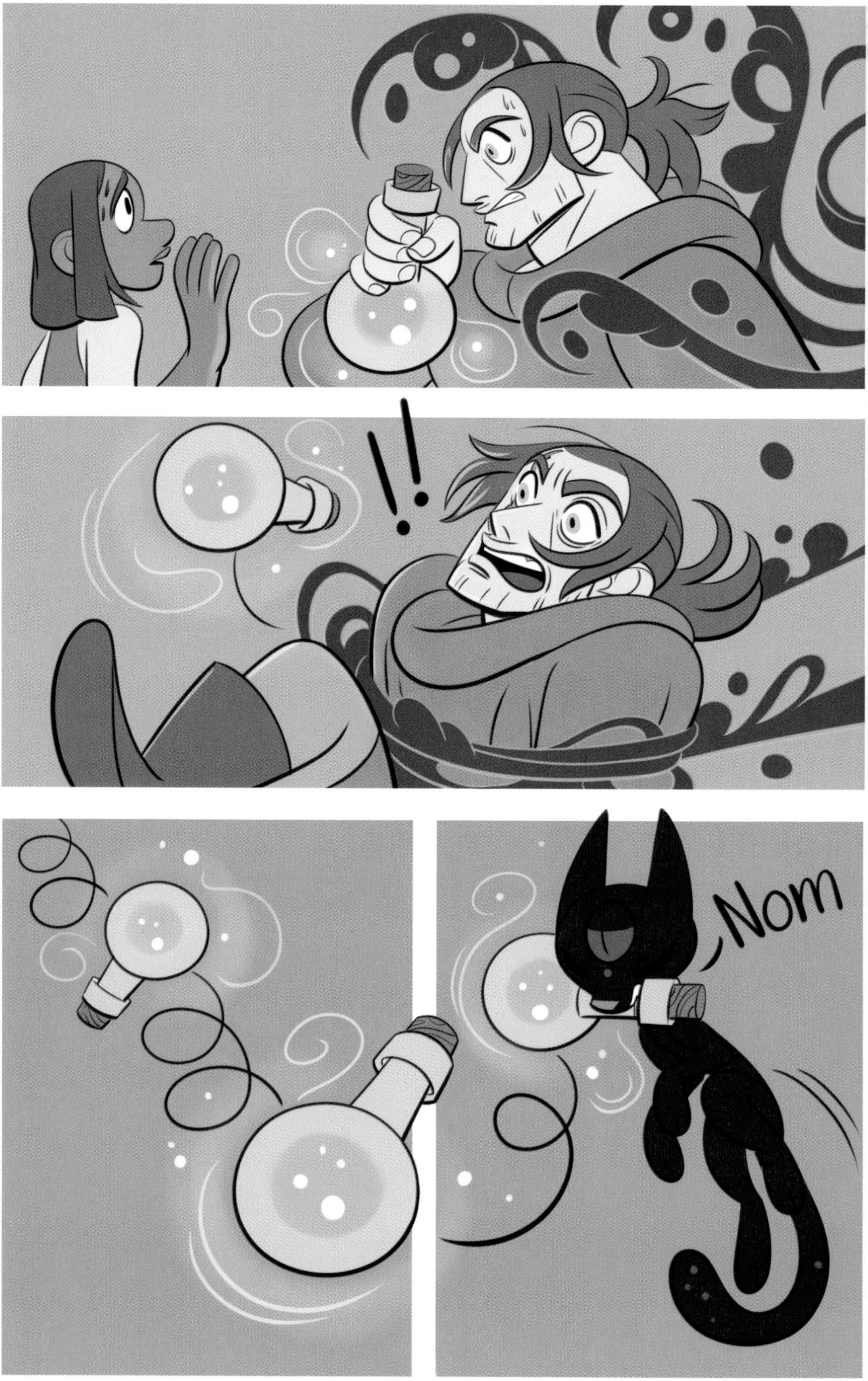
!!
Nom

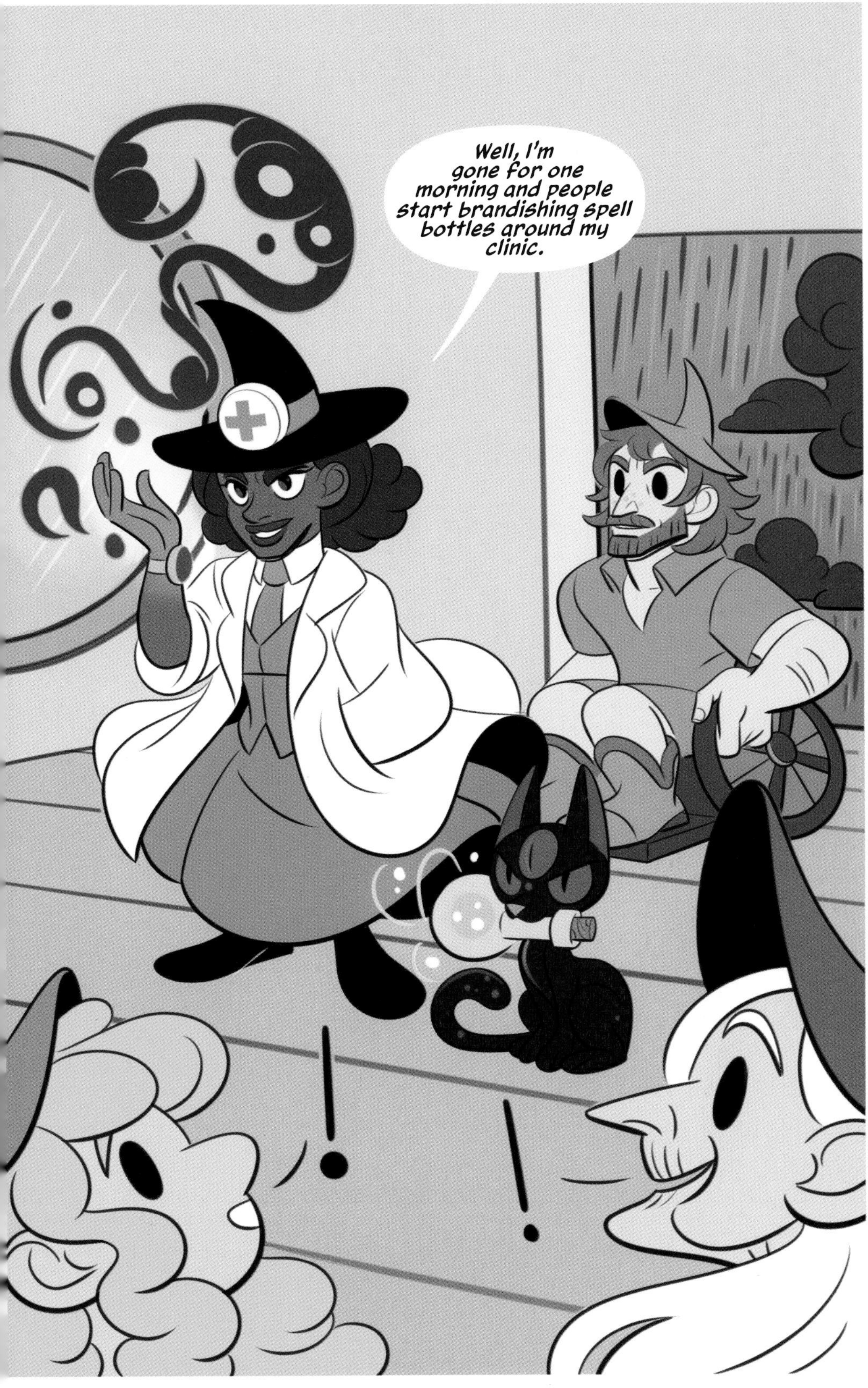
Well, I'm gone for one morning and people start brandishing spell bottles around my clinic.
!
!

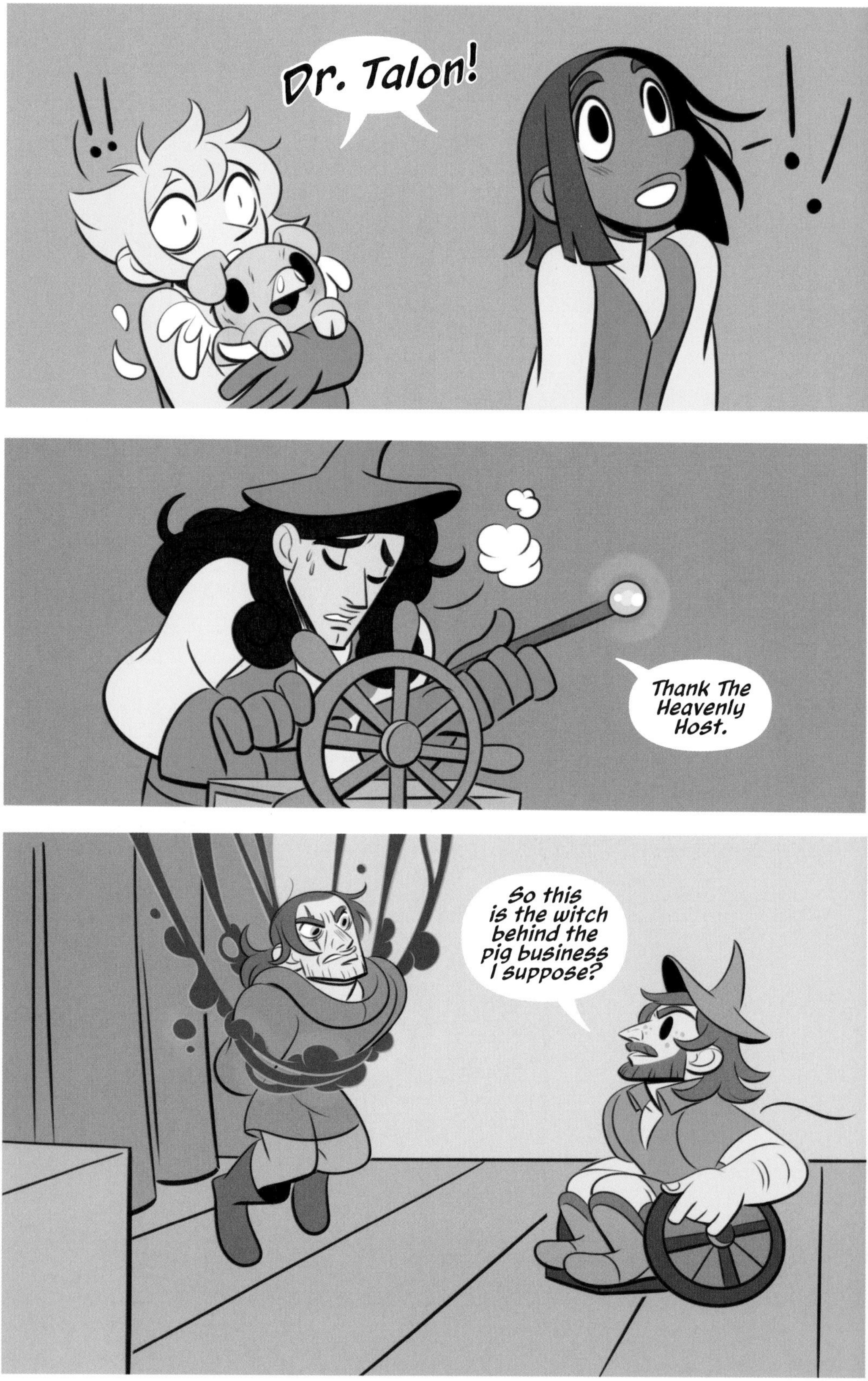
Dr. Talon!
Thank The Heavenly Host.
So this is the witch behind the pig business I suppose?

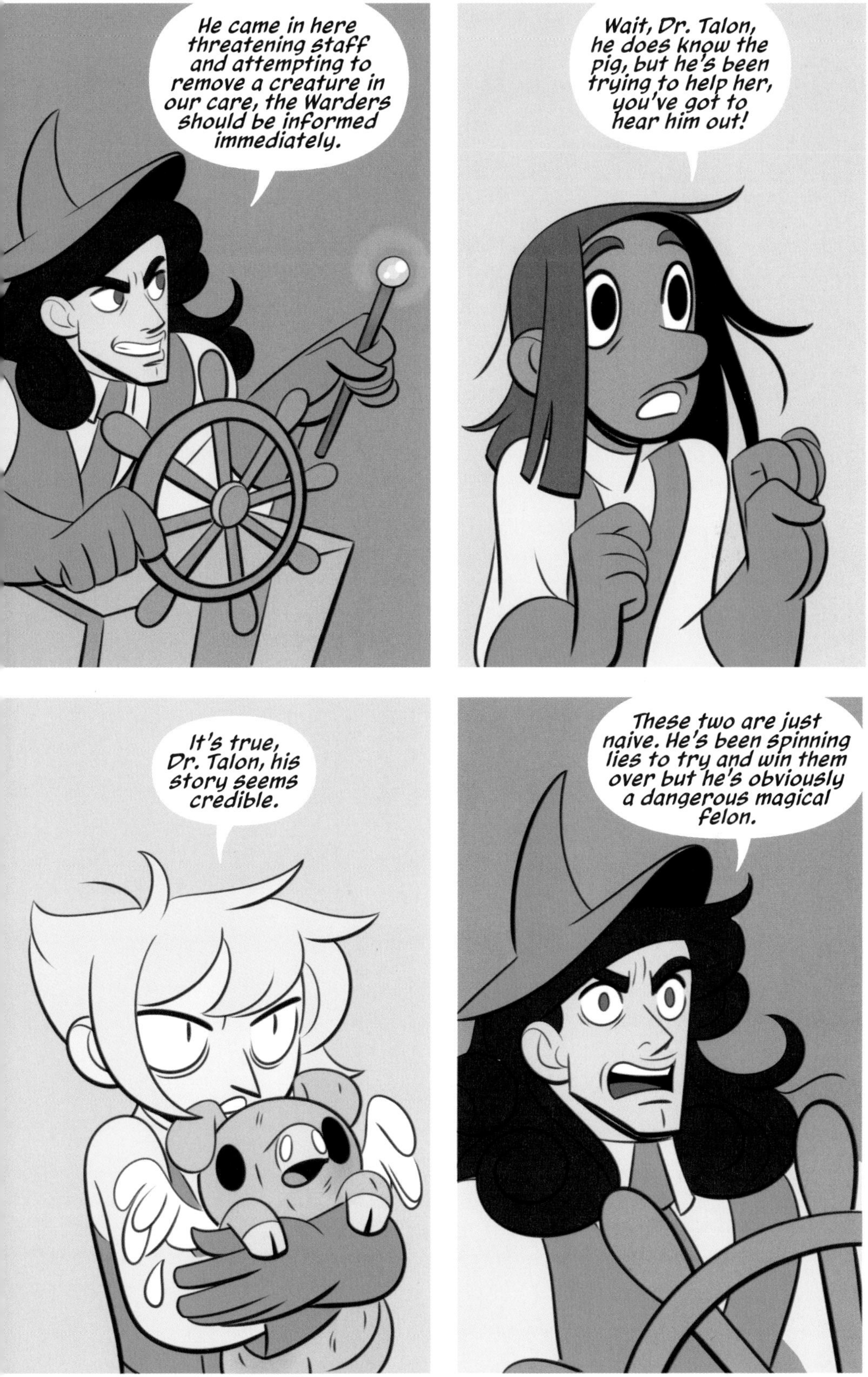
He came in here threatening staff and attempting to remove a creature in our care, the Warders should be informed immediately.
Wait, Dr. Talon, he does know the pig, but he's been trying to help her, you've got to hear him out!
It's true, Dr. Talon, his story seems credible.
These two are just naive. He's been spinning lies to try and win them over but he's obviously a dangerous magical felon.

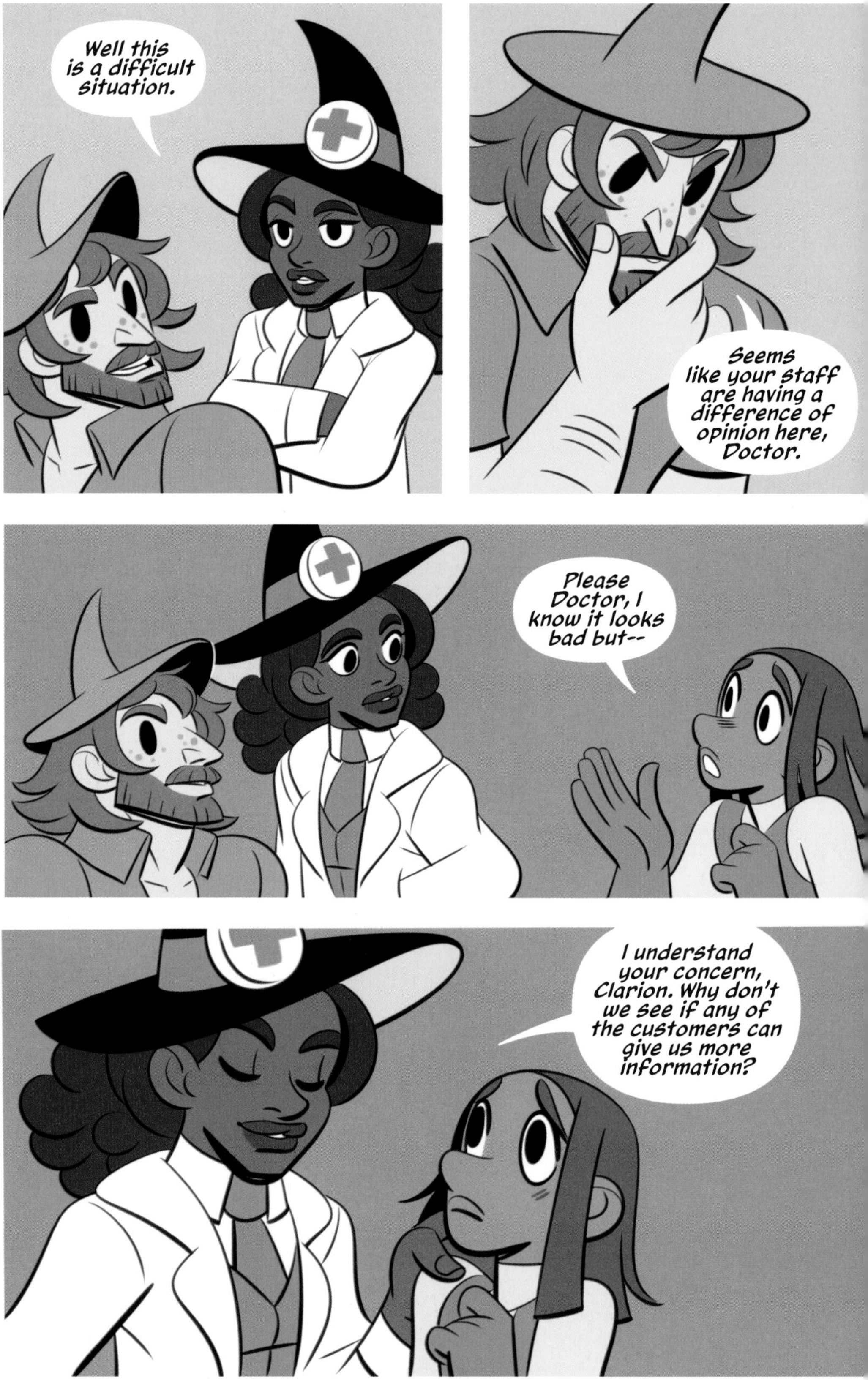

Well this is a difficult situation.
Seems like your staff are having a difference of opinion here, Doctor.
Please Doctor, I know it looks bad but--
I understand your concern, Clarion. Why don't we see if any of the customers can give us more information?

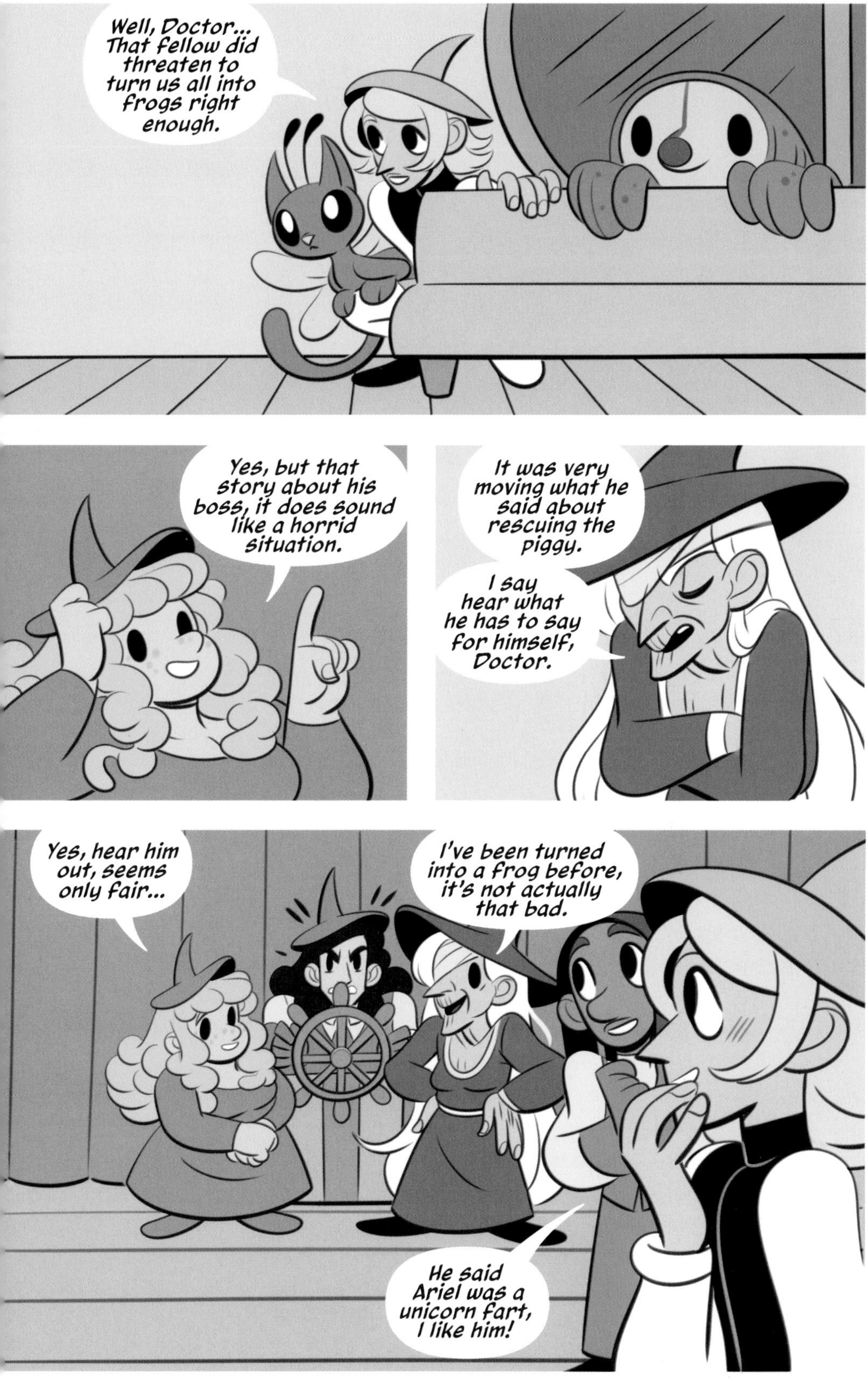

Well, Doctor... That fellow did threaten to turn us all into frogs right enough.
Yes, but that story about his boss, it does sound like a horrid situation.
It was very moving what he said about rescuing the piggy.
I say hear what he has to say for himself, Doctor.
Yes, hear him out, seems only fair...
I've been turned into a frog before, it's not actually that bad.
He said Ariel was a unicorn fart, I like him!

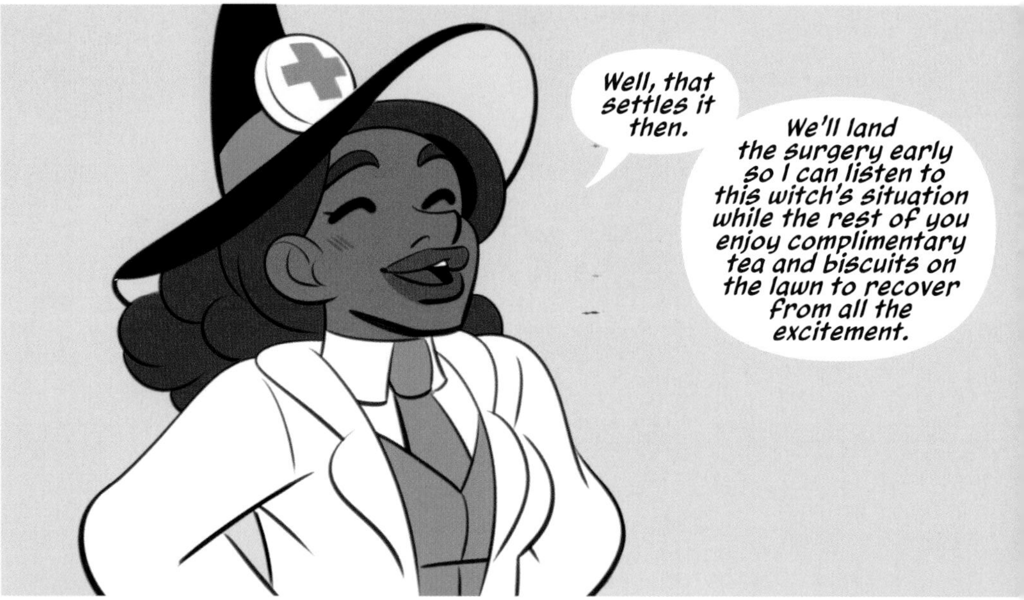
Well, that settles it then.
We'll land the surgery early so I can listen to this witch's situation while the rest of you enjoy complimentary tea and biscuits on the lawn to recover from all the excitement.

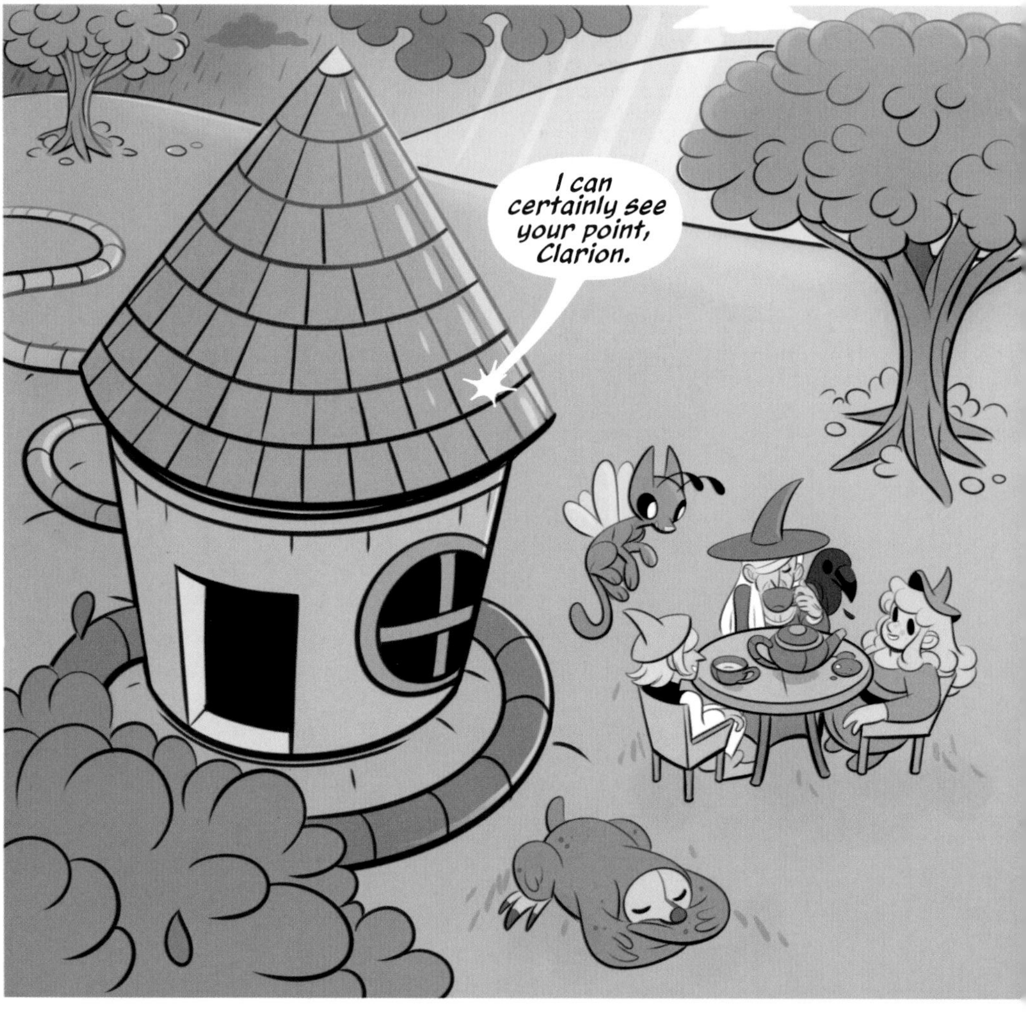
I can certainly see your point, Clarion.

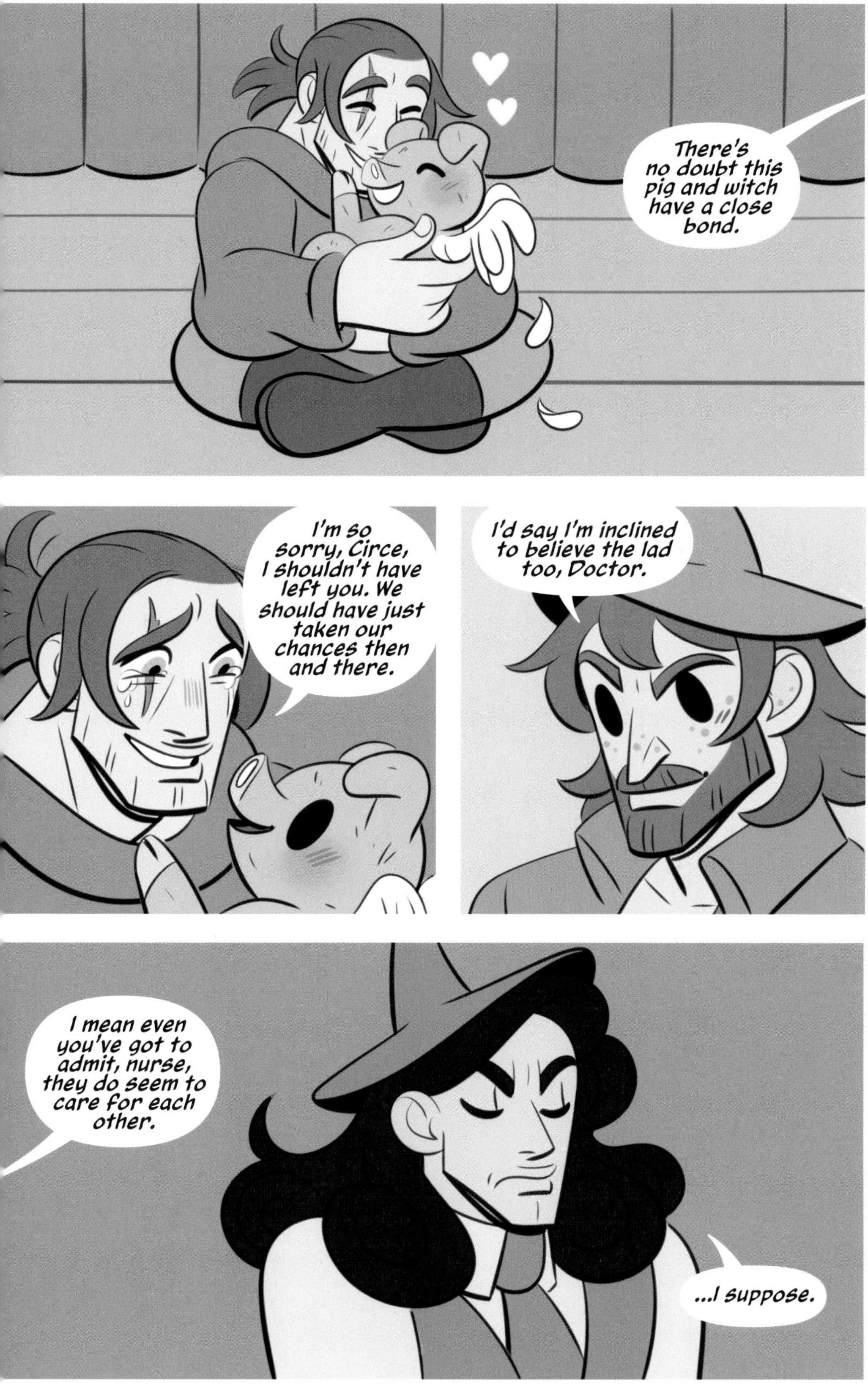
There's no doubt this pig and witch have a close bond.
I'm so sorry, Circe, I shouldn't have left you. We should have just taken our chances then and there.
I'd say I'm inclined to believe the lad too, Doctor.
I mean even you've got to admit, nurse, they do seem to care for each other.
...I suppose.

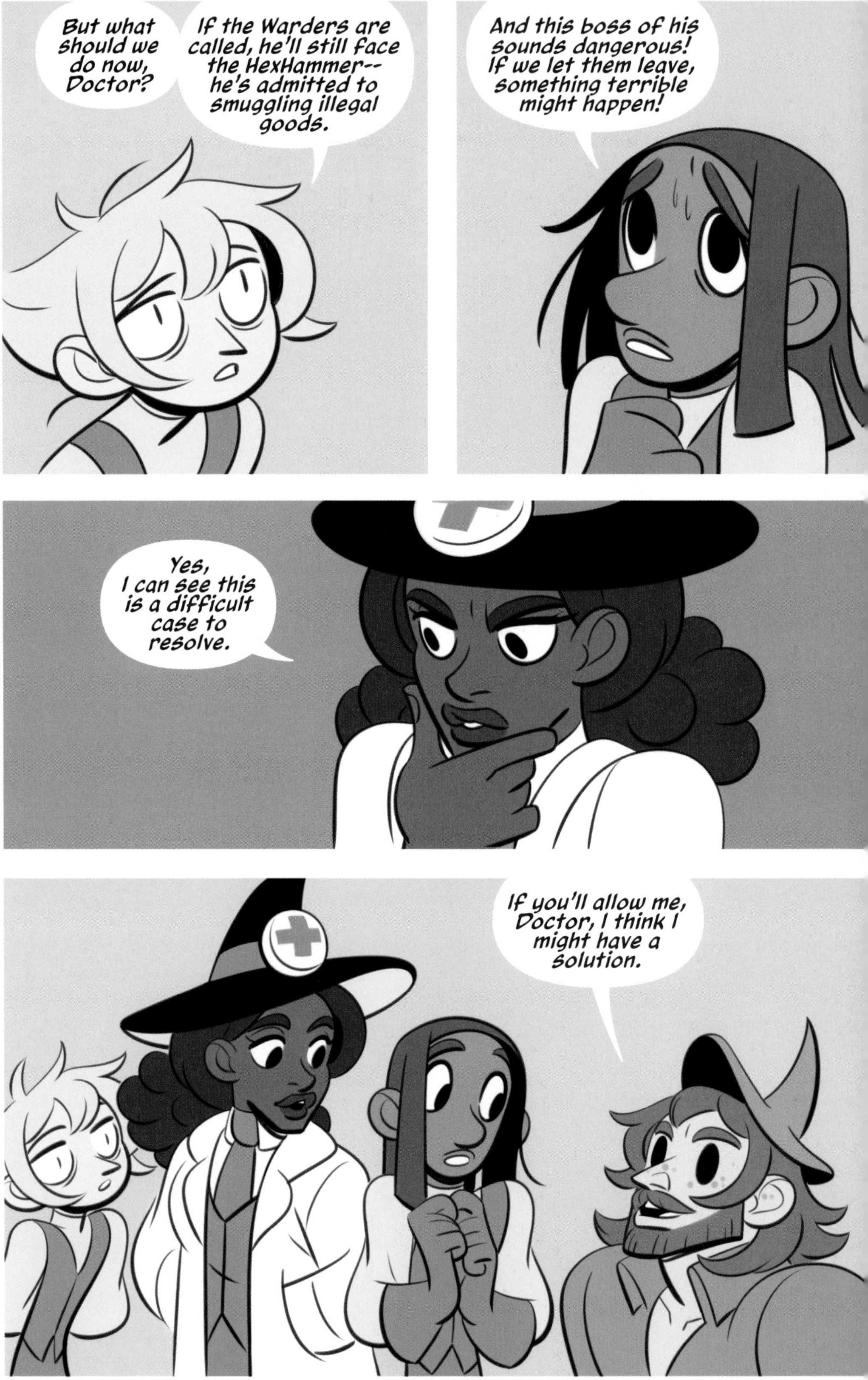
But what should we do now, Doctor?
If the Warders are called, he'll still face the HexHammer-- he's admitted to smuggling illegal goods.
And this boss of his sounds dangerous! If we let them leave, something terrible might happen!
Yes, I can see this is a difficult case to resolve.
If you'll allow me, Doctor, I think I might have a solution.

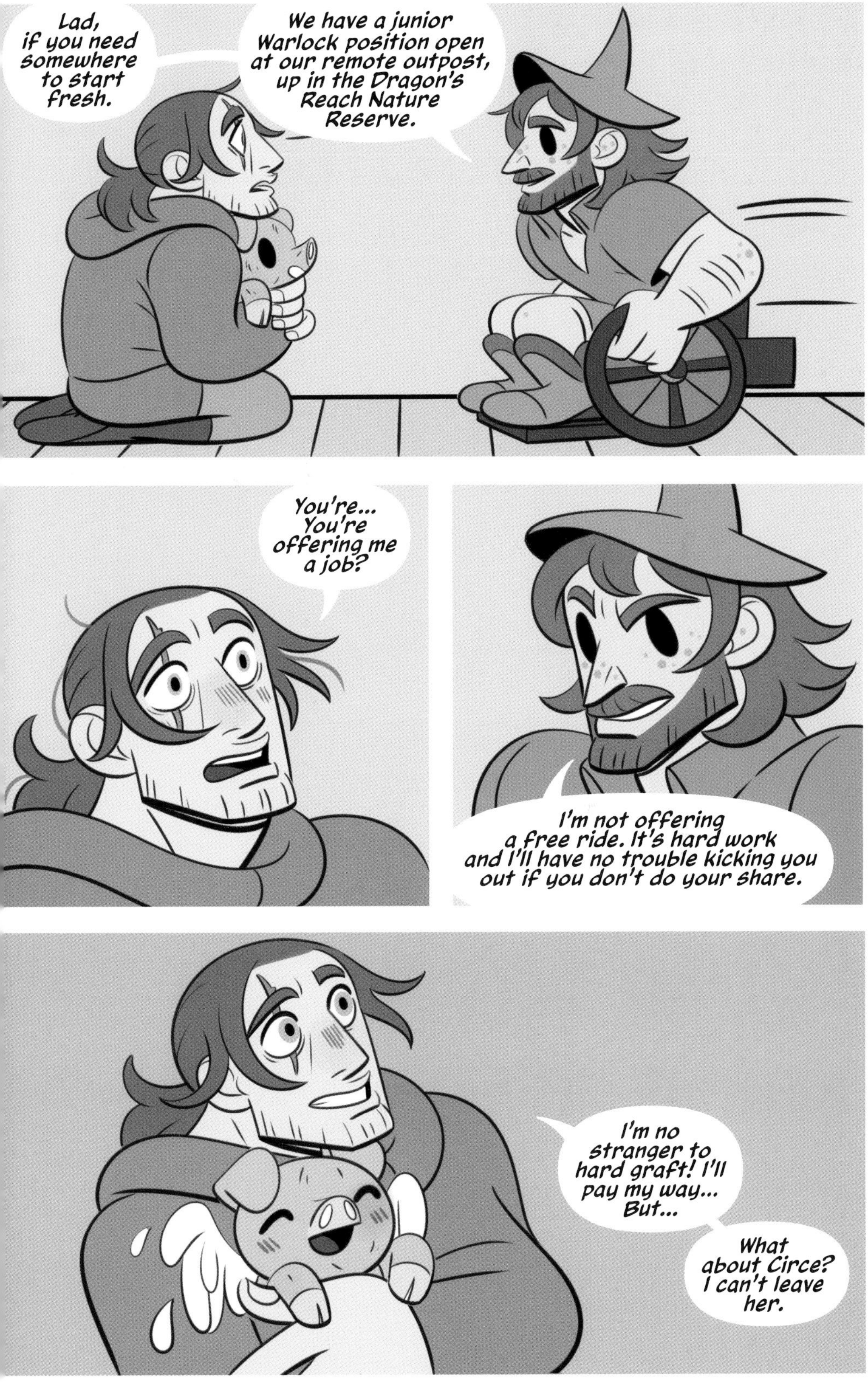
Lad, if you need somewhere to start fresh.
We have a junior Warlock position open at our remote outpost, up in the Dragon's Reach Nature Reserve.
You're... You're offering me a job?
I'm not offering a free ride. It's hard work and I'll have no trouble kicking you out if you don't do your share.
I'm no stranger to hard graft! I'll pay my way... But...
What about Circe? I can't leave her.

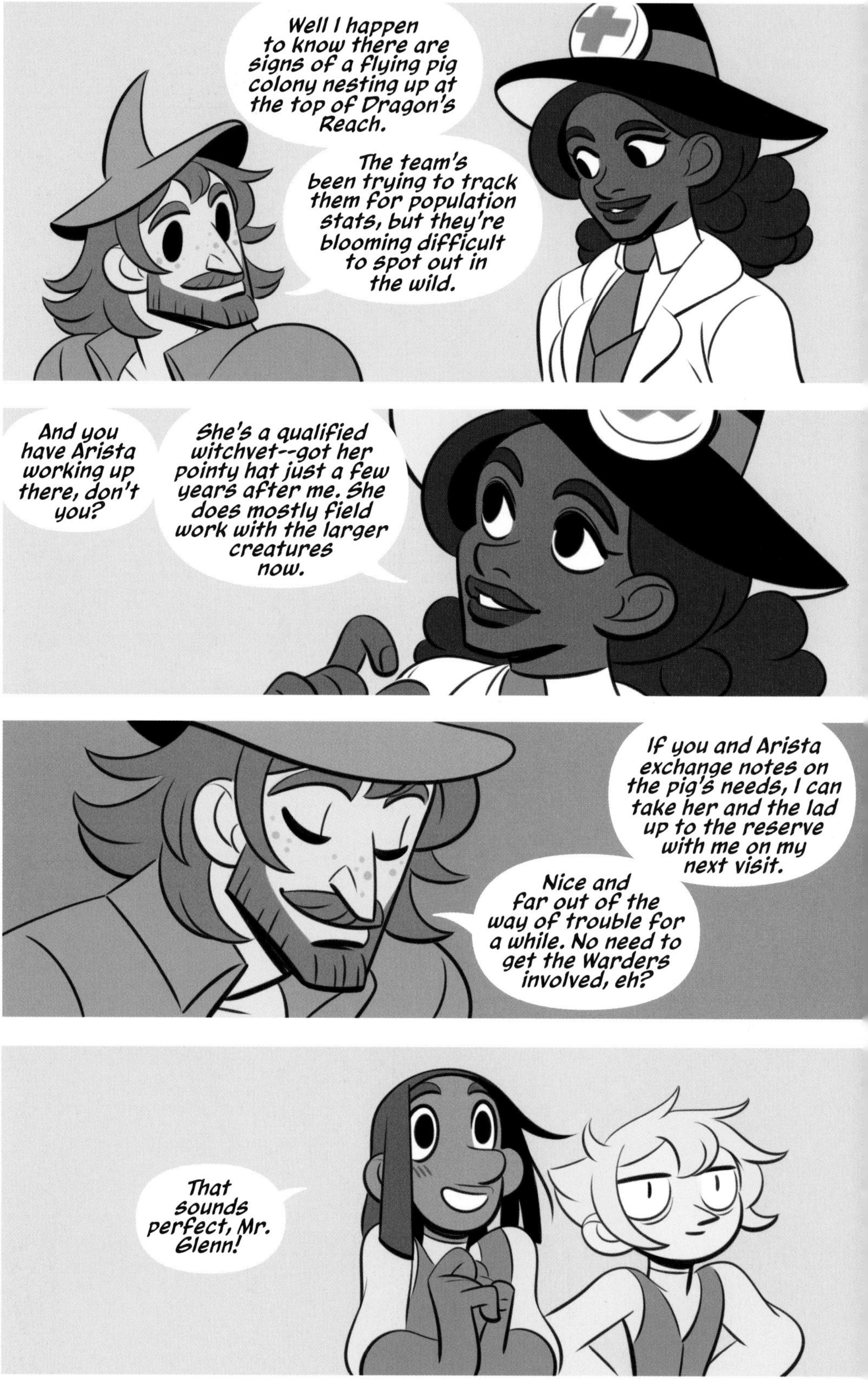
Well I happen to know there are signs of a flying pig colony nesting up at the top of Dragon's Reach.
The team's been trying to track them for population stats, but they're blooming difficult to spot out in the wild.
And you have Arista working up there, don't you?
She's a qualified witchvet--got her pointy hat just a few years after me. She does mostly field work with the larger creatures now.
If you and Arista exchange notes on the pig's needs, I can take her and the lad up to the reserve with me on my next visit.
Nice and far out of the way of trouble for a while. No need to get the Warders involved, eh?
That sounds perfect, Mr. Glenn!

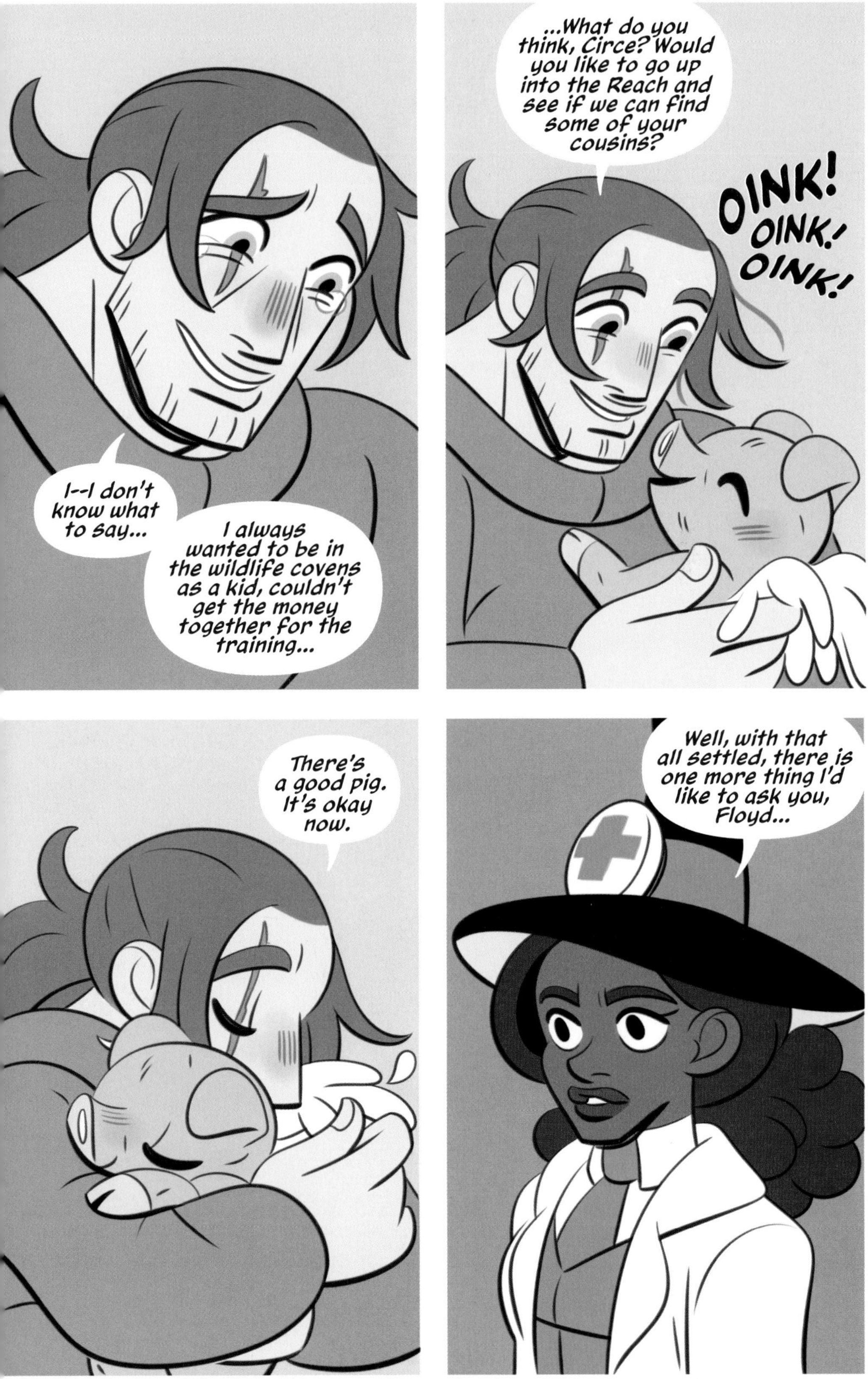
I--I don't know what to say...
I always wanted to be in the wildlife covens as a kid, couldn't get the money together for the training...
...What do you think, Circe? Would you like to go up into the Reach and see if we can find some of your cousins?
OINK! OINK! OINK!
There's a good pig. It's okay now.
Well, with that all settled, there is one more thing I'd like to ask you, Floyd...

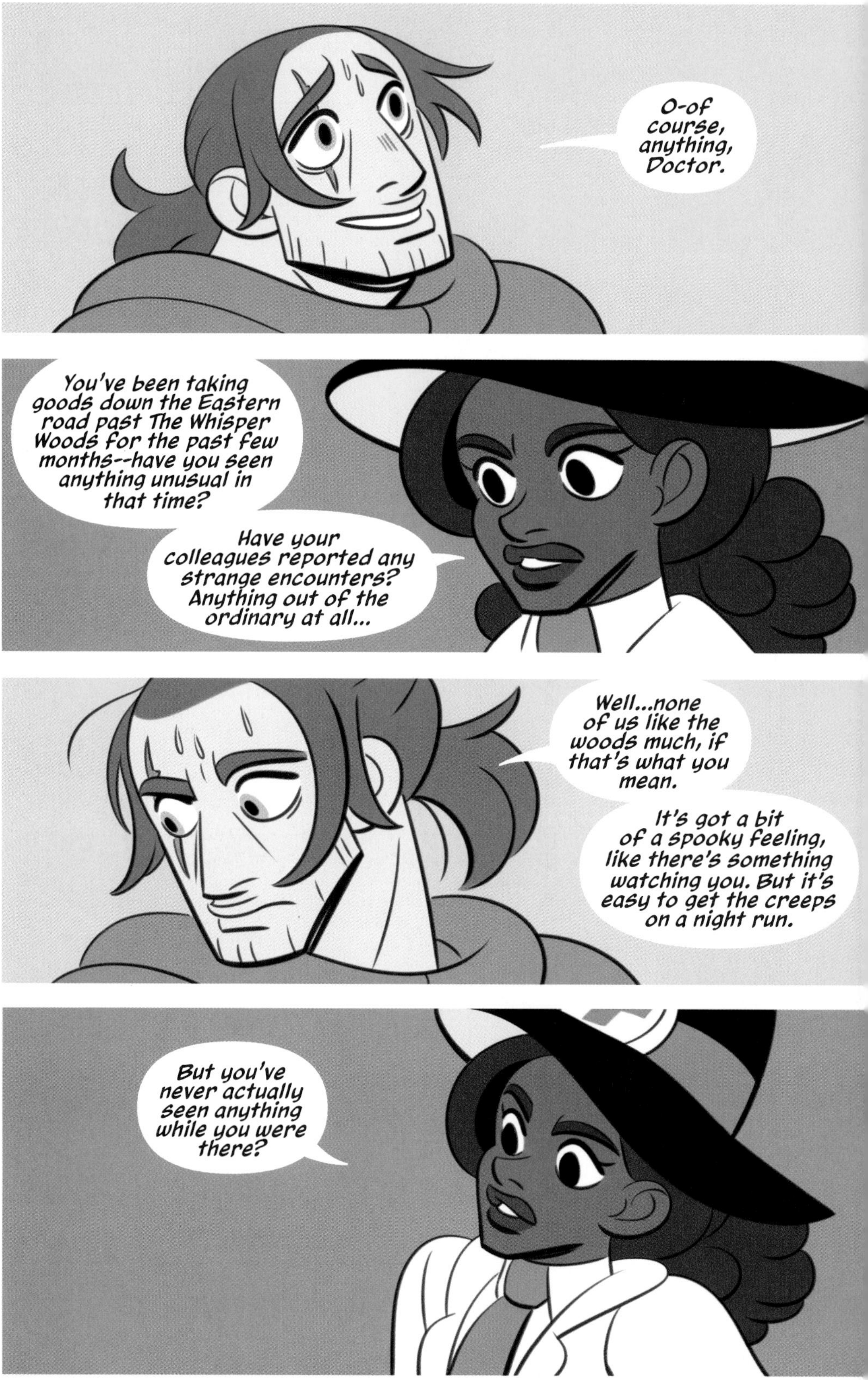

O-of course, anything, Doctor.
You've been taking goods down the Eastern road past The Whisper Woods for the past few months--have you seen anything unusual in that time?
Have your colleagues reported any strange encounters? Anything out of the ordinary at all...
Well...none of us like the woods much, if that's what you mean.
It's got a bit of a spooky feeling, like there's something watching you. But it's easy to get the creeps on a night run.
But you've never actually seen anything while you were there?

There was this one night, I was driving through with Little Sue. We had a shipment of horrible old bones some necromancer had ordered in the city, so we were already a bit on edge, mind you.
I thought I saw this dark shape moving through the trees a couple of times, keeping pace with us. At first, I thought I was imagining things, but then Little Sue suddenly swerved the coach and we almost went over into a hedge row.
When I got my breath back I asked her what happened. She said something huge ran across the road--something "black, blacker than the sky behind it" was what she said.
She was shaking something terrible. I had to drive the rest of the way--she was that spooked.

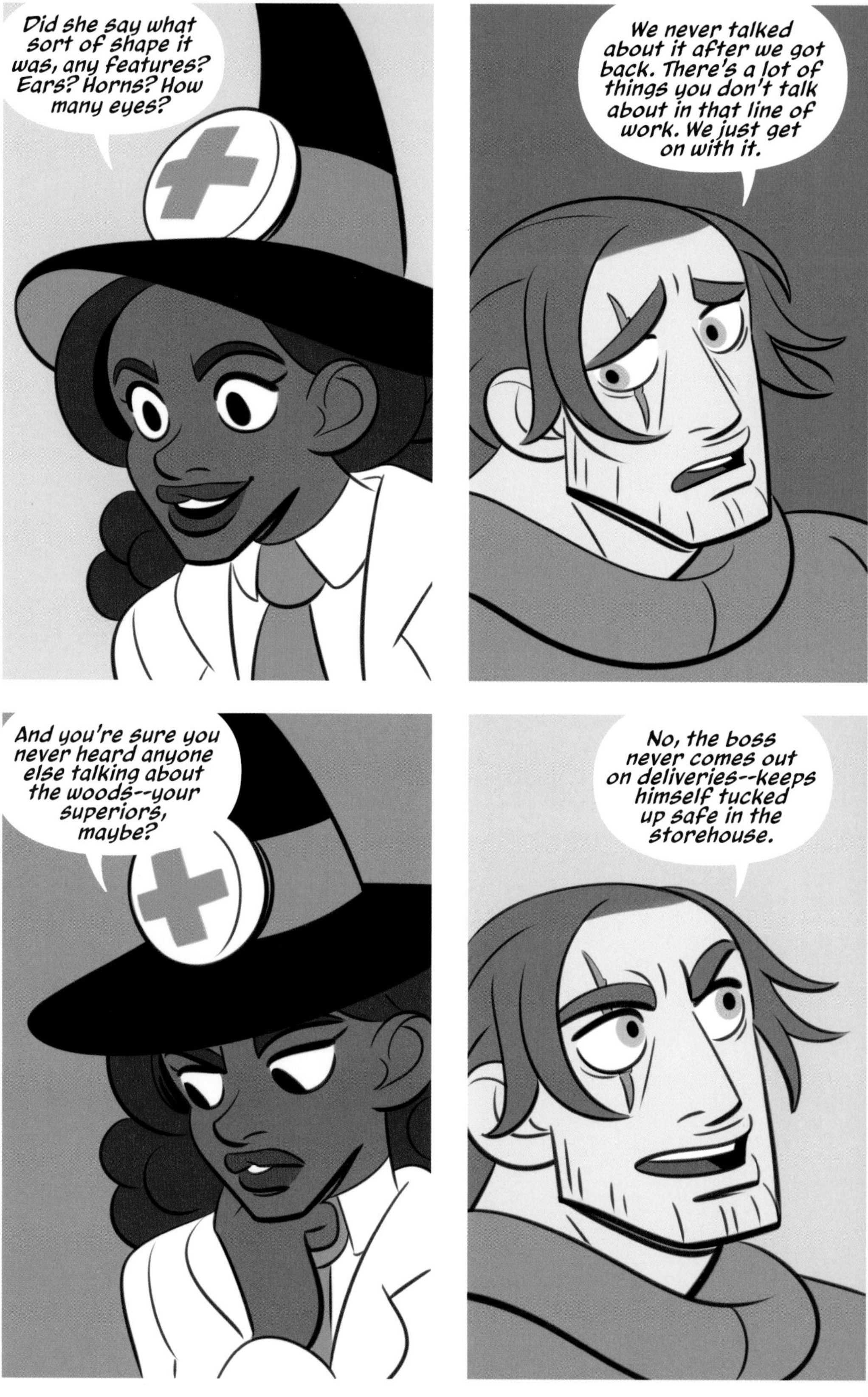
Did she say what sort of shape it was, any features? Ears? Horns? How many eyes?
We never talked about it after we got back. There's a lot of things you don't talk about in that line of work. We just get on with it.
And you're sure you never heard anyone else talking about the woods--your superiors, maybe?
No, the boss never comes out on deliveries--keeps himself tucked up safe in the storehouse.

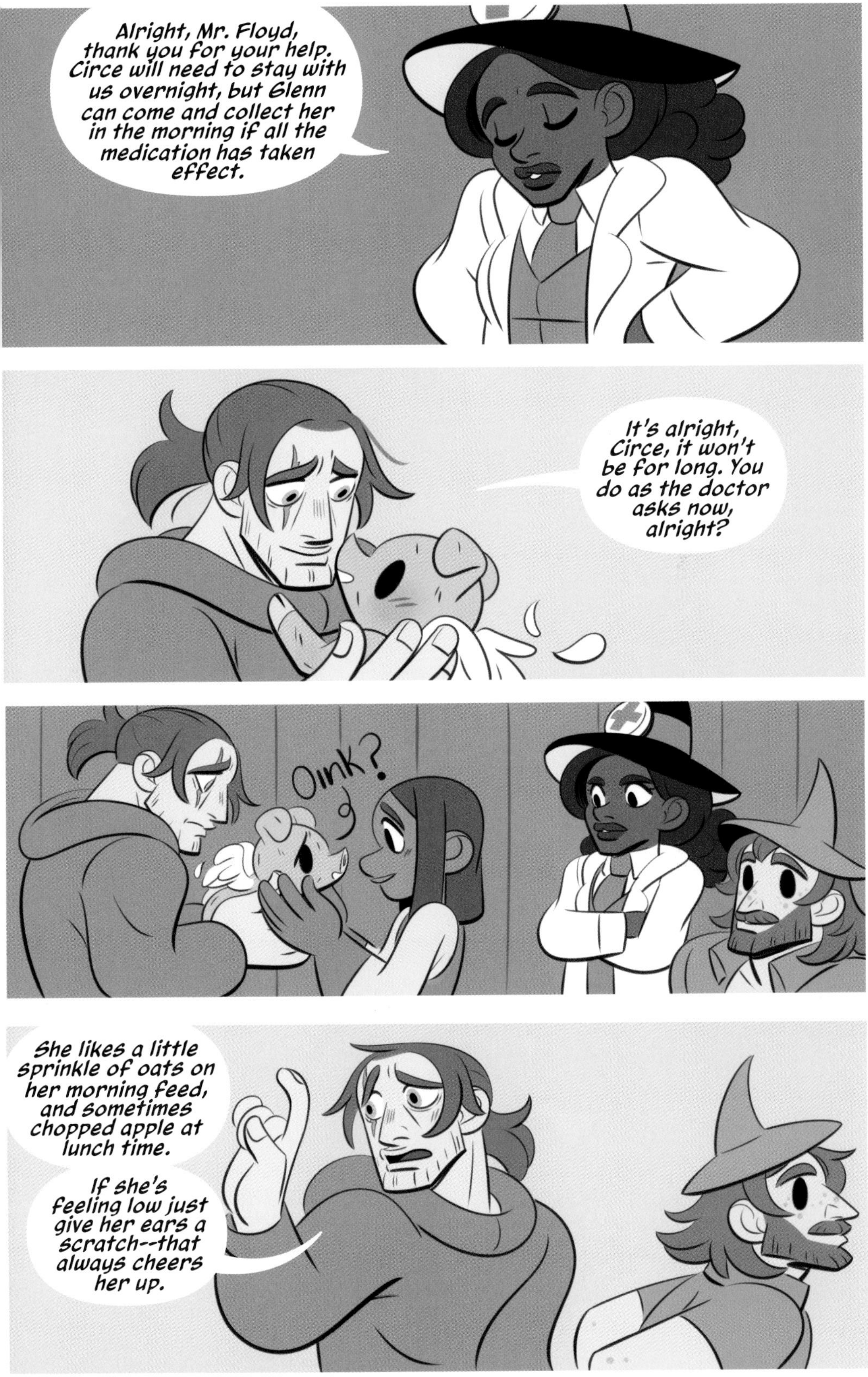
Alright, Mr. Floyd, thank you for your help. Circe will need to stay with us overnight, but Glenn can come and collect her in the morning if all the medication has taken effect.
It's alright, Circe, it won't be for long. You do as the doctor asks now, alright?
Oink?
She likes a little sprinkle of oats on her morning feed, and sometimes chopped apple at lunch time.
If she's feeling low just give her ears a scratch--that always cheers her up.

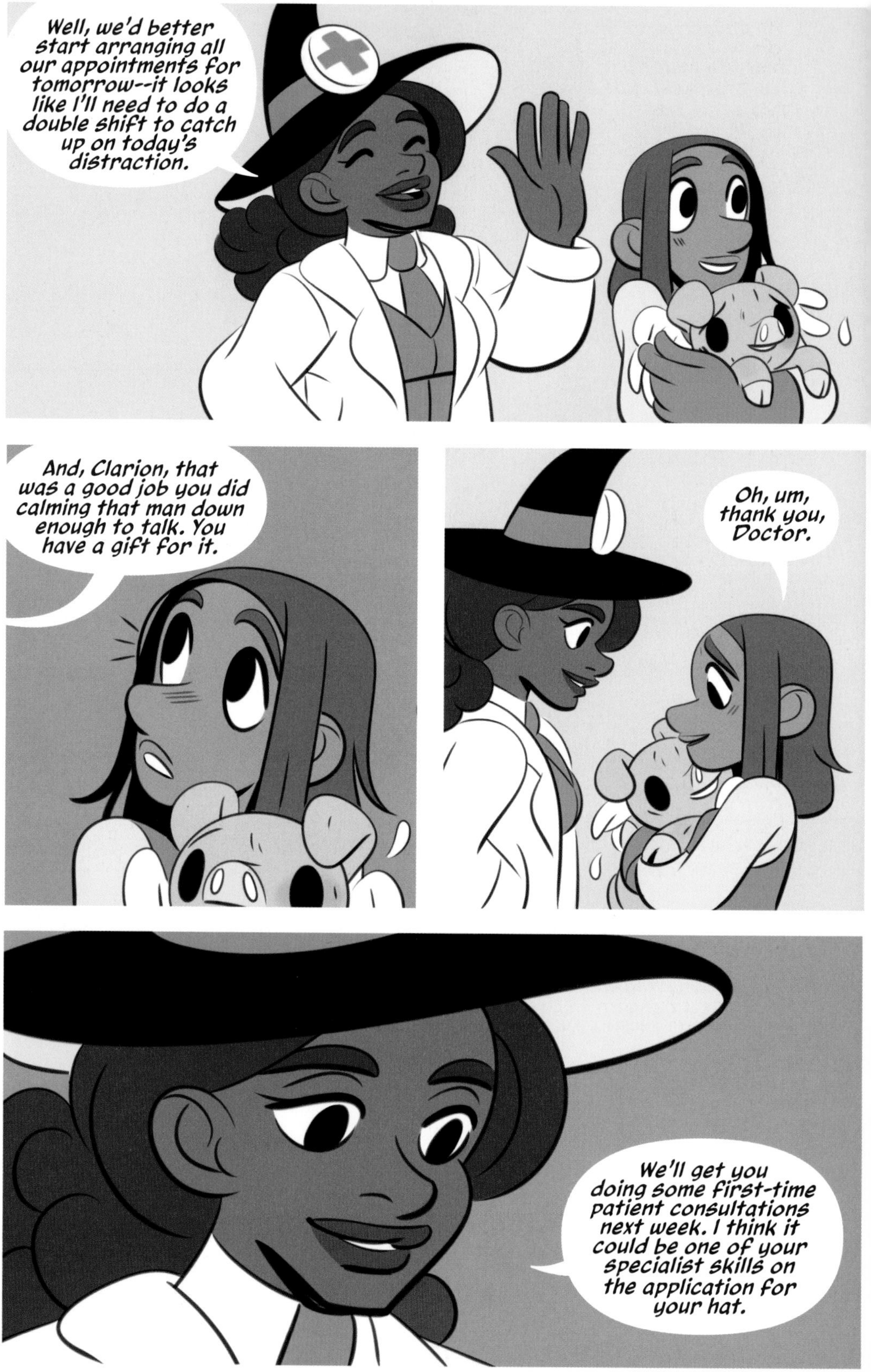
Well, we'd better start arranging all our appointments for tomorrow--it looks like I'll need to do a double shift to catch up on today's distraction.
And, Clarion, that was a good job you did calming that man down enough to talk. You have a gift for it.
Oh, um, thank you, Doctor.
We'll get you doing some first-time patient consultations next week. I think it could be one of your specialist skills on the application for your hat.

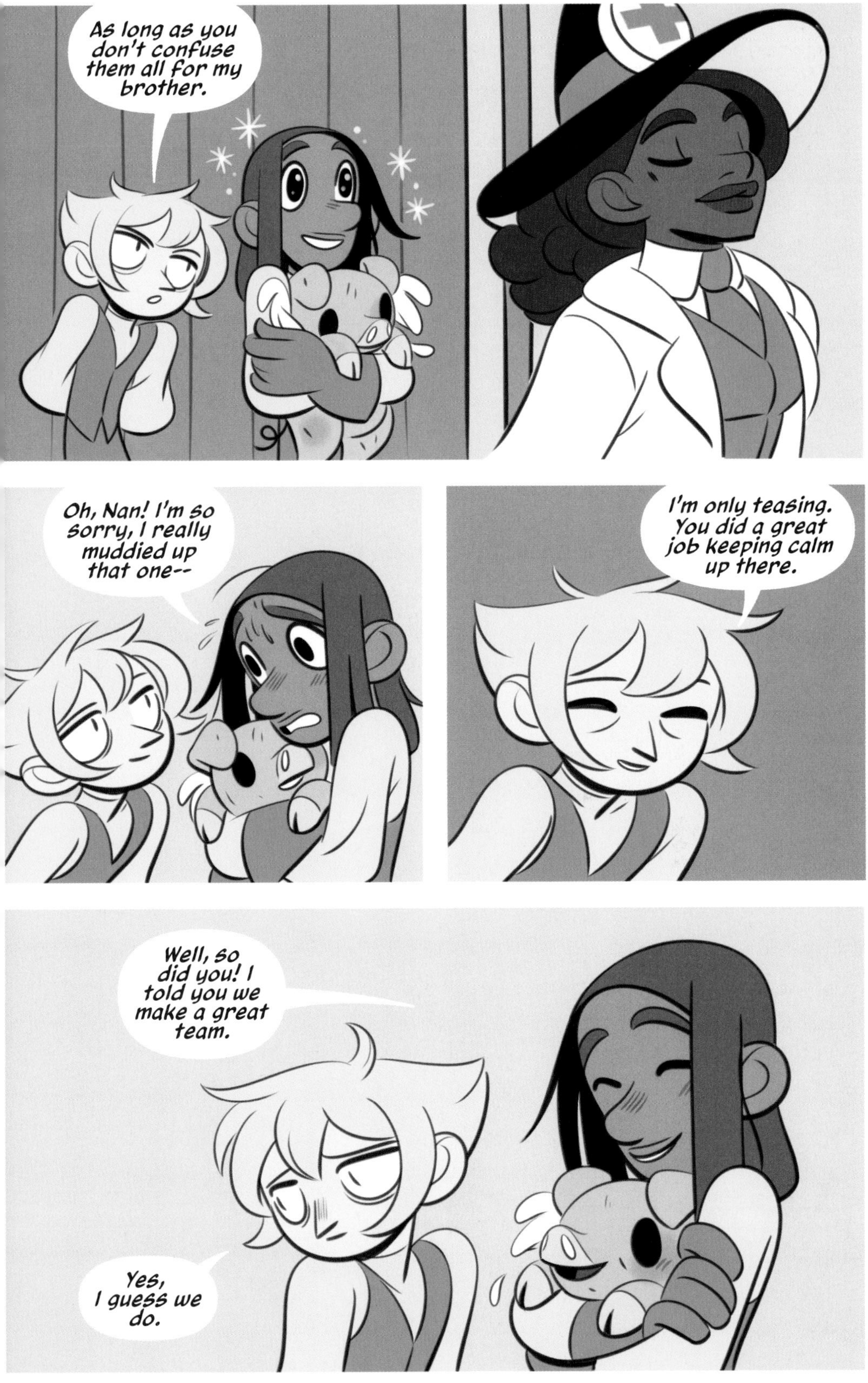
As long as you don't confuse them all for my brother.
Oh, Nan! I'm so sorry, I really muddied up that one--
I'm only teasing. You did a great job keeping calm up there.
Well, so did you! I told you we make a great team.
Yes, I guess we do.

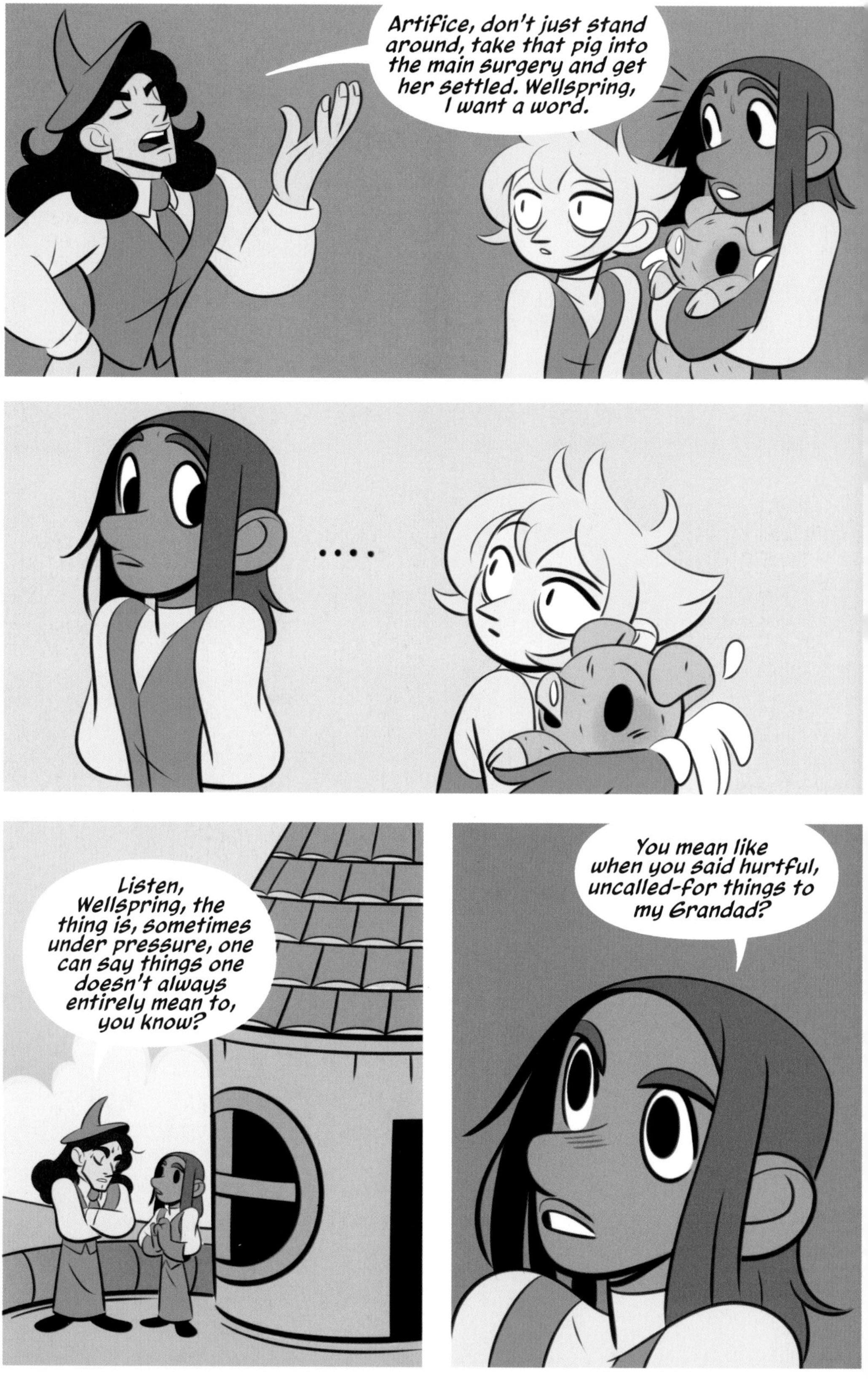
Artifice, don't just stand around, take that pig into the main surgery and get her settled. Wellspring, I want a word.
....
Listen, Wellspring, the thing is, sometimes under pressure, one can say things one doesn't always entirely mean to, you know?
You mean like when you said hurtful, uncalled-for things to my Grandad?

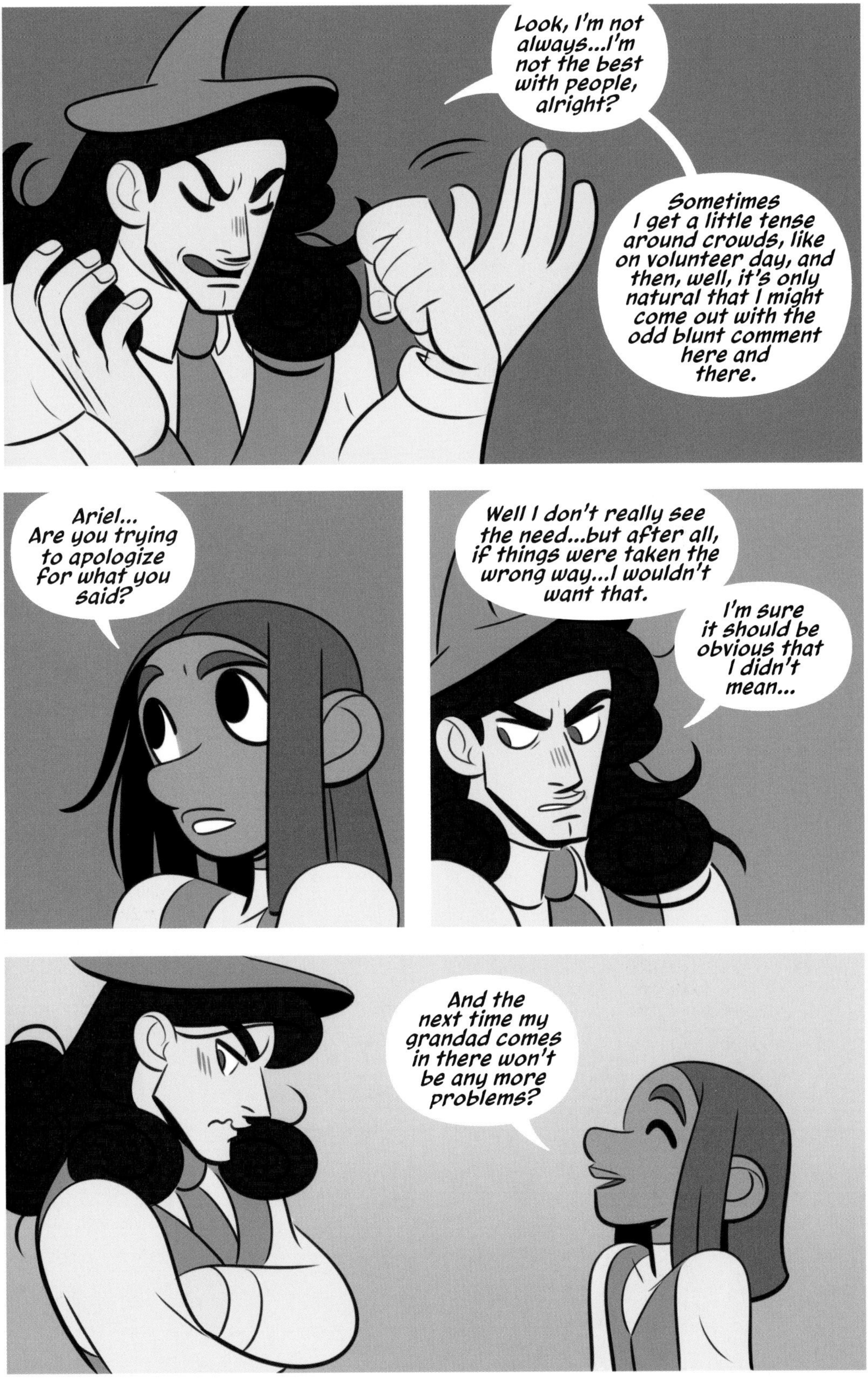

Look, I'm not always...I'm not the best with people, alright?
Sometimes I get a little tense around crowds, like on volunteer day, and then, well, it's only natural that I might come out with the odd blunt comment here and there.
Ariel... Are you trying to apologize for what you said?
Well I don't really see the need...but after all, if things were taken the wrong way...I wouldn't want that.
I'm sure it should be obvious that I didn't mean...
And the next time my grandad comes in there won't be any more problems?

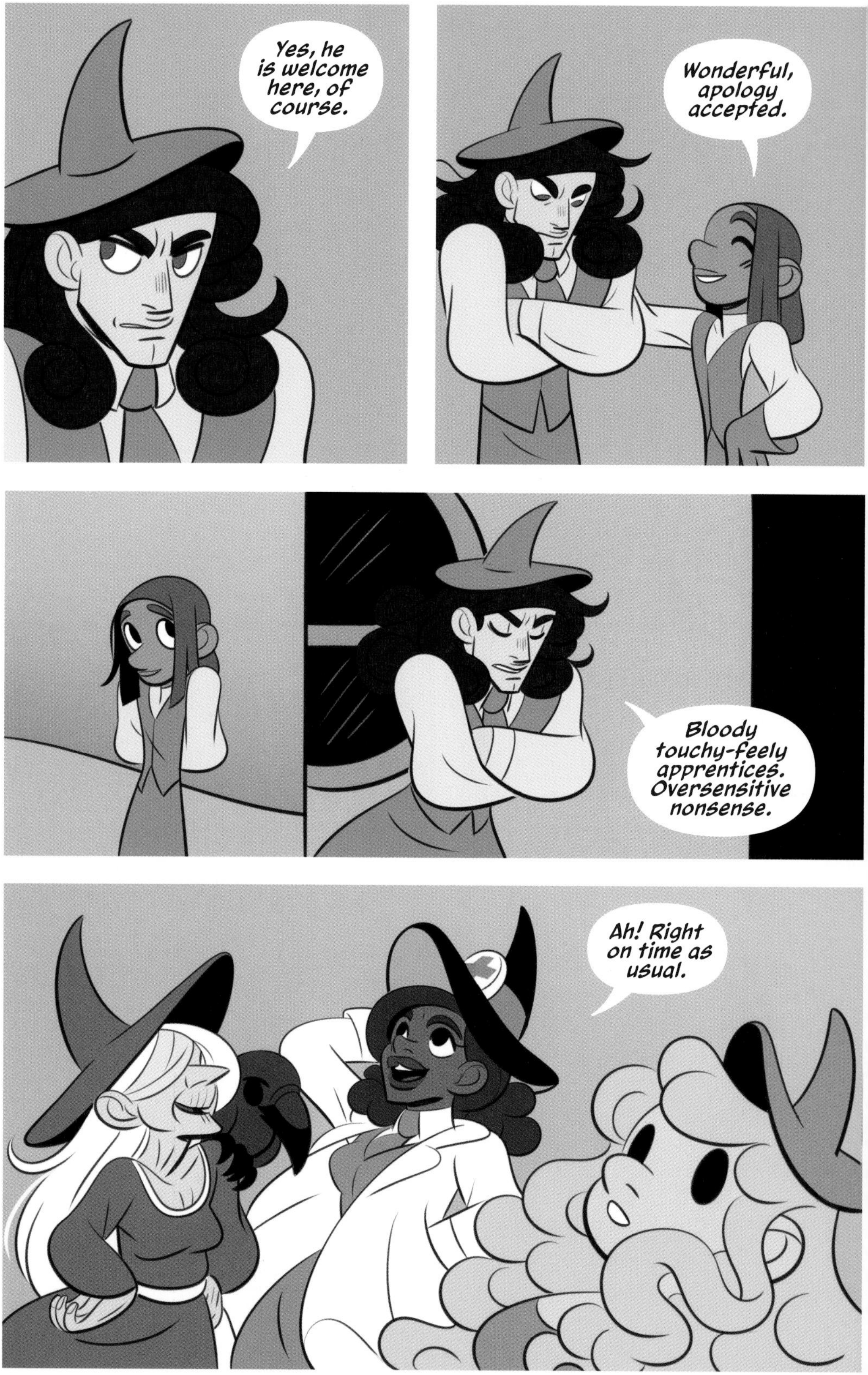
Yes, he is welcome here, of course.
Wonderful, apology accepted.
Bloody touchy-feely apprentices. Oversensitive nonsense.
Ah! Right on time as usual.

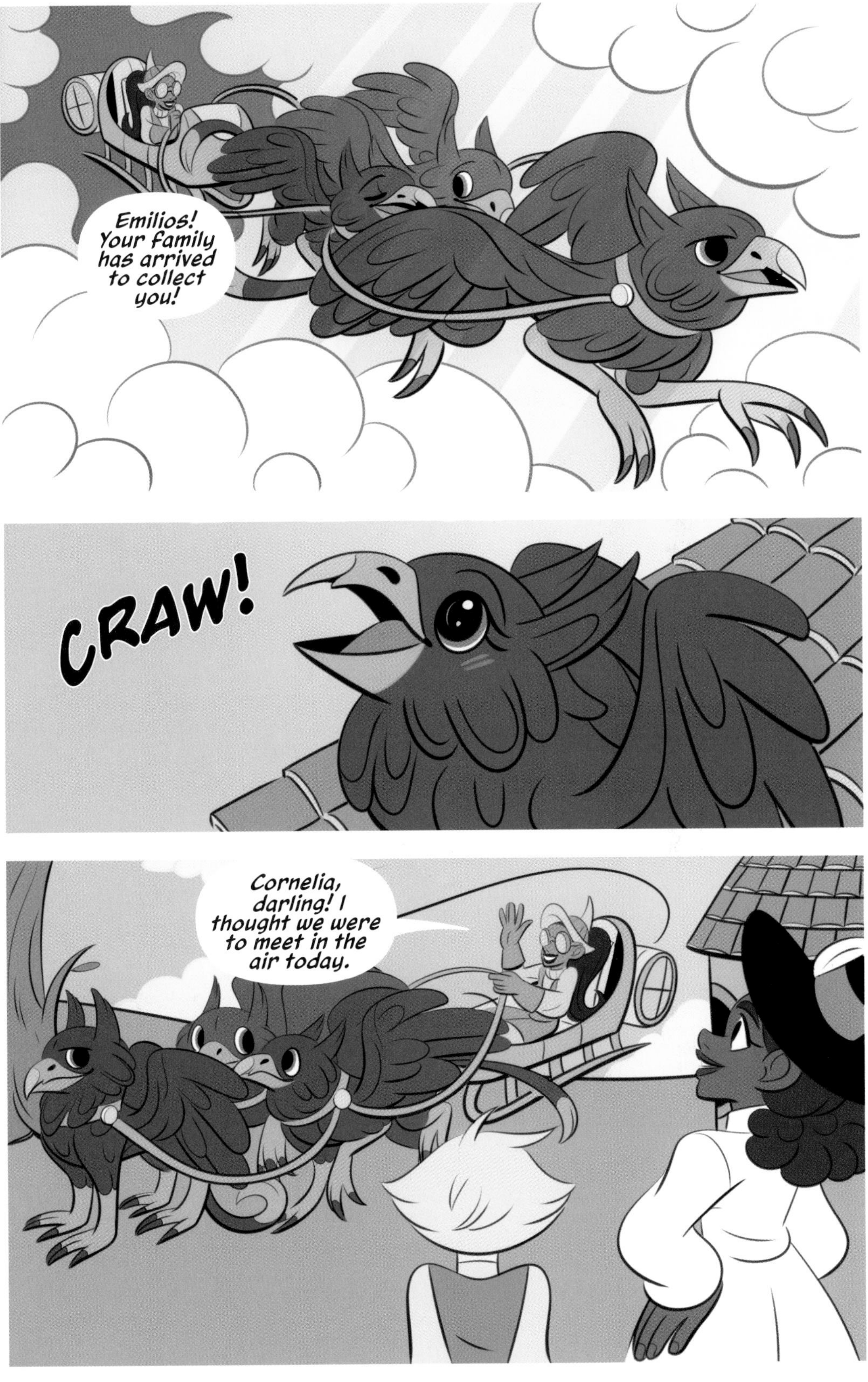
Emilios! Your family has arrived to collect you!
CRAW!
Cornelia, darling! I thought we were to meet in the air today.

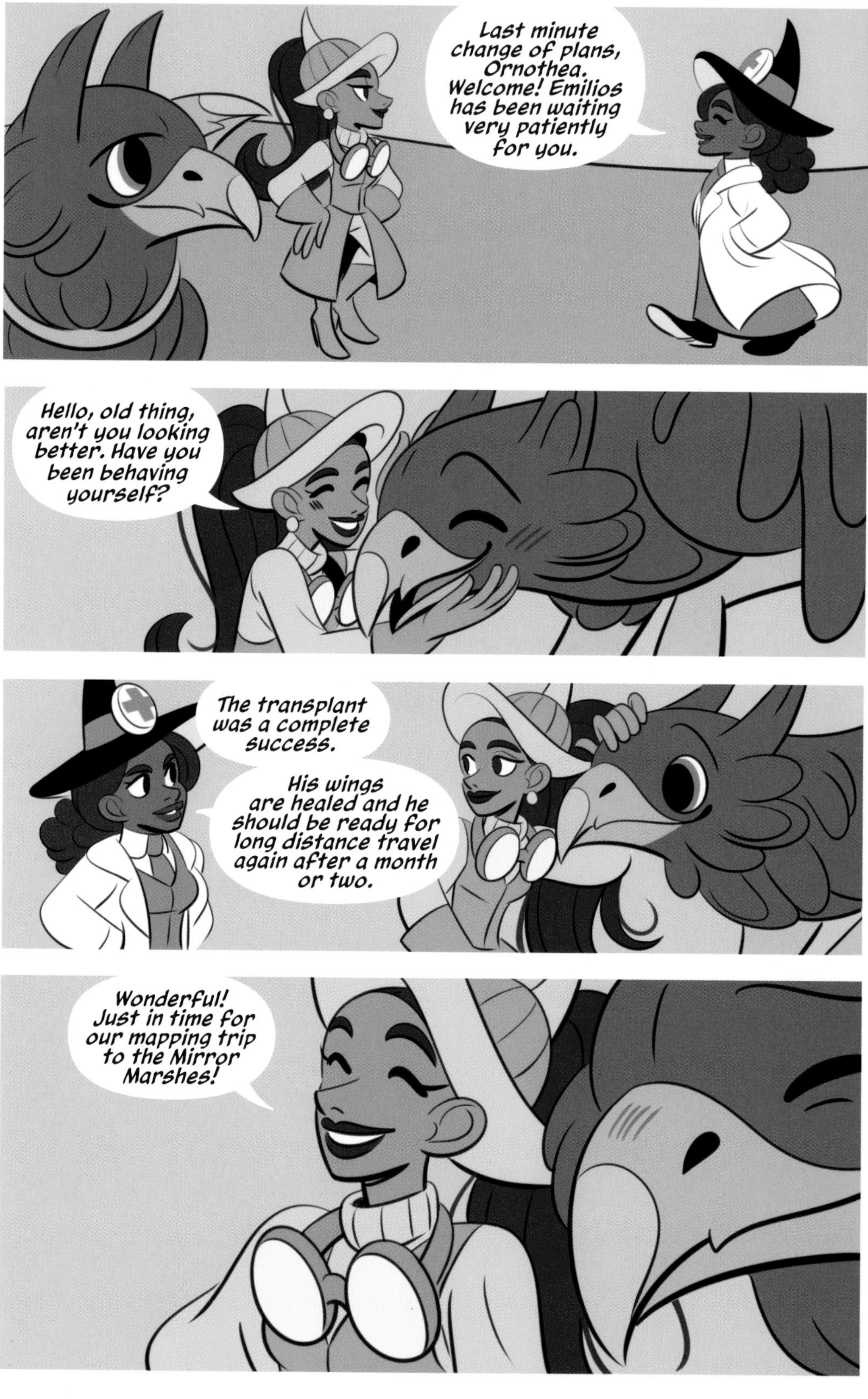
Last minute change of plans, Ornothea. Welcome! Emilios has been waiting very patiently for you.
Hello, old thing, aren't you looking better. Have you been behaving yourself?
The transplant was a complete success.
His wings are healed and he should be ready for long distance travel again after a month or two.
Wonderful! Just in time for our mapping trip to the Mirror Marshes!

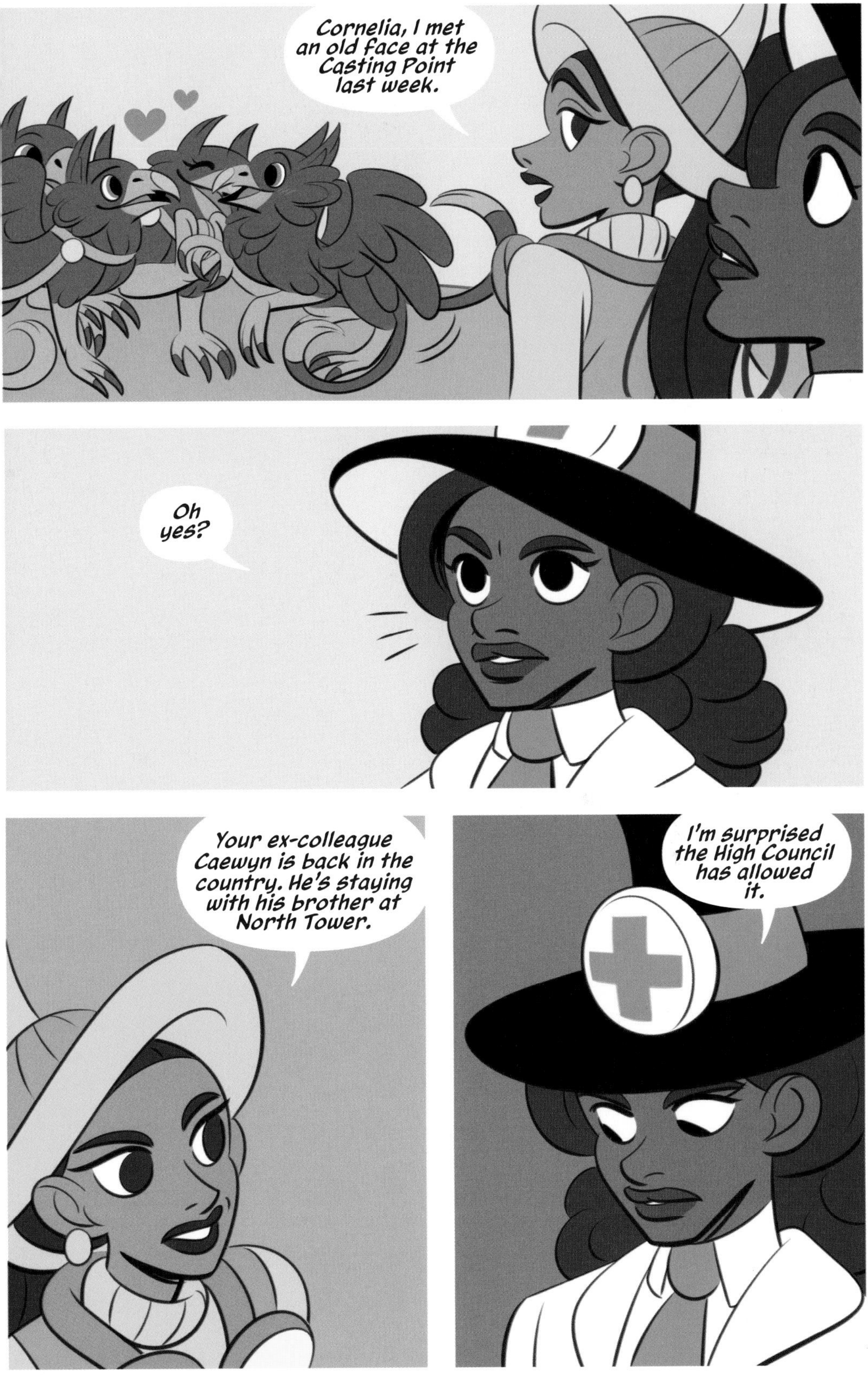
Cornelia, I met an old face at the Casting Point last week.
Oh yes?
Your ex-colleague Caewyn is back in the country. He's staying with his brother at North Tower.
I'm surprised the High Council has allowed it.

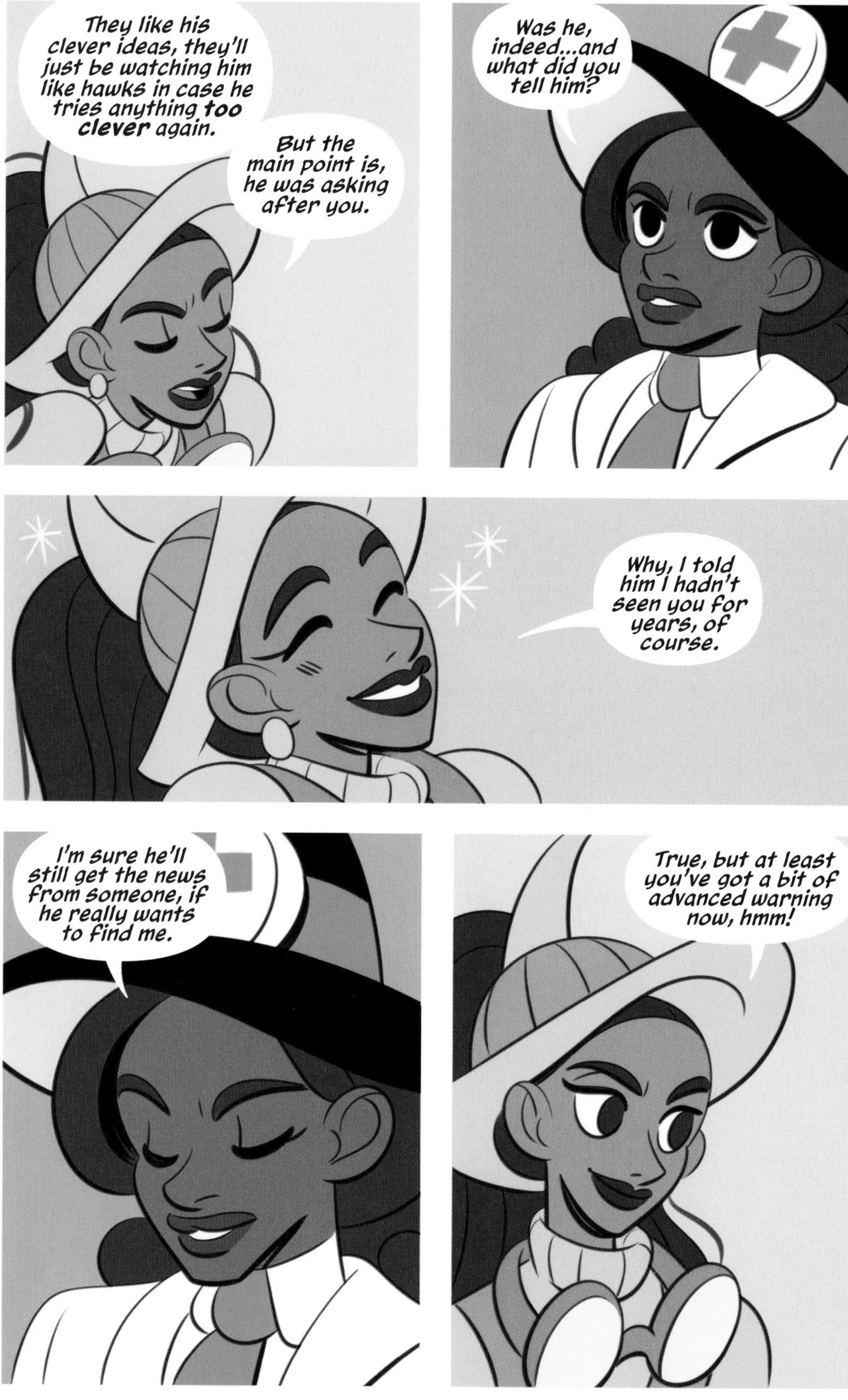
They like his clever ideas, they'll just be watching him like hawks in case he tries anything **too clever** again.
But the main point is, he was asking after you.
Was he, indeed...and what did you tell him?
Why, I told him I hadn't seen you for years, of course.
I'm sure he'll still get the news from someone, if he really wants to find me.
True, but at least you've got a bit of advanced warning now, hmm!

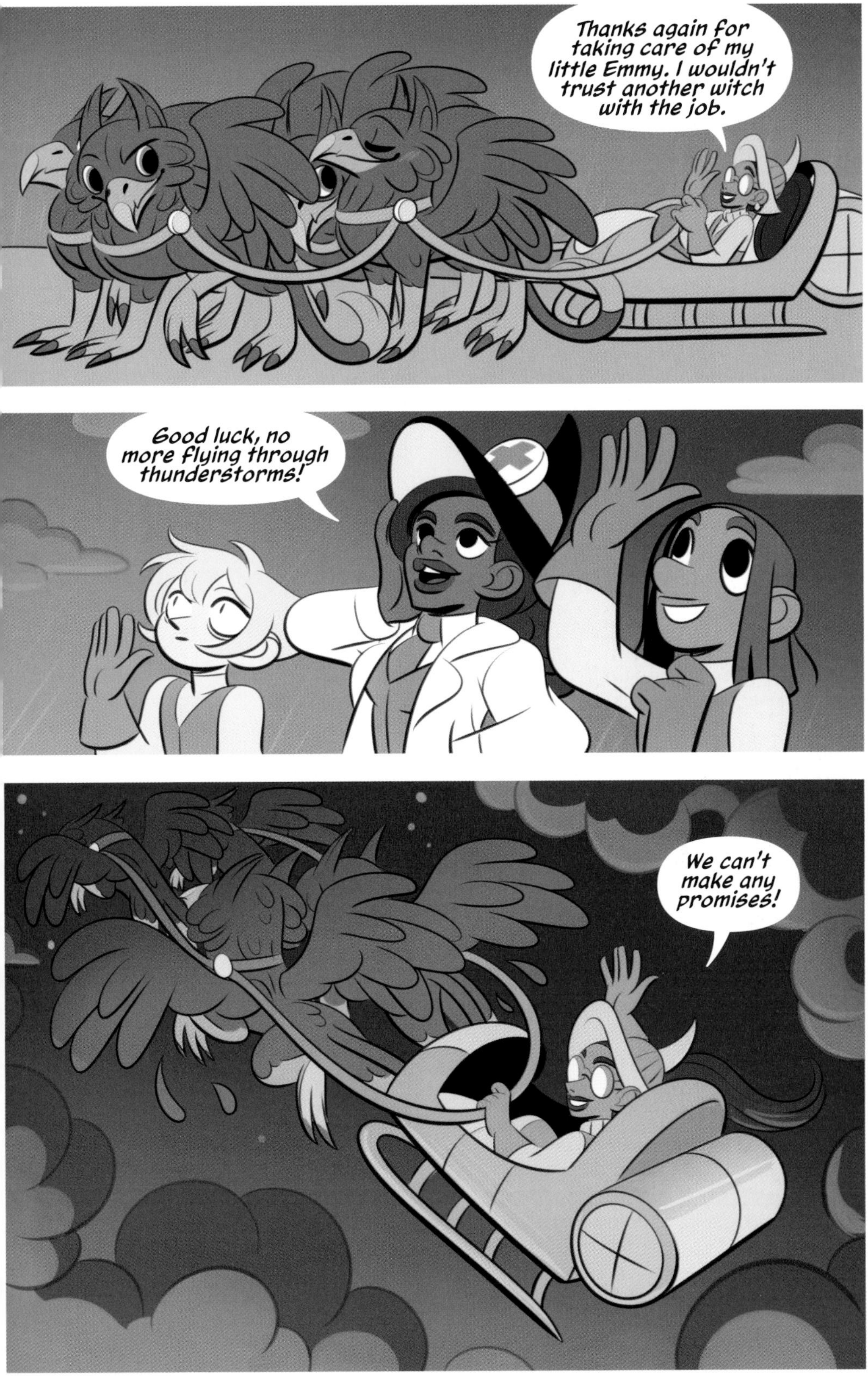
Thanks again for taking care of my little Emmy. I wouldn't trust another witch with the job.
Good luck, no more flying through thunderstorms!
We can't make any promises!

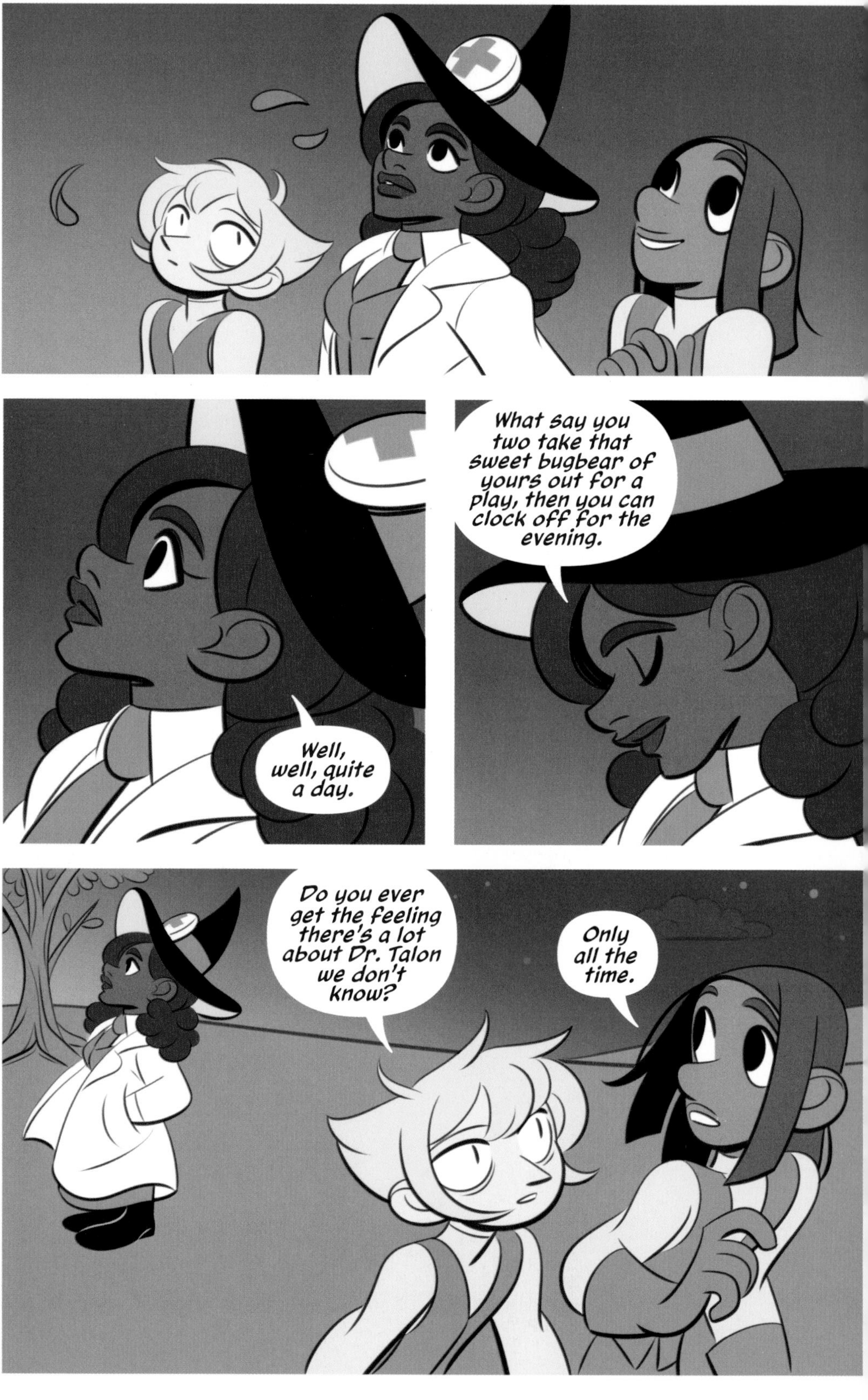
Well, well, quite a day.
What say you two take that sweet bugbear of yours out for a play, then you can clock off for the evening.
Do you ever get the feeling there's a lot about Dr. Talon we don't know?
Only all the time.

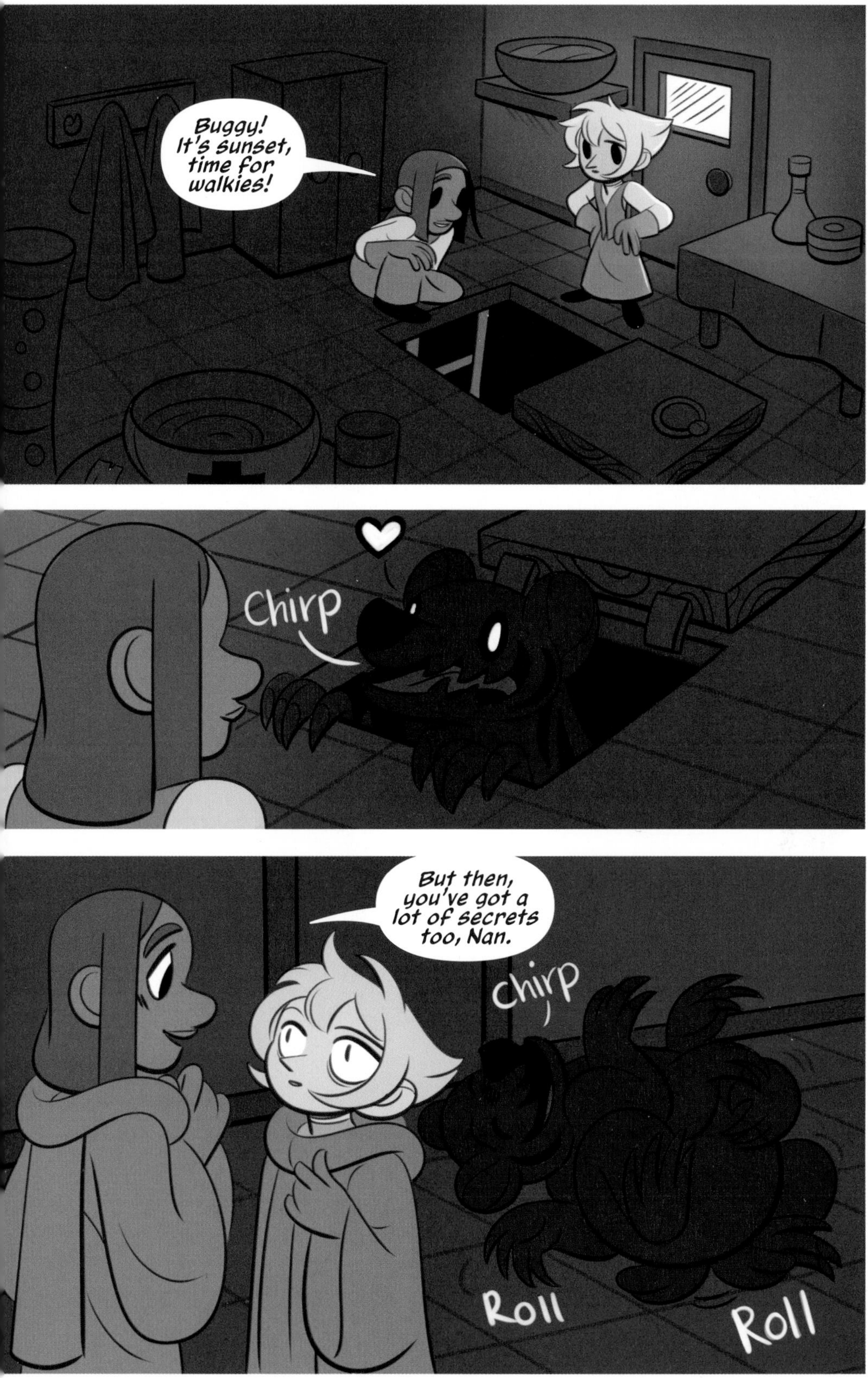
Buggy! It's sunset, time for walkies!
Chirp
But then, you've got a lot of secrets too, Nan.
Chirp
Roll
Roll

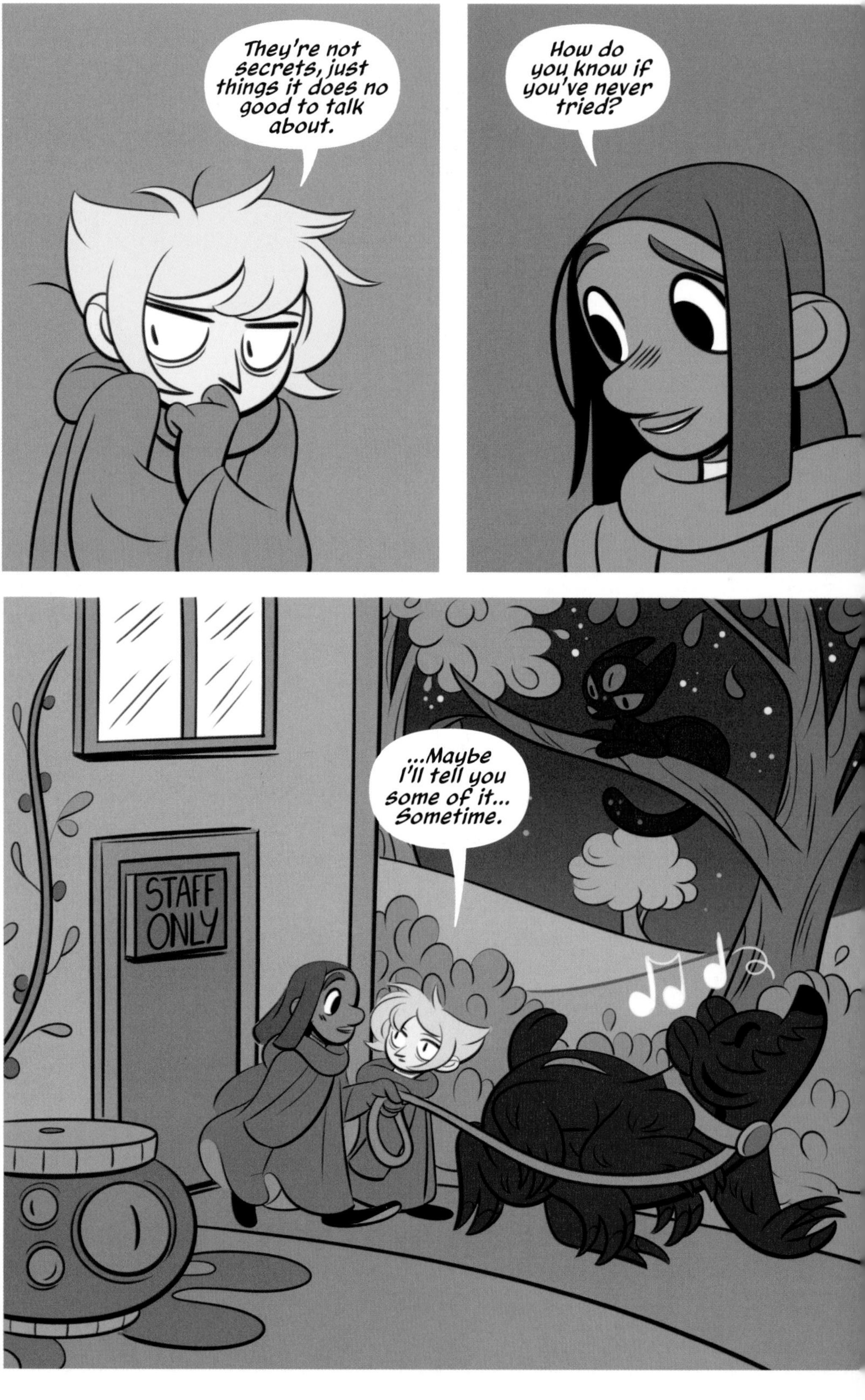
They're not secrets, just things it does no good to talk about.
How do you know if you've never tried?
STAFF ONLY
...Maybe I'll tell you some of it... Sometime.

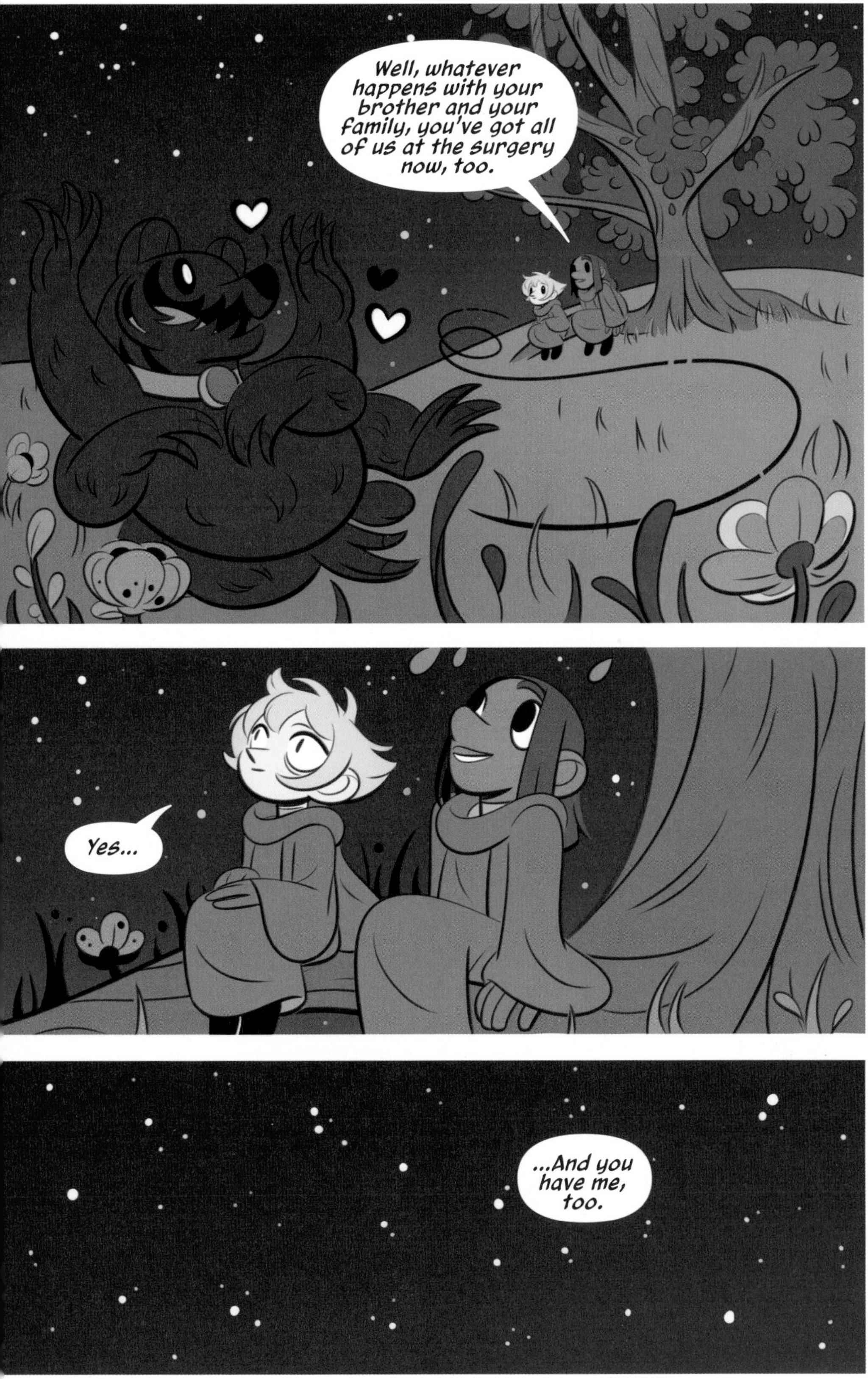
Well, whatever happens with your brother and your family, you've got all of us at the surgery now, too.
Yes...
...And you have me, too.

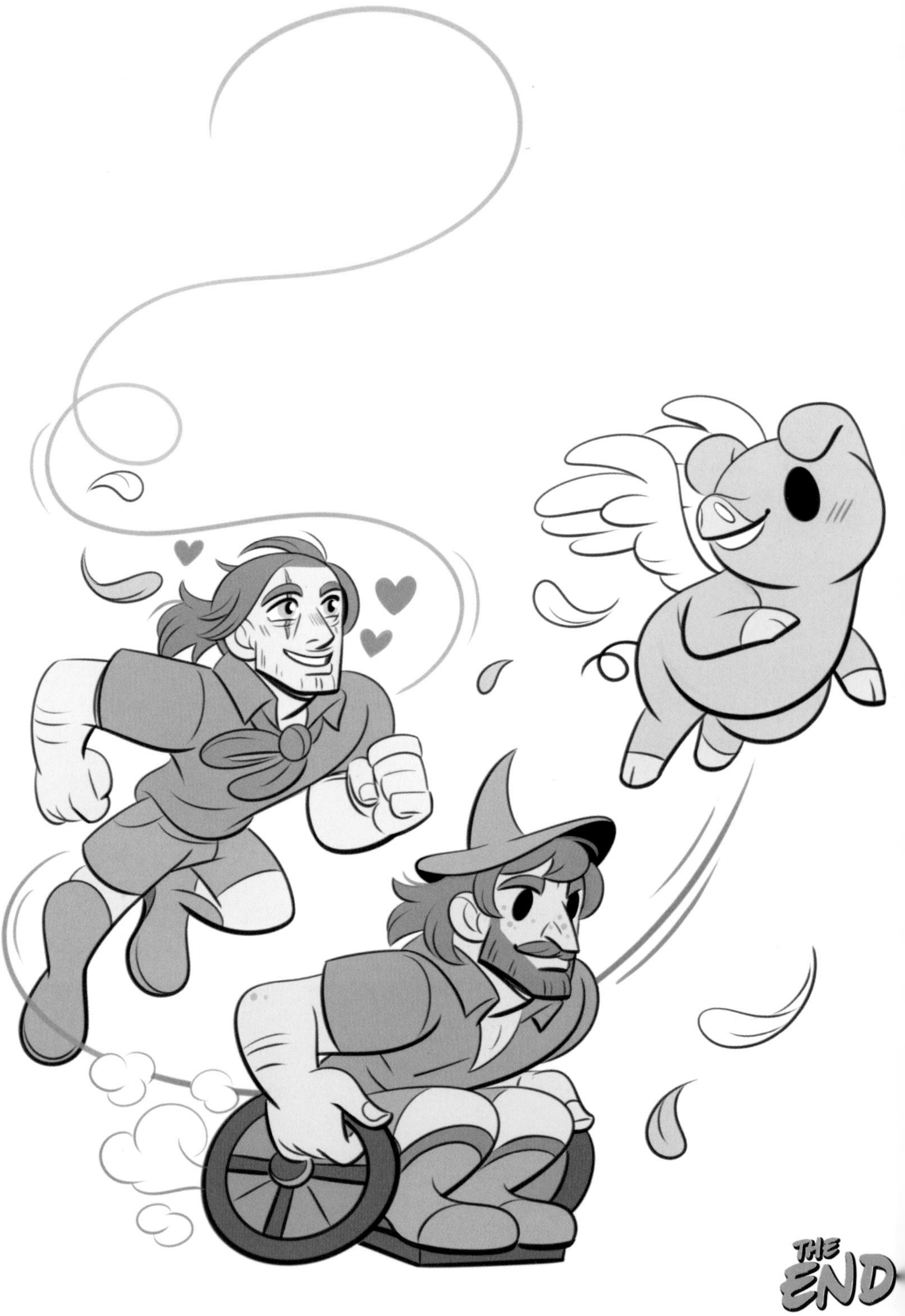
THE END

Author Bio

Sam Davies is an illustrator and comic artist living somewhere in the UK countryside, probably near some ducks. She's best known for her online silent all-ages comics series *Stutterhug* which currently has over 160 strips and will probably keep going until someone stops her. If you meet her in person she likes talking about ghost stories and animal species that don't exist. *Hex Vet: The Flying Surgery* is her second graphic novel, following *Hex Vet: Witches in Training*, and she hopes you have a good time reading it.

DISCOVER
EXPLOSIVE NEW WORLDS